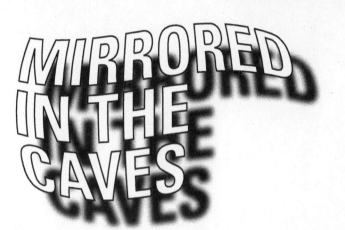

MIRRORED IN THE CAVES

MIRRORED IN THE CAVES

A NOVEL BY **BARBARA D. JANUSZ**

inanna poetry & fiction series

INANNA PUBLICATIONS AND EDUCATION INC.
TORONTO, CANADA

Canada Council   Conseil des Arts   ONTARIO ARTS COUNCIL
for the Arts   du Canada   CONSEIL DES ARTS DE L'ONTARIO

We gratefully acknowledge the support of the Canada Council
for the Arts and the Ontario Arts Council for our publishing program.

We are also grateful for the support received
from an Anonymous Fund at The Calgary Foundation.

THE CALGARY
FOUNDATION

Cover design: Val Fullard
Interior design: Luciana Ricciutelli

Library and Archives Canada Cataloguing in Publication

Janusz, Barbara D.
        Mirrored in the caves / Barbara D. Janusz.

(Inanna poetry & fiction series)
Issued also in an electronic format.
ISBN 978-1-926708-62-1

        I. Title. II. Series: Inanna poetry and fiction series

PS8619.A6785M57 2012   C813'.6   C2012-903111-9

Printed and bound in Canada

Inanna Publications and Education Inc.
210 Founders College, York University
4700 Keele Street, Toronto, Ontario, Canada M3J 1P3
Telephone: (416) 736-5356 Fax: (416) 736-5765
Email: inanna.publications@inanna.ca
Website: www.inanna.ca

for Olek and Garry

All is a continual flux upon the earth. Nothing in it keeps a form constant and determinate; our affections — fastening on external things — necessarily change and pass just as they do. Ever in front of us or behind us, they recall the past that is gone, or anticipate a future that in many a case is destined never to be. There is nothing solid to which the heart can fix itself.

— Jean-Jacques Rousseau, "Musings of a Solitary Stroller," 1777

1.

THE SOFT RESONANCE OF THE SEA displaces the mechanical rattle of the automobile motor. It's not the roar of an ocean, but like the hypnotic whisper that spills out of a seashell held against the ear. Elizabeth emerges from the driver's seat, tunes in to the rhythmic sound of the surf wafting over the dunes. She scrambles up the rise, leans forward to counteract the density of the sand. Standing on the crest of the mound, she now catches the interceding whisper of the waves as they recede back to sea. She takes a deep breath, draws in the scent of the salty air infused with a tinge of the earth.

A pair of pelicans roost upon the water, rock back and forth with the gentle surf. The sea birds remind Elizabeth of a surfer, lying face down on his surfboard, waiting for the next big swell — the cue to assume a bipedal, but slightly bent over stance; his arms, limberly outstretched, yield him that perfect balance — a prowess to ride, like a gull hoisted upon an updraft. The surfer then lets go, trusts with wild abandonment the climax of an unrestrained wave.

Stepping out of her sandals, she savors the heat of the sand on the soles of her feet, treads downwards through the dunes towards the water's edge. Her feet sink into the sand and her calf muscles contract with each step, invoking an image of trudging laboriously through a fresh bed of deep snow, many decades ago, when she was a child and the seasons were still markedly defined by weather.

Cormorants and seagulls waddle along the shoreline, stopping every now and then to turn their heads for a peripheral view of their surroundings. Wading in up to mid-calf, Elizabeth relishes the warm salty water caressing her legs. Without warning, the marine fowl alight, inciting the pelicans to shake off their catatonic state.

The fluid horizon, north of Tecolote Beach, is reined-in by Isla Espiritu Santos, an uninhabited, pastel-hued mound of rock. Where the island collides with the shimmering turquoise waters of the Sea of Cortez, Elizabeth can just barely make out an ivory strip of sand. Turning her back to the sea, she studies the mountains beyond the dunes that fragment the desert from the beach. They appear darker than from the floor of the canyon, and the dissecting ribbon of asphalt that she'd followed to its abrupt end, alongside the dunes. The late morning angle of the sun illuminates red patches of iron in the rock. On the summit of one of the highest rock faces she discerns the white cross that, only minutes earlier, she'd caught sight of while gearing down to skirt the mangrove wetlands on the west side of the highway. As the christened towering peak had receded through her rearview mirror, a peaceful, almost spiritual feeling had enveloped her. Just as suddenly, she'd conjured an image of Spanish soldiers scaling the volcanic scree, staking the white cross onto the summit on behalf of the Jesuits bent on converting the natives to Christianity. While zealously attempting to eradicate the existential belief system of the Aboriginals, the Spanish conquistadors ironically had routinely adopted pagan places of worship as their own religious sanctuaries.

In what seems like an eternity, Elizabeth feels, for the first time, as though there is nothing hanging over her head — no dark, hovering clouds, no ceiling with jarring fluorescent lights — only the sky and a cloudless one at that. Shifting her body westwards, she catches, through the corner of her eye, a person walking briskly toward her, along the water's edge. In anticipation of meeting him or her, perhaps even exchanging a few words with the only other human being on this desolate stretch of beach, her heart begins to pound. Surmising that the approaching beachcomber must be a foreigner, like herself, she perceives, as the figure draws nearer, broad shoulders and narrow hips — unmistakably the dimensions of a man. Out of precaution, Elizabeth wades out of the water to stand back on shore.

Stopping within a hundred meters of her, the man, in turn, wades out into the water before nodding to her. Hesitantly, she raises her hand and waves back.

"Hope you don't mind my invasion of your solitude."

"I was going to say the same thing." Taking in his long hawkish nose and blond, greying moustache, she stops herself from sizing him up further.

"I'm Richard." Wading toward her, he switches his sandals to his left hand before extending his right one for her to shake.

"Elizabeth." Sensing the warm firmness of his grip, she asks, "Where are you from?"

"San Diego. And you?"

"Canada. Calgary."

"What brings you to La Paz?"

"I'm on sabbatical to study the cave murals of the peninsula."

"Wondered whether I might run into one of my colleagues here on the beach. You're Dr. Thiessen."

"Yes. And you're Dr.... I'm sorry. I'm very bad with names."

"Wellington. Richard Wellington." Breaking into a restrained smile, he takes off his sunglasses and runs his forearm across his forehead. Before propping his glasses back onto his nose, Elizabeth catches the blue hue of his eyes, and the tiny wrinkles that jut out, like crow's feet, from their corners. "Do you want to take a walk over to Palapa Azul and join me for a beer?"

"Sure. But what about my rental car? I've parked it beyond the dunes." Elizabeth turns and points behind them.

"Should be okay. Is it locked?"

"Yes, but I should get my bag out of the baggage compartment."

Reaching the car, she flinches at the scorching hot chrome handle on the front baggage compartment. Heaving it open, she throws her purse and sandals into her beach bag, before slinging it over her shoulder.

The thump of the closing trunk jars Elizabeth's memory back to the past weekend — her brother, Michael, stowing her suitcase in the trunk of his car. Her mother, Krystyna, prone to tears when saying good-bye, had, for Elizabeth's sake, put on a brave face; though, at the last minute, she caused Elizabeth to second guess her decision to go back into the field.

"Aren't there deadly snakes and scorpions in that desert, over there?" Krystyna had gasped. "And you'll be sleeping in nothing but a tent!"

"But I thought you were glad for me!" Looking back at how her tone had risen into a protest, Elizabeth wonders whether her mother had waited to catch her at that most vulnerable moment — the definitive moment of parting, when she'd fall into the trap of reinforcing her status as a child. But she'd managed to regain her composure, by asking, "Haven't you been worried about me becoming such a recluse?"

Retracing her steps to the beach side of the dunes, she notices that the wind has picked up, and the tidemark has shifted towards the sea. She winces from the sting of the sand being flung against the back of her legs. With each gale, the receding surf washes the sand underfoot into a cool compact surface, prompting Elizabeth and Richard to pick up their pace.

Richard raises his voice to be heard over the shrieking gulls and thundering surf. "Where're you staying?"

"At the Los Arcos. And you?" Elizabeth has fallen slightly behind her new companion. She notices the hamstrings of his thighs tighten with every stride. For a man whose temples are visibly graying, he appears quite fit although his abdomen has begun to develop the proverbial middle-aged sag.

"Decided on La Concha. To take advantage of the beach there. But today, thought I'd come out here. Like to walk. At La Concha the beach isn't very long."

"I thought I spotted some coral reefs when approaching La Concha on my drive here."

"Yes. In the little cove, in front of the hotel. Haven't done any snorkeling though. Water's a little cool for that right now. Further up the beach, there," he points ahead of them, to a rocky plateau, beyond Isla Espiritu Santos. "Around that point, at Playa del Coyote, there are some reefs. After a good storm, a lot of coral gets washed up on the beach."

"The clerk at the car rental agency thought I was crazy to be coming out here this time of year. I guess the natives don't start going to the beach until after *Semana Santa*, the week after Palm Sunday."

"It's a little cool for the locals too but, no doubt, hailing from Calgary, you probably find this downright balmy." Richard grins at her and extends his hand towards the *palapa* restaurant.

An oversized, grey-weathered piece of plywood with the name, Palapa Azul, painted fittingly in cerulean blue, graces the crest of the thatched roof. Constructed of the trunks and fronds of palm trees, the restaurant and its outbuildings have displaced the dunes on the leeward side of the asphalt road that abruptly ends at a stone wall. A dozen metal tables with chairs are neatly arranged in three rows out front, on the beach, but prudently set back from the watermark. Claiming one of the tables nearest the water's edge, Richard orders a round of beer.

"Since you live on the border, you've probably been to Mexico before," Elizabeth remarks, sinking into the backrest of the chair that faces the ocean.

"I know the Baja well." His thin lips break out into a smile, but again, it's a controlled smile, not a teeth-revealing one.

A story must lie behind that stifled smile, a story with a

woman. If she'd been asked the same question and recalled a previous tryst with a man, she too might smile like that — gluttonously, yet covertly.

The waiter returns with their beer and a basket with tortilla chips and salsa.

"*Gracias.*" Richard takes her glass and beer and pours it for her. "Thiessen. That's Dutch isn't it?"

"Yes. My ex-husband's background is Dutch. Mine's Polish, though."

"Thought I detected a bit of an accent."

"English is my second language. My father was a strict disciplinarian, insisted that we speak Polish at home. I also picked up a bit of French in school."

"That's right. You guys are bilingual up there in Canada."

"Not so much in Calgary, but yes, you'd have a tough time getting around Quebec, particularly the northern parts, without a little French." She thinks back to the summer just before her daughter, Patricia, had enlisted in the armed forces. They'd spent two weeks touring Montreal, Quebec City, and the Gaspé Peninsula. As they'd ventured further away from the cities, they encountered fewer and fewer people who could converse in English. "So we're to meet now, Monday morning, at the department — in the boardroom for our orientation."

"Yes, typical Mexico. Hurry up and wait. Don't be surprised if Guzman contacts you between now and then and tells you the meeting's been postponed until the middle of the week. When did you speak with him?"

"This morning. My room at the hotel had only been reserved for two nights, until Saturday."

"So you had them extend the reservation until Tuesday?"

"Yes."

Taking a hefty gulp of his beer, Richard leans back in his chair. "When I had the chance to leave the country for awhile, I jumped at it. This recession is turning pretty ugly."

Elizabeth nods. "How much debt have you guys accumulated over Iraq and the war on terrorism?"

"An obscene number in the trillions."

"People must be terribly angry"

Richard lets out a chortle. "It's funny how everyone thinks of us as harbouring so much anger."

"Everyone, as far as I know, from watching the news and reading the papers, is still very afraid. Anger is a secondary emotion. Beneath anger, there's usually fear or shame. Or both."

"No question they're trying to control us with fear. But I don't buy that anger stuff."

Through the dark lenses of his glasses, Elizabeth can sense Richard scrutinizing her. She should have changed the subject when he'd mentioned the U.S. economy taking a nose dive. She recalls having seen him at conferences but somehow they'd never been drawn to introduce themselves to one another. Now, under his intense scrutiny, she wonders whether he'd intentionally avoided her. The hand that lifts his glass to his lips doesn't bear a wedding band. Perhaps he's gravitated towards the younger anthropologists on the symposium circuit.

"Would you like another beer?"

"Sure. But first I need to find a bathroom."

Stepping into the cool shade of the palm-fronded roof, Elizabeth removes her sunglasses. There's a young woman seated on a stool behind the bar with a stack of receipts and a calculator. *"El baños?"*

The woman points to a back door. *"A la fuera."*

Nodding, she heads in the direction indicated, when she's caught by the images on a television suspended from the rafters of the bar. The volume has been muted. Recognizing the CNN logo, she absorbs the text flowing across the bottom of the screen. "Three Canadian soldiers have been taken hostage by Taliban insurgents, including a female intelligence officer."

Elizabeth groans, slumps onto a stool at the end of the bar. *Patricia. Please God, no!*

"*Que pasa Senora?*"

"*Agua. Necesito aqua.*" She feels numb, outside of herself, like someone else is observing the woman reach for a glass, pour water out of a pitcher. Taking a few sips of water, she rises unsteadily from the bar stool. The woman again points toward the back door.

Blinding sunlight hits her like a lightning bolt. A sharp pain erupts in her head, followed by a wave of nausea. The aftertaste of beer makes her want to retch. Groping for the door handle, she staggers into the bathroom.

She places her head between her knees to combat her nausea. She's so tense that she can't relieve herself. Willing herself to conjure up the sound of the surf, Elizabeth imagines, instead, dark faces with black scarves tied across their mouths and noses. The televised footage of the dusty street outside the village elders' quarters from where the hostages were kidnapped looms like a relentless image from a nightmare. The only female intelligence officer posted in Afghanistan, she's certain that Patricia is among the hostages. Easy prey. Women have always been easy prey. She bursts out crying, heaves up sobs.

Splashing water on her face, she looks at herself in the mirror. Terror. It's no longer her face that's reflected in the glass, but the face of terror. Richard's words, "I don't buy that anger stuff," comes to mind. She pulls her sunglasses over her eyes. Her hand shakes as she grips the doorknob. The white cross on the mountain summit hovers ominously overhead.

She goes around the building to avoid encountering the woman with the pitying, dark brown eyes, hastily makes her way back to the table where Richard, like a statue, soaks up the sun's rays. Slinging her beach bag over her shoulder, she blurts out, "I must get back to La Paz."

"Why? What's happened?"

"My daughter. She's been taken hostage by Taliban insurgents."

"What?" Richard's face drops into a stunned expression.

"She's in intelligence, with the armed forces." Elizabeth turns to go.

"Let me go with you." Gripping her shoulder, he steers her toward the dunes, to the road that severs the desert from the beach.

2.

"JUST GIVE ME A MOMENT. I don't want to lose my train of thought." Commanding herself to concentrate on the words on the computer screen, she tries blocking out the figure of her eighteen-year-old daughter looming within arm's length at the corner of her desk. No sooner than Elizabeth fixes her attention back to the hypothesis that she's so painstakingly formulated for her latest, long-overdue publication, she hears her office door slam and Patricia's footsteps recede down the hall to her bedroom.

"Fuck! Is it possible for an eighteen-year-old to have less patience than a preschooler?" She clicks the "Save" command, rolls her chair away from her desk and follows her daughter to her bedroom. After all these years, you'd think she'd have some inkling of how hard it is to stay abreast of all the new scientific theories coming down the pipe!

Applying her knuckles to the door in quick succession, Elizabeth heaves in a deep breath before opening the door. "What do you want?" she asks, forcing herself to hide her exasperation.

Standing at the window, Patricia's shoulders are tensely raised, but she's turned her head toward the door, Elizabeth's cue that it's all right for her to sit down on the edge of the bed. "I'm so sorry Patricia! I just needed to get it down before it turned into sludge in my poor middle-aged brain."

The late afternoon light imbues her daughter's strawberry

blond hair with a reddish metallic luster. Turning from the window, Patricia's green-grey eyes seem to rival the gleam of the dusky sky. Thankfully, they convey disappointment rather than anger, prompting Elizabeth to muster up the confidence to ask, "What did you want to talk to me about?"

Patricia's hesitancy in answering tells her that whatever it is, it's serious. "I don't know whether we should talk about it here. How 'bout a cup of tea?"

"That serious, eh?"

"It's not earth shattering, but it's pretty important, Mama."

Elizabeth rises from the bed and crosses the hardwood floor to take her daughter in her arms.

"I'm not pregnant, or anything like that!" she protests, releasing herself from her mother's embrace, and striding purposefully into the kitchen.

Elizabeth trails behind and heads toward the counter where the kettle sits. Pouring water into the kettle, Elizabeth places it onto the stove, rinses out the teapot, and throws in two tea bags. These mundane tasks out of the way, she crosses her arms and turns towards her daughter who's retreated into the corner of the breakfast nook. "Okay, let's have it."

Like her mother, Patricia has wrapped her arms defensively across her chest. "I've joined the armed forces." To reinforce that there's no changing her mind, she raises her chin slightly and projects it, challengingly, toward Elizabeth.

"When did you decide this?"

"Two weeks ago, just before graduation. Remember, I told you that there was a career fair at school?"

Elizabeth frantically jogs her memory, vaguely recalls something about the armed forces recruiting, not just prospective graduates, but youngsters barely sixteen years of age. Confident that Patricia had her heart set on studying psychology, after taking a year off to work and travel, she hadn't given it a second thought.

"You can't stop me. I'm eighteen years old."

"I know." Elizabeth sits down across from her and lets Patricia attend to the whistling kettle and the teapot. "But what about *Dziadzio?*" She thinks of her father, a Second World War veteran. As he'd grown older, on rare occasions, when watching a newscast reporting on the latest war casualties, he'd comment on the senseless carnage of both military personnel and civilians in Iraq and Afghanistan.

"That was sixty years ago, Mama! We're not in Nazi-occupied Poland and I'm not joining the Polish underground, like *Dziadzio* did."

"But Canada is engaged in Afghanistan, fighting Muslims!"

"And those women and children over there deserve to live a good life too."

"Nothing is ever going to change over there. You're not even fighting money like your grandfather did, which was a losing battle anyway. You'll be fighting on the side of money, not to better the lot of the average Afghani!"

"Everyone is entitled to their opinion. I can't bury my head in the sand like you."

Patricia's last remark cuts like a knife. Having always prided herself on sustaining a strong sense of social consciousness despite public opinion shifting increasingly to the right, Elizabeth feels a surge of indignation rising to her throat. Wait a minute, count to three. Am I going to counter self-defensiveness by being self-defensive? "But female recruits in the Canadian armed forces are engaged in combat. Did you know that the Israelis don't even allow that anymore? That they've determined that Muslims have a tendency not to retreat when they're facing women in combat? It's their culture. It would be extremely humiliating for a Muslim to retreat when confronting a woman in combat. I didn't raise you only to lose you to a phony war on terrorism."

"Would you like some honey?"

"Don't change the subject." She shakes her head. "Going

into combat over there is the same as Muslim women joining the ranks of suicide bombers! How many of your girlfriends have been recruited?"

Patricia tilts the teapot so as not to spill any tea on the pinewood tabletop. "None. I'm the only girl. But three guys signed up."

"Gregory?"

Patricia shakes her head.

"Have you told him?"

"No. He wouldn't approve either."

"What are his plans?"

"He's going to U of A. He's been accepted into the faculty of engineering."

"So you and Gregory are done?

"Mama, times have changed. No one marries their high school sweetheart anymore. Besides, I'm not interested in getting married."

"Who said anything about marriage?"

"I'm not interested in marriage, period. Not now, not ever."

My, God! Is this what my protracted selectiveness over a partner has given rise to? Elizabeth thinks back to the men she's dated over the years after her divorce, Patricia asking what happened to Stephen or Thomas or David when the telephone calls and weekend sleep-overs suddenly ceased.

Her daughter retreats back into the corner of the breakfast nook and while she stirs a spoonful of honey into her tea, Elizabeth tries to imagine what Patricia will look like with cropped hair, a helmet and army fatigues. The sun has shifted. It unleashes its slanted rays through the kitchen window and throws an oblong flood of light onto the hardwood floor. She shakes her head at the memory of her daughter sitting at the window, watching the sun set over the Rocky Mountains, while she cooked dinner after returning home from the university. What happened to Patricia's dreams of becoming a mother and a career as a psychologist? Perhaps the divorce and all the subsequent failed relationships had affected Patricia more profoundly than Elizabeth had realized.

"Have you told your father yet?"

"Of course not!"

"I was only asking." She wonders whether, despite her good intentions in never pitting her daughter against Bernard, she'd unwittingly instilled in Patricia the propensity to keep the so-called patriarch in the dark. Her own mother had intentionally sheltered Elizabeth's father from the normal, mundane problems that families in the sixties and seventies had encountered with their rebellious teenaged sons and daughters. The basis for such subterfuge had never been articulated but instinctively understood. Stanislaw had come out of the war irreparably damaged and too fragile to cope.

On the eve of taking her marriage vows, Elizabeth had vowed not to follow in her mother's footsteps. She'd taken great pains to keep Bernard apprised of what was on her mind, and despite his protests, had succeeded in prying out of him his anxieties about landing a partnership with Baker & McCaffery. But not long after Patricia was born, she began to withdraw from Bernard, keeping more and more of her anxieties to herself. As he rose up the ranks in the legal profession, Bernard began to exhibit the same impatience and self-absorption Elizabeth had witnessed in her father. His reluctance to lend her a sympathetic ear — not over Patricia, who'd proven to be easygoing and less demanding than other children her age — but over her nebulous position in the hierarchy of the halls of higher learning, had left her feeling overwhelmed by the demands of motherhood and the rigours of an academic career. Perhaps she'd unwittingly misplaced her anxiety, projected it resentfully, albeit silently, onto Bernard, causing a rift between them that eventually proved impossible to bridge.

"Is it about money?"

"What do you mean?" Patricia throws her a look of bewilderment.

"You don't want to be dependent upon a man. Let's face it. Most women, even these days, are in the unenviable position of having to beg. He who controls the money, calls the shots. You don't want to be controlled. I don't blame you."

Elizabeth considers whether Patricia feels trapped. Today's competitive marketplace dictates that young women embrace a career, but having witnessed the frenetic home front-workplace juggling act that put her own generation of women practically over the edge, is it any wonder that today's new generation of liberated young women are having second thoughts? Hadn't she read somewhere about a recent trend of young women choosing motherhood over a career, demanding, like their grandmothers in the fifties and sixties, that they be supported by their husbands?

Patricia's pretty, oval face draws a blank. "I've never considered not having a career."

"Of course not, but what happened to psychology?"

"I'm not interested in pandering to neurotics. Luxury problems. That's what the healing professions are concerned with in this part of the world, while women and children, elsewhere, are deprived of the basic right to literacy and the necessities of life."

"When do you report for duty?"

"July 15th."

"So after our trip to the Gaspé?"

"Yeah. We won't even have to change our travel plans." Patricia reaches across the table to grasp Elizabeth's hand. "Mama, it'll be like old times. Just you and me and the open road."

3.

"BERNARD, IF I COULD HAVE STOPPED HER from going over there, I would have, you know that!" A torrent of static erupts over the line. "Hello! Are you still there?"

"Yes, I'm still here." Elizabeth hears him heave a heavy sigh. "Sorry, Liz. I know I shouldn't be blaming you. I'm mad at myself, really. And thoroughly pissed off at our government for even getting involved in that mess over there."

"Should I come home?"

"Hell, no! What could you do here that you can't do there?" He hesitates before answering his own question. "Except worry. Thank God they're refusing to release Patricia's identity."

"Have you told your partners?"

"Yes, of course. They know that Patricia's in intelligence and they would have connected the dots sooner or later. I haven't exactly been myself since I learned about this."

"Well, at least the bastards had the decency to contact you." Through the corner of her eye, Elizabeth notices Richard raising his eyebrows at overhearing the word, "bastards." Turning away from him, she adds, "Did they indicate how they intend to resolve this?"

"Yeah, right. They would have laughed in my face had I asked. It's all in the name of security these days and you and I both know what that means. They can fuck up all they want and no one will know any better."

"Did they say whether there are any terms for the soldiers' release?"

"The usual. Canada's withdrawal of its troops."

She hears another call coming in on his office line. "Listen, Bernard. We're not leaving for the sierras for another week. I'll e-mail you my telephone number at the hotel and I'm thinking I'll ask the department to equip me with a cell phone. I'll pass that onto you when I'm connected."

Hastily bidding him farewell, Elizabeth hangs up even before hearing the disconnecting click.

"What'd you find out?" Richard asks.

She shakes her head. "Not much. Patricia left two emergency numbers. The defense department contacted Bernard late last night."

"Wasn't meaning to eavesdrop, but I take it they're not disclosing what they're doing to try and have the hostages released."

"No. That's right. All in the name of homeland security and the war against terrorism!"

A knock on the door stops Richard from proffering a response. While he rises from the armchair to answer it, Elizabeth turns towards the balcony. Out of the corner of her eye she sees the waiter set down a tray on the table, but her focus is upon the cove that skirts the crescent-shaped resort complex. A panga veers alongside the pier. The deepening twilight has transformed the dock, vessel, and disembarking passengers into silhouettes. The tranquility of the scene only makes her more agitated. How can she be surrounded by such exquisite beauty and tranquility while her daughter's life is being held ransom? Abruptly standing up, she begins pacing the room, until the sight of Richard hovering over the tray on the table proves enough of a distraction to momentarily soothe her frayed nerves. "What have you got there?"

With an exaggerated flourish he pulls the checkered napkins off two plates of grilled fish, refried beans and salsa, and then, as though he himself had cooked the whole shebang, he steps back, extends his hands, palms facing outwards. A second knock on the door spurs him back across the room. "That must be the wine."

While the waiter positions the ice bucket beside the table and eases the cork out of the bottle, a severe case of sheepishness takes hold. On their drive from Tecolote Beach to Richard's hotel, she'd cut into him for suggesting that she call Bernard rather than trying to contact someone in Ottawa. She'd finally relented, but not before she'd torn a strip off the poor guy.

Setting the table with cutlery and the plates of food, he asks, "How's Bernard?"

"Worried. He gave me shit for allowing Patricia to go over there. But you were right to suggest that I call him. He needed to unload on someone. Better me than taking it out on a client or one of his partners."

"Let's eat something."

"I'm not very hungry."

"Then drink." Richard hands her a glass of white wine.

"The way I'm feeling, I'm sure to get totally pissed."

"Then you'll have to eat something. How's your head? Did the aspirin help?"

"Yes, better, thank you."

He clinks his glass against hers. "*Sante.* To you."

Another wave of despair washes over her. Elizabeth sets down her glass. Rising from the table, she retreats into the bathroom. She pulls a tissue out of the dispenser in the bathroom, and she dabs the corners of her eyes. *Thank God I'm not alone.* But her gratitude becomes quickly displaced by a torrent of anger. She hates feeling so vulnerable and out of control, and then she imagines the worst again — Patricia with a blindfold drawn tightly across her eyes, like the hostages she's viewed on television newscasts, their kidnappers cradling automatic weapons, holding them menacingly over their victim's shoulders. Victimization. That's what terrorism is all about. And vengeance. An eye for an eye.

"You all right?" Richard calls out from the room.

Turning off the bathroom light, Elizabeth glimpses a shadow of herself in the mirror before returning to the table and sliding back into her chair.

Richard sets down his fork and knife, leans over to gently rub her shoulder.

His touch feels soothing, but makes her want to cry again. She lowers her head and picks up her cutlery. "I'm okay. But I don't know what to do. I have to call my parents at some point. Patricia is my father's favourite grandchild. He was so proud when she joined the armed forces. He's eighty-seven years old. I don't want to have to say, 'I told you so,' but it's time he finally admitted that war is a poor excuse for securing our standard of living, maintaining the status quo."

Richard's crinkled brow indicates that some clarification is in order.

She swallows hard before launching into her father's life story and leans back in her chair. "My father graduated from a military academy in Poland in 1939. Within weeks he was on the front line, facing German tanks. It was all over, of course, in a matter of days — the Nazi invasion and Poland's occupation. He joined the resistance. In '43, while working for a German dairy farmer as a chemist — he took a crash course in pasteurization when the Nazis ordered every able-bodied German male to report to the eastern front — he was arrested and ended up in Mauthausen concentration camp. He was liberated by the Americans in May of 1945."

"So, he's a war hero. But with the Communist takeover of Poland after the war, he must have questioned whether it was worth it?"

"And will absolutely not admit that the U.S. is a war-mongering nation. The Americans liberated his camp and so they can do no wrong. Before I decided against law school and switched into anthropology, I majored in Political Science. This was back in the mid-'70s just at the end of the Vietnam War. My professors were not exactly right-wing conservatives and the concepts that I came home with every evening to share with the family around the dinner table didn't exactly lend themselves to uncontroversial small talk. My mother acted as a mediator and when I look back on that time, I realize that she encouraged me to stand up to my father. She lacked the credibility, herself having only a Grade 10 education, to put him in his place. She lived vicariously through me, as parents often do."

Assuming a wide-eyed expression, Richard asks, "Are you going to call your parents?"

"At some point, yes. I don't know that I should call them right away. It's doubtful, but perhaps this will be over before I need to worry them."

Richard's facial expression is steeped in doubt. "More wine?" Raising the perspiring bottle out of the ice bucket, he points it toward her.

"Sure, why not. Boy, I could use a cigarette."

"Do you want one?" Quickly rising from the table, he throws open the closet doors to retrieve a plastic duty free bag from the shelf.

"You smoke?"

"Not anymore, but when they were coming around with the duty free goodies on the plane, thought I'd buy a carton just in case. Figured since I'd be working in Mexico, it might not be a bad idea to have some on hand. Just in case I get stressed out." Returning to the table with a package of Marlboros, he peels off the cellophane and offers her one, before taking one himself. "Now for a light."

"By the phone." Elizabeth points to an ashtray with a book of matches.

"Thank God we're in Mexico. It's become very politically incorrect to smoke in California. I'm telling you, fascism is lurking around every corner. No wonder the world is in such a fucking mess!" Taking a deep drag off his cigarette, Richard leans back his head, puckers up his lips and blows out a succession of smoke rings. Smiling smugly, he says, "Was wondering whether I could still do that."

As the last rays of sun drop into the sea, a pall of silence descends upon the room. Butting her cigarette in the ashtray, Elizabeth rises from her chair. "I have to go. Sorry about the imposition. All my troubles."

"No. No trouble. Please don't go yet. Stay and have another glass of wine."

"No. I'm going to go. I feel very tired. Thank you for everything."

"Can I call you tomorrow?"

"Yes. Yes, of course." Elizabeth's voice trails off.

"Let me walk you to your car."

"No, please. I just want to be alone." Opening the door, she hesitates before saying goodnight, catches the look of expectancy on Richard's face, and then abruptly shuts the door behind her.

4.

JULIO GUZMAN'S HANDSHAKE IS FIRM and self-assured. "*Bienvenidos, Doctora* Thiessen. It's a pleasure to see you again. How long has it been?"

Peering into his dark brown eyes, Elizabeth strives to glean from their depth some inkling as to how he's likely to react to her news about Patricia being taken hostage. "Four years ago, at the conference in San Francisco."

"*Si, yo recuerdo.* "Guzman nods. Of medium height, and slight build, Guzman appears to have aged since Elizabeth last made his acquaintance. His ebony hair, now streaked with grey, underscores the olive tinge of his complexion. "You gave a presentation on North American Indian adolescent vision quests."

Elizabeth stifles an urge to smile at Guzman's pronunciation of "quests." Despite Guzman's almost flawless English, he pronounced the "qu," as is customary in Spanish, like a "k."

"Yes, that's right. My daughter, Patricia, accompanied me to the vision quest sites in the Southwestern Rockies. She even took some of the photos that were in my PowerPoint presentation."

"And how is your daughter?"

She can hardly believe how their conversation has seamlessly flowed toward the topic that, on the one hand, she'd prefer to avoid, but that, under the circumstances, she's compelled to broach. An insomniac for over twenty years, typically awakening at 3:00 a.m., as though her brain was hardwired to go off like an alarm clock, Elizabeth had tossed and turned the night before, coaching herself to refrain from exhibiting too much emotion when disclosing her situation. She'd also attributed her middle of the night anxiety to having agreed to give Richard a lift to this morning's orientation. Consoling herself with the truism that the tongue-wagging she could anticipate would be a small price to pay for Richard's kindness, she'd finally had to seek solace in a two-ounce bottle of scotch from the mini bar.

She peripherally observes the rest of the team at the opposite end of the boardroom. As though on cue, Richard excuses himself to join the other scientists.

After clearing her throat, Elizabeth explains, "*Doctoro* Guzman. I thought I should inform you. My daughter is in Afghanistan with the Canadian armed forces, working in intelligence, and was kidnapped a few days ago, with two other officers, when negotiating with some village elders to garner support for the new government."

Guzman's eyebrows extend like Eiffel towers over his eyes. A shiver runs up and down Elizabeth's spine. Had Guzman's eyes been blue, they would have emitted a cold steeliness.

"Do you wish to withdraw from the project, *Doctora*?"

A wave of panic engulfs her. She can't imagine that Guzman would ask this of a male colleague. She musters up the courage to say, "I'm not sure what to do. What would you do?"

"Are you in contact with anyone in Calgary about your daughter?" Guzman's eyes dart back and forth in their sockets, like in a game of tennis. The only cultural anthropologist on the team with expertise in shamanism, Elizabeth knows that she is indispensable to the realization of Guzman's life-long aspiration to unearth the secrets to the Baja California cave murals. The funding of this project had undoubtedly been a significant coup for the small university to which he's devoted his entire academic career.

"Yes. Her father is a lawyer in Calgary and he is in contact with Foreign Affairs in Ottawa." She hates having to air her dirty laundry but adds, "Bernard and I have been divorced for ten years, but we are on good terms with one another."

Evidently this is a satisfactory answer as Guzman's pumped up chest seems to have deflated by several centimeters and his shoulders have fallen back from their guarded raised posture. Family. Why, of course. Mexicans regard family as the foundation for all social and political affairs.

"Let me introduce you to my secretary, Isabela Toledo. Perhaps Isabela can maintain contact with your husband. *Pardone me*, your ex-husband, while we are in the sierras. She is a very conscientious person," he adds, extending his arm outwards toward a door at the opposite end of the room from where they entered. As he guides her toward it, Elizabeth notices that the door is almost camouflaged by the interior wood-panelling.

"Isabela, I would like you to meet *Doctora* Thiessen, from the University of Calgary."

Isabela rises from her chair and extends her hand toward Elizabeth. "*Mucho gusto.*"

"*Igualmente.*"

"Isabela, *Doctora* Thiessen has suffered a personal tragedy. Her daughter has been taken hostage by Taliban *terroristas* in Afghanistan."

"*Lo siento, Doctora! Que lastima!*" Isabela's otherwise cheerful demeanor drops into one of sympathy and worry as two distinct creases form across her broad forehead. Her large dark eyes, which are set far apart from one another, convey sensitivity and empathy.

Elizabeth avoids Isabela's eyes and looks past her at a poster of the central mural in the cave overhang of the Sierra de San Francisco. Symbolic geometric forms and crude drawings, predominantly of deer, but also of bobcats and turkey vultures, encircle the string of four oversized human figures, whose heads are adorned with deer antlers. The words, *Cueva Flecha*—cave arrow — printed on a diagonal, beneath the figures' feet, refers to the arrows penetrating their torsos and extremities.

"We will have to maintain contact with *Doctora's* family in Calgary during our time in the sierras," Guzman instructs.

"Perhaps after the orientation, *Doctora*, we could call your family," a suggestion that garners a look of approval from Guzman.

"Actually, *Doctoro* Guzman, I was hoping that the department might be prepared to provide me with a cell phone. I agree that Isabela should call my ex-husband, but I've practically become a hostage myself, since this happened."

Venturing out only sparingly to take a brisk walk along the Malecon or for a bite to eat, since leaving La Concha on Friday evening, Elizabeth had confined herself within the four walls of her room waiting for Bernard's phone call, and any news that he might have about Patricia.

"Isabela, *por favour*, call the telephone company and find out about cell phones, whether we can expect any reception in the sierras."

"*Muy bien, Profesoro.*"

Guzman extends his arm back toward the door and follows Elizabeth into the conference room where he promptly seats himself at the head of the table. At his behest the orientation commences with introductions. "Doctora Thiessen, *por favor*, if we could start with you."

Still feeling shaken by Guzman's reference to her plight as a personal tragedy, his choice of words having reinforced for her the seriousness of her situation, she begins in a barely audible voice. Accustomed to projecting her voice with confidence when addressing an audience, she senses her face becoming flushed and practically chokes upon her enunciation of, "*Hola.*"

Taking a deep breath, she draws solace from a nod from Guzman, but speaks uncharacteristically rapidly. "I'm Elizabeth Thiessen, from the University of Calgary. I specialize in the subspecies field of anthropology, known in some academic circles as the Anthropology of Religion, and I've published several papers on shamanism." Exhaling with relief over having accomplished this perfunctory task without breaking down, she then forces herself to zero in on her other team members' introductions.

On Guzman's left, Maynard Brigham, from the University of British Columbia in Vancouver, waves his hand in greeting. "*Buenas dias.* As you can tell from my accent, I need a lot of practice with my Spanish." Maynard, who appears to be the youngest of the group, smiles self-consciously before adding, "I lecture predominantly in the field of Psychological Anthropology. I'm looking forward to working with all of you on this exciting project."

Sandwiched between Brigham and Richard, directly across the table from Elizabeth is Bartlomiej Tomaszewski, from the Jagiellonian University in Krakow, Poland. Striking in a rugged yet polished manner, she notices that Bartek, as he likes to call himself, is in the habit, when speaking, of energetically gesticulating with his hands. "I don't know whether you are aware that, recently, at the Jagiellonian University, we formed a committee to honour the seminal contributions made by the late anthropologist, Bronislaw Malinowski. He was tenured with the London School of Economics, but was a graduate of the Jagiellonian University before studying abroad. I've been elected chair of the committee and look forward to discussing with some of you how applicable Malinowski's functionalist approach is to our study of *las pinturas rupestres*."

Richard's turn reveals that, coincidentally, the focus of his doctoral thesis was Malinowski's functionalist approach. "I too look forward to working with all of you in deciphering the myths that the Indigenous peoples wanted to immortalize in the cave overhangs. But frankly, I'm here not only because of what I think my expertise can bring to the table, but because of my love for the Baja. Residing so close to the border, I've vacationed here many times and I couldn't imagine passing up the opportunity to participate in such an exciting project."

"*Muchas gracias. Doctoro* Wellington. *Si, la Baja* is very special. We only became a state in 1974, when the highway was completed. Before that we were still a *territorio*." Guzman shifts his body to the right, toward *Doctoro* Raul Gutierrez, who he introduces as the head of the Archeology Department at *La Universidad Autonoma* in Mexico City.

Gutierrez explains that he has organized a team of three graduate students to study the artifacts that they hope to recover from the cave site. "We have also recruited an artist, who is very adept at drawing anything that we pull out of the ground. Carolina Madero is also an accomplished photographer but I like to have drawings of artifacts to supplement the photographs. She will be arriving a little bit later, and I think that *Doctora* Thiessen will welcome a little female companionship."

Upon hearing her name, Elizabeth's heart begins to knock irregularly in her ribcage. Smiling feebly, she nods toward Raul and then shifts her attention upon the last team member to introduce himself — Pierre Miguerre from the Sorbonne in Paris. Confirming his recent doctoral thesis on cave art and particularly the famous mural of Lascaux, he pulls a few strands of hair from the side of his head, before adding, "My greying hair confirms that I am no longer a young man. This is my second career. Before returning to study anthropology, I was a dentist in Lille, and as you all know, there is a connection through the teeth," he breaks into a tooth-revealing smile at this point, "between anthropology and dentistry."

The spotlight then reverts back to Guzman. "*Muy bien. Bienvenidos a La Paz y Baja California Sur*. As you can see, we have convened a diverse group of academics for this project, which will be officially inaugurated one week from today, when we leave in two jeeps for the village of San Ignacio, north of Santa Rosalia. The hamlet of San Francisco will be our base camp for the three-month period that we've scheduled for data gathering and the conducting of research. In June, it becomes very hot in the sierras, and the surrounding desert. So I hope that we can conclude our work before the onset of summer.

"I've made six copies of all the academic papers which this department has on file. We've organized them in a binder, together with maps." Guzman passes three binders each to Maynard and Raul to pass around. "Please bring these materials with you next Monday morning."

"Do we have any assignments, apart from these reading materials, for the rest of the week?" asks Miguerre.

"*Si*. I was just going to explain that. Even though the focus of our study is on *las pinturas* near San Ignacio, I thought it might be useful to team up in groups of two and conduct some supplementary studies of cave art in other parts of the peninsula. In your materials on page 129." Guzman pauses to allow everyone to flip to this page. "I have listed four sites that could be studied. Take a few minutes to study the maps that follow the list and let me know before you leave this morning which site you'd like to investigate. The Department has rented jeeps for your disposal. Please see my secretary, Isabela, for the keys and documentation. And there are documents that each of you must complete for your work visas. I hope that you all brought your passports and tourist visas."

Elizabeth catches Richard's eye from across the table. No sooner than she lowers her chin slightly to let him know that she'll pair up with him, he deposits himself over her left shoulder. Pointing to a site on the map, near the tip of the peninsula, he suggests, "Let's do *La Concepcion*."

"Do you know it?"

"I've only heard about it. But I know the east and west capes. And we could tour the golden triangle while we're at it."

"Okay." Elizabeth's heart resumes it irregular knocking. She leans her head against her right hand, checking to see whether her cheeks are flushed. Her eyes scan the faces of colleagues.

Thankfully they're engrossed in studying the maps of the cave sites. She's never felt so panicky before at an academic meeting. She's experienced anxiety at social functions, particularly after her separation from Bernard, but has always managed to alleviate her discomfiture by heading to the bar for another drink. Feeling as though she's going to faint, crumple like a rag doll onto the floor, she imagines these strangers having to rush to her side with a glass of water, slapping her cheeks to rouse her from semi-consciousness. Her mouth is very dry, but she doesn't dare take a sip of the coffee that Isabela has poured for her, afraid that the caffeine will push her over the edge. She has the urge to flee but feels glued to her chair, the muted voices in the room resound, surreally, like an echo. It's as though she's not present, but standing outside of this windowless room, on the other side of a permeable wall.

"Excuse me, Dr. Guzman," says Richard. "Where are the washrooms located in this building?"

Giving Richard directions, Guzman suggests that they take a break.

Once inside one of the cubicles, Elizabeth lowers her head between her knees and gulps in air. Staring at her sandal-clad feet, she considers what time of month it is. She's suffered the odd hot flash in front of the classroom but never anything like this before. *Stress. I'm stressed out.*

Splashing water onto her face and around her neck, she applies lipstick to her lips, draws two diagonal lines down her cheeks and then rubs the coral colour along her cheekbones to camouflage the paleness of her face. She takes two more deep breaths and returns to the boardroom, where her colleagues have since abandoned their chairs and stand casually chatting with one another.

Overhearing Richard discuss his travels in the Baja with "Bartek" Tomaszewski and Raul Gutierrez, she avoids joining them so as not to encourage speculation about she and Richard becoming too close. Pierre Miguerre and the young

Canadian from Vancouver, Maynard Brigham, draw apart to include Elizabeth in their discussion about petroglyphs in Western Canada.

"Last summer, I had occasion to visit Writing-on-Stone Provincial Park, in southeastern Alberta, along the Milk River," Maynard says. "There too, I studied some petroglyphs. Not that old, mind you, but interesting from the point of view of Plains Indian culture."

"I would think that some of the symbols at Writing-on-Stone are synonymous with those at San Francisco," suggests Elizabeth, brushing the left lower lid of her eye with her index finger.

"How so?" asks Brigham.

"The Plains Indians were nomads, following the buffalo herds, much like the Huichols of Baja California tracked the deer herds of the peninsula."

"The Writing-on-Stone petroglyphs include horses and are, therefore, much more recent. We're talking about a difference of five thousand years."

"And on the west coast of British Columbia, the Haida focused on carving their mythic images onto totem poles," interjects Pierre, who reaches into his shirt pocket for a package of cigarettes and offers one to Elizabeth and Maynard.

"No, thanks," Maynard shakes his head. "I don't smoke. The west coast Indians were somehow less interested in preserving their legacy than in ensuring that their carvings were recycled back into mother earth. They'd simply allow the totems to collapse onto the old growth forest floor. In our humid climate, the slugs and other bugs, in no time, begin the process of breaking down the softwood."

"Yes," Elizabeth replies, leaning her body towards the flame of the match held out by Pierre. Exhaling, she picks up the thread of Maynard's last comment. "The west coast Aboriginals evolved more trust in their capacity to survive, a product of a more benevolent climate and the fecundity of their coastal environment. Their culture is a magnificent reflection of their ability to rely on the oceans and forests to provide them with a reliable food source."

"So you and Wellington have claimed *La Concepcion* as your pet project for the week?" Maynard says.

"Yes. Apparently the west and east capes are spectacular. And you two have formed a team?" She detects a tinge of competitiveness in Maynard's remark and recalls her mother's words of encouragement when she'd first mentioned her plans to take a sabbatical.

"You are still a young woman and must think about your future, Elizabeth. Go. You've become too much of a homebody. Go out into the world. It's been years since Patricia has been out of the house. You need to make a life for yourself. You don't want to be alone for the rest of your life." Krystyna had then added that some older women were taking up with younger men. Elizabeth had scoffed at the idea but Maynard Brigham, she guesses, must me at least ten years her junior, and she can't help but sense some attraction for her on his part.

"Yes," answers Pierre. "We've chosen a site west of Santa Rosalia, just south of La Sierra de San Francisco."

"So how do you feel about being the only female on the project?" asks Maynard.

"But I'm not. Carolina Madero will be joining our team."

"Well, yes, Gutierrez mentioned that, but she's just part of the support staff." Brigham's ruddy complexion and red hair seem to have ignited out of embarrassment for being corrected.

"She's a professional like us, but an artist instead of a scientist." Shifting her body slightly so as to sever the face-to-face stance that Maynard has initiated with her, she asks Pierre, "So for how many years did you ply the trade of a dentist?"

"Ten. It was very stressful. People hate going to the dentist and some have a very low tolerance for pain. In France many people don't bother going to a dentist until it is too late and I had to pull out a lot of teeth. Sometimes I felt like the butcher of Lille." Pierre lets out a guffaw. His pun, however, completely mystifies Maynard, who is evidently too young to be particularly well versed in Second World War European history. Elizabeth, out of courtesy, laughs. His witty reference to the infamous French Nazi collaborator unleashes a pang of anxiety over her parents still being in the dark about Patricia.

As though reading her mind, Pierre asks, "Did you leave family back in Calgary?"

"Yes. I have a daughter, but she is overseas at the moment. And you?"

"I am divorced and my son is studying engineering."

"And I'm single without attachments," Maynard interjects.

"So what about the famous central mural at San Francisco called *Cueva Flecha*?" Not waiting for an answer, Elizabeth adds, "I think its most significant features are the different colours, or variations of colours, that the Indigenous peoples used in painting the human figures. Some are painted black, or red, others white and red, black and red."

"Black is the colour of the uninitiated in both shamanic and adolescent tribal initiation rites of some extant Aboriginal tribes," Pierre offers. "White is usually reserved for shamans. But what about the name of the mural?"

"Could it be that when the Jesuits dragged the Cochimis out of their caves to recruit them in building the missions, they didn't give it much thought?" Brigham suggests. "Being so arrogant about the superiority of the Christian faith, they might have simply zeroed in on one of the features of the murals — the arrows — and named it cave arrow."

"But in doing so, they unwittingly validated the Aboriginals' culture, not unlike the adoption by the Spaniards of spiritual sites." Elizabeth suppresses the onset of a shudder at the thought of the white cross on the mountain peak at Tecolote Beach. "The arrows and the animals, predominantly deer, represent a hunt. The shamans, by being penetrated, figuratively speaking, by arrows derived spiritual power in guiding the tribe to fertile hunting grounds. And of course, the nomadic treks in pursuit of the deer herds that migrated north in the summer, and south in the winter, were crucial for their survival."

Elizabeth turns and notices Guzman opening the wood-panelled door leading into the reception area. Excusing herself, she picks up one of the binders of materials from the conference table and checks her wristwatch. It's just about noon — a good time for Isabela to try and catch Bernard at his office.

5.

"HOW DO YOU KNOW where the cave paintings are located?" Elizabeth asks, projecting her voice so as to be heard over the roar of the motor.

Tearing his eyes momentarily off the winding road to meet hers, Richard yells back, "I don't. We'll have to ask around in San Bartolo for directions. All I know from one of my trips down here is that the cave of *La Concepcion* is accessible from San Bartolo and located on someone's ranch."

"Do we have to pay the rancher anything for taking a look?"

"Apparently these *vaqueros* are unbelievably hospitable. We can expect an invitation to spend the night and they'll put on a spread that'll include everything from their pantry. They act as our guide to the cave site, but when we leave them some money we need to stress, so as not offend them, that we're paying them for guiding and not their hospitality."

A sign announcing their arrival to the village of El Triunfo prompts Richard to shift into a lower gear. Colonial-style buildings line the highway, the most prominent of which is a church painted bright yellow with pinkish red trim. On the right hand side of the road a *tienda* advertises the sale of local handicrafts. Beside it stands a café, its open door revealing a rustic, deserted interior. The elongated branches of blooming orange and magenta-coloured bougainvilleas drape the palm-fronded, thatched roofs of the villagers' small adobe dwellings and detract the eye from the otherwise drabness of grey rickety fences and monotonous backdrop of pale green cacti forest.

"This used to be a gold and silver mining town, but the mines have been shut down for eighty years. See the two smoke stacks over there." Richard points to the right. "That's where the ore was smelted. The metal was shipped across the sea to the mainland, and from there transported to the Gulf of Mexico, and onto ships bound for Spain."

Elizabeth nods and then shifts her focus to the left. Through the windows of a half dozen small buildings, arranged in a semi-circle in a school yard, she sees classes in session. Feeling a pang of regret at having relinquished her position at the front of the lecture hall, she yearns for the predictability and security that she'd derived from the methodical teaching of a set of concepts, reduced into a curriculum. Now, particularly with the uncertainty over Patricia, she feels uprooted, like a sailor lost at sea.

Past El Triunfo, the road becomes steeper and even more serpentine. Gone are the barren mountain faces that hem in La Paz. Here, the hills are laden with vegetation, predominantly ferns; but as the road ascends over a pass and skirts a mountainside of rock seams with saplings clinging to veins of soil, Elizabeth can't help but wonder how anything can thrive in such hostile conditions. Every few kilometers, weather-beaten road signs warn of the potential for rockslides; indeed, now and then, Richard swerves into the opposite narrow lane to avoid a boulder or cluster of rock that has given way from above.

Descending into the farming community of San Antonio, located in a verdant valley of cultivated farmsteads, they hardly have a chance to blink before the road climbs again, winding around mountainsides until it cuts through a palm-lined canyon, within which is nestled the village of San Bartolo.

Richard abruptly veers in front of a *palapa* restaurant, on the left hand side of the highway. "We'll ask here for directions to *La Concepcion*. And besides," he adds, grinning, "I could use a cold *cerveza*."

The proprietress, attired in a faded, cotton print, sleeveless dress, asks them if they want something to eat.

"No, *gracias*," Richard replies, wiping his sweat-lined brow with his shirt sleeve. "*Solamente dos cervezas, por favor.*"

Elizabeth's body releases an involuntary quiver.

"Are you all right?" Richard runs his hand along her shoulder.

"Yes. I just felt a bit chilled. It's amazing how much cooler it is in here."

"You know the saying, necessity is the mother of invention. They've built this little place right up against the mountainside, so it's naturally air conditioned by the rock."

But there's another reason behind her shudder. The rustling of palm fronds overhead jolted Elizabeth's thoughts back to the afternoon at Tecolote Beach, when she'd caught the CNN footage of the village in Afghanistan from which Patricia and her fellow officers had been whisked away by Taliban insurgents. And then the next image that came to mind was of her cell phone, lying inside the jeep's console. Should she be carrying it with all the time? How ironic that in targeting the industrialized world's technological way of life, she of all people, who had resisted becoming a slave to technology, had now become the terrorists' latest victim, feeling compelled to arm herself with a technological tool that keeps her connected 24/7.

The woman sets down two bottles of beer, glasses, and a small bowl of lime quarters.

"*Gracias. Con permiso, Señora*, we're looking for the cave paintings, located north of here, on a ranch."

"The road is very bad."

Richard nods obligingly and points outside towards the jeep. "We're prepared for bad roads."

"Do you have a map?"

He unfolds it onto the table and gestures for her to sit down.

Returning to the bar for her eyeglasses, *la Señora* takes the chair across from Elizabeth. Studying the map for a minute, she points to a broken red line to the southwest of San Bartolo, traces it with her index finger to a small circle, beside which, in italicized letters, are printed the words, *La Concepcion*. She then points out another broken red line extending from San Antonio to the same destination and explains, "The distance from San Antonio is greater, but the road is better, and you might get there faster."

"But we can get to *La Concepcion* from here?" asks Richard.

"*Si*," she nods. "The road begins just after the *llantera*, on the opposite side of the highway."

"What does the small circle signify?" asks Elizabeth.

"*Rancho*," answers Richard. "How many kilometers is it from here?"

Rising from the table, *la Señora* cups her chin in her right hand. "Probably twenty-five. About a two-hour drive. Mario!" She calls out toward the kitchen, on the other side of the bar. "I've never been there but my husband has."

A short, burly man in a white undershirt and a pair of worn, cotton, navy-coloured trousers pulls back a set of drapes from behind the bar.

"*La Concepcion?* These people are asking about the road and how long it will take them to get there."

"*Muy malo*," Mario replies, shaking his head.

"Will we get there by nightfall?" asks Richard.

El Señor checks his wristwatch, hesitates before nodding.

"With time to spare?" Richard asks, looking at his wristwatch and taking a gulp of his beer.

"You can make it there before sunset but you would not be able to make it back before dark."

"Is there a hotel here in San Bartolo?" asks Elizabeth.

"There's nothing here. We're too close to the east cape. The rancher will put us up. We'd better drink up if we want to find our way before nightfall." Richard drains his glass and strides cowboy style to the bar, reaches into his back jean pocket for his wallet. Pulling out a twenty peso note, he deposits it, together with his empty glass, onto the counter.

"The Carcamo family owns *La Concepcion* ranch. José Miguel Carcamo." *El Señor* painstakingly enunciates the surname.

"Carcamo," Richard repeats back. "*Bueno. Muchas gracias. Hasta luego.*"

"May you journey well," *la Señora* calls out after them.

"Do you think it's all right to take this road?" asks Elizabeth, fastening her seatbelt. "Maybe we should backtrack to San Antonio and take the better road."

"These people don't drive the road because their vehicles are falling apart. We'll be all right."

The road behind the tire shop looks like it's made more for burros than cars. They pass several dwellings separated from one another by the ubiquitous, dilapidated, grey fences. Chickens clear the path in a cacophony of clucking. Judging by the diminutive items of clothing hung out to dry in the hot desert sun, the residents of San Bartolo are a prolific lot. Many of the doors to the adobe dwellings have been left ajar, the dark interiors gaping like toothless smiles. The deserted dirt yards bespeak the heat of the day, when everyone, it seems, has receded indoors to savour a siesta.

The road climbs out of the valley and becomes rutted with large boulders. They are advancing through a stream bed, the sun-baked vertical ridges bear out the torrential force of water that descends and then runs downwards during the rainy season. It's a rough, bumpy ride, and the speedometer needle barely rises above twenty kilometers per hour.

Richard points to flocks and solitary flights of black, broad-winged frigate birds. "Those frigates are also known as man-of-war birds."

"Why?"

Richard shrugs. "I don't know. Maybe because of their predatory instincts."

When not soaring above the mountain peaks, the frigates, like turkey vultures, are in the habit of perching themselves onto the crests of cordon cacti, their small sleek heads frozen in the moment, their roving eyes scan the surrounding landscape for any movement by prey.

Richard breaks the monotony by pointing every now and then to a snake slithering across their path or a jackrabbit jumping through the cacti forest.

A dwelling comes into view. Unlike the modest, adobe houses in the village of San Bartolo, it has a large wooden veranda.

"I think we should stop and tell the ranchers where we're headed."

"Okay." Sitting up, Elizabeth readies herself to spring into action.

A woman with a small child propped on her hip stands on the porch. Elizabeth alights from the jeep and points up the mountain. "We're headed for *La Concepcion.*"

"Keep to the right. Further on, the road has a fork in it. Continue travelling north." Pointing, she rocks her baby in a gentle, swaying motion. "The next ranch is located just past the fork."

Richard is stretched out across the front seats, his back wedged against the driver's door and his knees bent, forming an arch, over the console.

"That doesn't look very comfortable," Elizabeth waits for him to maneuver his body back around into the driver's seat, before opening the door.

"Just thought I'd try it, in case *Señor* Carcamo doesn't offer us a bed for the night." Grinning, Richard shifts into drive and affectionately rubs Elizabeth's arm.

The rocking of the vehicle makes Elizabeth feel sleepy and for the first time in days, her thoughts have slowed. She plays back in her mind's eye random images of the other team members at the orientation and of the serpentine roadway that plunges into arroyos before ascending again onto plateaus and skirting the flanks of the sierras.

"All these ranchers probably share the same water source." Richard turns his head and pauses to ensure that he has her attention. "Did you know that a hundred years ago ranchers like these inhabited Southern California? Now, it's one huge conglomerate of freeways, subdivisions and shopping malls and we're relegated to piping water from the Colorado River and from underground aquifers that are quickly running dry."

Elizabeth dodges Richard's angry diatribe about the ecological trials and tribulations of Southern California. "Yes, Dr. Guzman told me yesterday that the ranchers of the Baja high sierras operate like a cooperative." *Yesterday. Was it only yesterday that we were at the orientation?* She glances at Richard before picking up her cell phone to check whether the tiny light is flashing.

"Any messages?"

Elizabeth shakes her head.

"Did you call your parents?"

"Yes. I called them."

"How did they take the news?"

"I got shit, of course, for not calling them right away. It was like being back at home. My mother understood why I didn't call sooner. My father, Stanislaw, focused instead on the number of days since I'd heard about Patricia rather than on what's happening. A typical reaction of avoidance and denial from a concentration camp survivor."

"You sound pretty cynical about it."

"Some things never change. He's an old man. I didn't expect otherwise." Upon hanging up the phone, when the familiar pall of guilt had descended over her head, Elizabeth had reminded herself that no one can make anyone else feel lousy; that she was in charge of her own feelings. At the same time, though, she couldn't help but question the wisdom of all that psychological self-talk. Her father knew exactly what buttons to push to make her feel like shit. Narcissists are masters at that. They never feel whole, can never fill the black holes, the voids that their deep-rooted feelings of inadequacy have dredged up over unresolved survival guilt complexes.

A herd of longhorn cattle graze amongst the cacti. Their thick ribs protrude through their sagging blond hides. Elizabeth questions how tender the meat from their carcasses can be with such sparse vegetation available for grazing. Higher up, in the hills, they observe a lone figure with a herd of goats.

As though reading her mind, Richard says, "The ranchers, when herding their livestock on horseback, wear heavy protective leather clothing." Arriving at the fork in the road, he abruptly applies the brakes.

"To the right. We're supposed to continue to the right."

"Are you sure?"

"Yes. The woman back at the ranch told me about this crossing."

Just past the fork in the road a ramshackle structure with a wooden front porch comes into view. This time an entire family has gathered to await their arrival.

"I bet these people up here communicate with one another by way of VHF radio."

Elizabeth hops out of the jeep and hurries up to the porch, extending her hand in greeting to the man and wife, three teenage sons and one younger daughter. Nodding in response to Elizabeth pointing up at the mountain, the man of the household alerts her to two more ranches up the road, before *La Concepcion*.

"No more forks in the road?" Richard asks when she climbs back into the jeep.

"Not that they advised me of."

"Look up there." Richard gestures toward a black cross on the summit of a mountain that, in their ascent, has come into view behind the one that has served as their vantage point. "Do you see a bearded face protruding out of the peak?"

Elizabeth studies the contours of the rock face, accentuated by the late afternoon angular light. The power of suggestion persuades her that she can make out the high forehead, heavy eyebrows, nose, and bearded mouth of a male face. As at Tecolote Beach, Elizabeth guesses that this must have been a sacred place for the Aboriginals and later for the missionaries who subjugated them.

"Do you ever feel as though regardless of what you do or what you think is going to happen, that fate or destiny is propelling you along?" Elizabeth asks.

"For sure. I'm not a religious person in a traditional sense. I recall having gone to church once, maybe twice with my parents when I was young. But, yes, I believe that there's a reason for things happening the way they do. The big picture. I'm not just here to study the cave murals. This is my path in life. For now, anyway."

Perce Rock. That's what this mountain with its strange facial profile reminds her of. There, on the beach, Patricia, like Richard just now, had assured her that the military was her path in life, at least for the time being.

"But what if things go terribly wrong? Do you still believe that it's your path in life? Don't you question whether the path you've chosen is the right one?"

Richard throws her a look of bewilderment. Elizabeth's voice has taken on a whiny tone. "I think it boils down to whether you believe that *you* chose the path or whether the path chose you."

"Destiny. The big picture." She intentionally projects her voice so as not to sound so needy.

Nodding, Richard pumps the brakes a few times while veering the jeep over a particularly deep rut in the road. "Have you considered that maybe it's her path and not yours? She's the hostage. Not you."

"To be honest, no. It can take a long time before a parent lets go. You become so conditioned to assume responsibility for them, their every quirk and neurosis, that when they leave the nest and choose to do something like join the military against your wishes, you still feel responsible."

"Why do you think she joined up?"

"A lot of young women are joining the ranks. I think that maybe they have no faith in the future. It's a suicide mission, really. No Muslim is going to retreat in the face of a woman. On some level, these young women must know that."

Dropping into an arroyo, the embankment envelopes them in shade until they emerge onto the perimeters of the third ranch. Elizabeth once again leaves the jeep to search out the inhabitants.

"I'm beginning to feel like a sprinter, jumping in and out of this jeep" she says, returning to the jeep.

"That was fast. Was anybody there?"

"Yes, the ranch wife with flour up to her elbows. She must have been making tortillas when she heard our motor. You're probably right about the ranchers communicating with each other by way of VHF radio. She simply waved me on."

The road becomes steeper and skirts a dugout.

"Here's where they collect their water for the longhorns." No sooner has Richard spoken than the road abruptly veers to the left and ensconces them onto the fourth ranch. Two men and a woman stand watch on the veranda. Richard maneuvers within a stone's throw of the house, and points toward the mountain. The older male throws his arm in the air in a gesture that suggests they should carry on. Pulling a u-turn, Richard installs the jeep back onto the road.

"Want a beer?" he asks, reaching behind the seat for two cans. "They're still a little cold," he encourages, applying one of the cans against Elizabeth's cheek.

"Oh, why not."

"That'a girl. Finally relaxing." Popping open his beer, he

takes a couple of long swigs. "I have to hand it to that Guzman. Not a bad idea that we take a break before settling down to work."

"Can we stop? My bladder is screaming for relief."

"Good idea. We can't be far now."

With the sun's descent behind the mountains, a soothing dry chill permeates the air. Tramping out into the thick cacti brush, the reddish dusty soil forms a powdery cloud beneath Elizabeth's sneakers. Choosing a thorn-free spot to squat behind an oversized yucca, she detects the odour of cow dung, commingled with the natural earthy scent that's become pronounced in the late afternoon shadow. She's struck by the stillness, save for the monotonous buzzing of flies, which her presence has attracted.

La Concepcion ranch is preceded by a steep incline. Purple and contrasting orange bougainvillaea swathes the roof of the Carcamo family ranch house. The magenta suffused dusky sky seems to augment the blooms' resplendence. Goats and chickens scratch the sparsely vegetated soil for something to eat. Before they even have a chance to alight from the vehicle, a tall, broad-shouldered man in his fifties, two older women, and a teenage boy and girl descend the stone steps to greet them.

Each family member in succession, beginning with *el Señor*, brushes their right cheek lightly against Elizabeth's left cheek and then repeats the gesture on the opposite side of the face. They then ceremoniously queue up side by side, opposite Richard and Elizabeth.

El Señor raises his right hand towards his expansive chest. "Miguel José Carcamo." His introduction is followed by his placing of his arm on the shoulder of a small, slightly stooped woman with silver hair combed back into a bun. "*Señora* Carcamo," and then pointing toward the second woman on his right, "*Mi esposa*, Maria Dorothea."

"*Mucho gusto*," his wife replies, bowing her head deferentially.

Extending his hand further down the queue, he introduces his son, Antonio Roberto and daughter, Teresa Margarita.

"My house is your house," *el Señor* declares, raising his hands in a manner akin to that of a conductor giving his orchestra the cue to strike the first note.

Catching a flicker of emotion in *el Señor's* dark brown eyes, Elizabeth senses butterflies in her stomach. There is a certain intensity surrounding this declaration of hospitality that makes her feel simultaneously at home and ill at ease. Even Richard, who she's come to regard as somewhat of a social butterfly, is uncharacteristically quiet.

El Señor places his hand on Richard's back to guide him up the steps to the house. *La Señora* loops her arm in Elizabeth's and wraps her other arm around the waist of *abuela*, *el Señor's* mother. The top of the steps opens onto a large veranda with a chrome table, covered with a plastic red-and-white checked tablecloth, which, in anticipation of their arrival, has already been set with seven place settings.

"You probably want to wash your hands after your long journey," *el Señor* suggests. "Just follow Teresa into the kitchen."

Separated from the veranda dining area by a curtain, the kitchen is long and narrow, with an open window at the opposite end above the stove. Half a dozen different aromas permeate the steamy air. Teresa hands Elizabeth a bar of soap and points to a towel hanging from a rack beside the large enamel sink.

After washing up, Elizabeth and Richard seat themselves next to one another, across from the *Señor* and *abuela*. Teresa excuses herself and quickly returns to the veranda with two large glasses of water which she sets in front of Richard and Elizabeth. Retreating back into the kitchen, Teresa returns with her mother, bearing plates and bowls of steaming food. *La Señora* asks Richard and Elizabeth whether they would like coffee.

"*Si, gracias,*" Richard replies.

El Señor points to a large satellite dish, anchored into the sloped ground behind them, against the roof of the veranda. "We get twenty-one channels on our television. *Señora,*" he points his chin in Elizabeth's direction, "maybe you would like to watch a *novela*? This is the hour when Teresa and Mama like to follow the intriguing lives of, I don't know their names, but they know them by heart. All the beautiful characters brought to life on the screen."

Elizabeth's brain gets stuck on the word *novela,* and she blushes upon realizing that *el Señor* is referring to soap operas. Richard gives her a light kick under the table as he passes her the plate of tortillas. "No, *gracias*. We have *novelas* on television back in Canada too, but I'm afraid that I'm usually too busy to be able to indulge in the pleasure."

The tortillas' circumference practically covers the entire surface of her white enamel, chipped plate. "These tortillas, they are thinner and larger than what I've eaten in restaurants in La Paz."

"La Paz!" *el Señor* chides. "Nobody in La Paz knows how to make tortillas anymore. Soon the usual fare will be *carnes con papas!*"

Elizabeth feels her face becoming flushed again with the image of her fellow Canadians sitting down every evening to a plate of meat with potatoes. What would *el Señor* say about the increasing number of working folk subsisting on ready-made frozen microwaved dinners? She observes him spoon some of the meat dish onto a tortilla, followed by a hefty helping of salsa, before folding the contents over into a crepe-like form and taking a bite out of one end.

"We are totally self-sufficient here," he explains, between mouthfuls. "We grow our own corn. Grind it into corn flour for tortillas. Raise our own cattle, sheep, chickens and goats. We have a variety of fruit-bearing trees — avocado, tomato, mango, orange, lime and even banana. A vegetable garden.

We make our own butter, cheese, yogurt. The oranges are now ripe and there are two trees by the guesthouse. *Por favor*, help yourselves. What is mine is yours," he says, passing Elizabeth a bowl of meat in a thick, dark brown gravy.

La Señora interjects by advising that the dish being passed to her is calves' liver, and she places on the table, next to Elizabeth, a second bowl containing another meat, swimming in a paprika-coloured sauce. "This is *carne*," she says in a soft-spoken voice.

"Goat meat," Richard adds, noting the puzzled look on Elizabeth's face. "It's delicious. Try some."

Teresa passes around mugs of coffee.

"We don't grow the coffee beans." *El* Señor's interjection gives rise to a snicker from Antonio and Richard.

A faded reproduction of da Vinci's *Last Supper* bears down upon them from the ranch house exterior wall. A plastic bouquet of red roses, badly in need of a vigorous dusting, is mounted at a right angle to the *Last Supper*. No other ornaments or pictures grace the hospital-green walls of the veranda.

"What do you do for water?' asks Richard, helping himself to a second helping of tortilla, *carne*, and salsa.

"We have a well," answers *el* Señor, not waiting to swallow the food in his mouth. "We've also dug a reservoir. You might have seen it on the drive up?"

"*Si.*"

"It's used by all the ranchers living southwest of San Bartolo. For the cattle," *el Señor* adds, spooning two heaps of sugar into his coffee and giving it a vigorous stir. "God has been good to us. We've had good rains for many years."

Abuela's ears perk up, upon hearing the word, "God." Nodding her head solemnly, she shyly looks up from the tortilla and small heap of calves' liver on her plate.

"This ranch belonged to my father, and to his father before that. I have two other sons, besides Antonio," in whose direction *el Señor*, points with his spoon.

Seated at the end of the table beside Richard, Antonio is tall for his seventeen years, lean, with a finely chiseled face and olive complexion. Like his father, his eyes are large, framed by long eyelashes and the irises are nearly black. He has the full lips of his mother and appears to have inherited her gentler, more refined demeanor.

"My older sons have a ranch further west of here, where they live with their families. My father died two months ago, at the age of eighty-two."

Elizabeth and Richard shift their gaze away from *el Señor* and in *abuela's* direction. "I'm sorry," says Elizabeth.

"It was his time," *la Señora* interjects, releasing a sigh and taking a seat at the opposite end of the table, beside Elizabeth.

"Antonio, it's time to light the lamp," *el* Señor commands.

Standing, Antonio carefully lifts the oil-burning lamp from the middle of the table and removes its glass cover. Retrieving a box of wooden matches from the pocket of his jeans, he strikes one along the rough edge of the table and lights the wick. The shedding of light chases away the solemnity brought on by the subject of death and prompts Antonio to maneuver himself into the conversation. He turns to Richard and asks, "*Señor,* you are from the United States?"

"Yes. From San Diego."

Antonio's thick lips stretch out shyly before he quietly asks, "And is it possible for *los Mexicanos* to get work in Los Angeles?"

It's Elizabeth's turn to nudge Richard with her foot under the table. Richard looks at *el Señor* before answering. "Many Mexicans have settled in the United States, but, of course, the life is very different from here." Looking over at *el Señor* again, as though seeking his approval, he adds, "Los Angeles is very crowded and busy. Most people are trying to get out of there if they can."

"Why?" asks Antonio.

"Son," *el Señor* interjects, "life in Los Angeles for simple people, and particularly *por los Mexicanos*, is not like in the *novelas*. They must travel very far from their homes every morning to work in a factory or a restaurant. They never see the sun shine. Only when it is setting. And by the time they get home it is almost time to go to bed because they must wake up very early the next day for work."

Antonio shrinks into his chair and leans over his plate of food with downcast eyes.

Teresa hovers over the guests, obligingly leaning over to offer them the sugar bowl and a glass of milk, for the coffee.

"These *frijoles* are delicious," Richard says, passing the dark beans to Elizabeth.

Elizabeth's first choice would be to eat with a knife and fork but *el* Señor's outspokenness has made her reconsider. The red paprika drenched goat meat that she's stuffed into her tortilla is less greasy than she'd anticipated. Casting her eyes toward *la Señora*, Elizabeth signals her appreciation.

"*Tu gusta?*"

"*Si. Es muy rico.*"

"*Gracias*," *la Señora* smiles gratefully

"What about schooling for the children?" asks Richard.

Antonio looks up from his plate and eyes his father out of the corner of his eye.

"The road is very bad. Antonio and Teresa and my other two sons used to stay with Maria's sister in San Antonio during the week. I drove them there on Sunday afternoon and picked them up on Friday. It's not possible to drive everyday, of course. We still go to town every week to buy sugar, coffee, salt and other necessaries. Every rancher now has a four-wheel drive, but in the early days we used to make the journey on horseback."

"And for how many years did the children go to school?"

"For eight years," *la Señora* interjects. "But Antonio last year completed his tenth year. He is very bright. I would like Antonio to go to La Paz to complete his high school and then maybe to study at the university."

"He's still too young for university." *El Señor* reaches for the toothpick dispenser, shakes one out and then leans back in his chair to pick his teeth. "Besides, I need him here on the ranch."

"José," *la Señora*'s otherwise mild mannered tone of voice has taken on an edge of admonishment. "Antonio must think about his future. We don't want him running across the Rio Grande when he's twenty, like so many of the boys in San Bartolo and San Antonio."

And what about Teresa? Elizabeth guesses that she's just fifteen, and for the last year and a half has been relegated to the drudgery of domestic chores.

A lump erupts in Elizabeth's throat. If only she could go back a decade, when Patricia was still Teresa's age, safe at home, just starting high school, insulated from the ugliness of adult life.

Richard clears his throat. "*Señor,* as you probably expected, we're here to study the cave paintings and we were hoping that you could show them to us."

El Señor discards his toothpick onto his plate and leans over the table. "Of course. We get visitors here every now and then but it has been, what?" He addresses his question to Antonio but doesn't wait for an answer. "Almost two years now since we've been up to the cave. I'll have to take along my machete to clear the path."

"How long does it take to get there?" asks Elizabeth.

"About one hour. How did you hear about the cave?"

"We're here for four months with La Universidad de Baja California Sur, to study *las pinturas* in the Sierra de San Francisco, near San Ignacio. We're part of a larger group of anthropologists and archeologists from other universities." Richard explains. "Elizabeth is from Canada. From the University of Calgary. But the expedition isn't departing for another week. We were assigned *La Concepcion* as a supplementary research project."

El Señor's eyebrows rise in a look of disapproval as he catches his wife's gaze. Evidently it never dawned on their hosts that their guests might not be married.

Elizabeth pipes up, "Would it be all right, *Señor*, if we stayed the night and viewed the cave tomorrow morning?"

"It would be an honour to have you. We have a room with two beds. Teresa will show you your sleeping quarters."

El Señor rises from the table and everyone follows suit. Elizabeth begins collecting the soiled plates.

"No, please, leave those." *La Señora* takes the stack of plates from her hands. "You are our guests. Go with Teresa. You must be tired after travelling all the way from La Paz."

"*Bien*. Thank you for the dinner, *Señora*."

"*De nada*. Go they are waiting for you." She gestures with her chin toward Richard and Teresa. "Sleep well."

"We must get our bags from the vehicle," Richard explains to Teresa.

Following Richard down the steps, Elizabeth is struck by the pitch-darkness, punctuated by thousands of stars. She immediately recognizes the Big Dipper, the North Star, and the constellation of Orion. Whenever she's been away from home on a conference or symposium, leaving Patricia in Bernard's care, she's often drawn solace from the night sky and its propensity to bridge her sense of longing for her little girl. She'd console herself with the thought that regardless of where she was, Patricia might be looking out the window gazing at the same constellations, if not at that very moment, then in a few hours. This time, though, she can't take that for granted and Elizabeth feels a sharp ache in her heart. Spotting a falling star, she makes a wish.

6.

TERESA HESITATES after lighting the oil lamp, and furtively surveys the room, as though embarrassed over its rusticity. Casting her eyes downwards towards the dirt floor, she bids her guests *buenas noches*.

Hearing Teresa's footsteps recede across the tiled patio, Richard parts the window curtains and peers out into the blackness. *El Señor*'s silhouetted figure reveals itself through the window of an alcove in the main house, directly across from them. Fiddling with the cloth, Richard attempts to draw the two pieces of fabric together. Discovering that the curtains are smaller than the window, he shakes his head in exasperation, and turns away from the window. "Did you see the look on their faces when they realized we weren't married? I bet *el Señor*'s ears will be bent in our direction all night."

"Hey, give it a rest. *El Señor* might prick up his ears during the night, but what's the chance he's going to sneak up on us and look through that slit in the curtains?" Pulling her arms through the straps of her knapsack, Elizabeth throws it onto the twin bed, furthest from the door. "Those poor kids. Did you see how he cowed poor Antonio into submissiveness?"

"Mexican society is still very patriarchal. I was surprised Dorothea stood up to her husband."

She checks her cell phone for messages. No news is good news, she tells herself, before laying it down on the bedside table. Leaning over to unlace her running shoes, she throws her hand behind her back before laboriously straightening herself. "Whew. Now that the ordeal with the dinner is over I can feel the ache in my poor spine. I wouldn't want to make that trip through that boulder-ridden streambed every day."

"Want a massage? Been told that there's magic in these here hands." Extending his arms, Richard flexes his hands a couple of times for emphasis.

Her instincts tell her that the source of this rumour is the same woman who provoked his subdued smile at the beach. Despite her three-in-the-morning agitation over her colleagues' anticipated prattle about she and Richard arriving together at the orientation, she's naively suppressed the idea of any intimacy developing between them. She can't imagine having teamed up with any of the others. But then again, perhaps Bartek. He was the only one, apart from Richard, and probably Guzman, who noticed yesterday morning that she was battling some kind of demon. On second thought, no, she'd never be able to go there. She had run into the Krakowian at a number of symposiums, just after the Wall came down. He'd always seemed edgy, but she'd ascribed his moody demeanor to the typical central European angst — the tendency to process even the most mundane, everyday occurrences, darkly and tragically.

"What I could really use is a shower. I feel like every pore of my body is suffused with desert dust."

"There's your shower," Richard chides, pointing to the enamel wash basin on the wooden table on the opposite wall of the small adobe hut. Save for the blue and red flower print curtains with an eyelet trim hung over the window, the guesthouse is starkly primitive.

"Where are we headed after this?"

"The capes. San José."

"A hotel with all the amenities?"

Richard nods.

"I think I'll hold off, then, on showering until tomorrow."

"My offer of a massage is still open."

Richard's mischievous smile provokes her to laugh. "Are you always so persistent?"

"Only when a lady is in distress."

Elizabeth rummages through her knapsack and retrieves a book. "Mind if I read?"

"No, go ahead. Could use a bit of a lie down myself."

A page and a half later, Elizabeth's concentration is severed by a nasal "hrumph" sound. Laying her book down, she leans across the narrow space between the beds to gently shake her roommate's shoulder, but Richard is so firmly anchored onto his back that her nudge only provokes an even louder snore.

Maybe if I sit on the edge of his bed, he'll turn over on his side, she thinks.

Richard's half-open mouth emits another "hrumph." So much for this Casanova's concerns about *el Señor* eavesdropping on them. Suddenly, a groggy Richard lifts his head and wraps his arms around her waist. "Was I snoring?" he asks in a sleepy voice.

"Sorry. I didn't mean to wake you." She tries to get up but he tightens his hold on her. Twisting her waist to free herself, she affirmatively adds, "Yes, you were snoring."

Sitting up, he throws her an unmistakably ardent look. "I should get out of these clothes and under the covers. You too." His last words are spoken imploringly.

"I'm not sure how to turn off this lantern."

Placing his hand on her shoulder for her to stand aside, Richard turns the knob that cuts off the oil. They watch the light slowly die. A tiny blue flicker engulfs the wick before it's extinguished, exhaling its final sizzle.

The darkness makes Elizabeth acutely aware of her own pulse. Her senses of sight, sound and touch are heightened. She can hear Richard breathing, the rustle of his advance.

Taking her in his arms, he cradles her head against his shoulder. She feels his heart pulsing against her chest. He kisses her, gently at first, little pecks on the mouth before exerting more pressure, pushing his tongue inside her mouth, enveloping her lips.

His hands begin to wander down to the waistband of her jeans. Pulling out her blouse, he runs his hands up her back, underneath her bra strap.

"Let's get out of these clothes," he whispers, then peels off his own shirt, and drops it onto the floor. Taking her hands, he guides her arms upwards and slips her blouse over her head. Her nostrils fill with the scent of his musky sweat. Her eyes having adjusted to the darkness, she watches him reach for her belt buckle. His fingers search for her zipper. As he pulls down, she feels herself throbbing, her desire escalating up her spine, travelling up her neck.

He guides her fingers to his own zipper. She releases him and feels the bulge through his shorts. Kneeling, he slips her jeans downwards, nuzzles his face in the fork between her legs, pushes his nose inside the crotch of her panties, inserts his finger, licks it, inserts it again, rises, and traces her lips with his finger. Taking her in his arms, he engulfs her mouth with his own, struggles with the clasp on her bra strap.

"Here, let me help you."

His body emits a tremor. Clasping the straps of her bra, he deftly draws the undergarment through her arms and flings it onto the floor. Taking her hand, Richard leads her to the bed and gently pushes down on her rib cage. Pulling back the crotch of her panties, he inserts his finger again. As she becomes dilated, he inserts a second finger, accelerates his strokes, adds his thumb. "Ooh, you're deliciously wet," he croons.

"Don't stop!"

"Sh." Placing two fingers against her lips, he emits another "sh" before prodding her to open her mouth, urging her to lick them, to savour her own secretions.

His hands are on the move again, caressing her stomach, fondling the curves of her body. He slips his fingers beneath the waistband of her panties and pulls them down. Hovering over her, she can feel him rub himself against her hip bone. Moving downwards towards her feet, like a cat, he runs his tongue up her legs, kneels over top of her, lifts her buttocks, cups them in his hand — like a bowl, tipped, readied to be emptied.

Closing her eyes, she spreads her legs. He plunges his tongue inside, runs his rough, unshaven cheeks along her inner thighs, returns with his tongue, sucks and licks, probes her with his two fingers, and carries her to a writhing, sweating pinnacle of pleasure.

He lays his head momentarily on her thigh, before sidling up to her side, reaches for her hand, guides it to his penis. She runs her hand back and forth, slides the foreskin up and down, imagines it inside her, impatient for it to fill her up. Shifting her position on the bed, she opens her legs.

"Not yet." He takes his cock in his hand, holds it as though he were riding a horse, rubs its tip against her nipple, strokes the other nipple before straddling her. Pushing her breasts together, he maneuvers himself back and forth within the flesh of her cleavage.

Raising her head, she sticks out her tongue and catches the tip on his forward thrust. Their eyes lock and she sees him smiling, nodding to spur her on. She pushes his hand away, takes his cock in her mouth. She sucks greedily, gives him a little bit of teeth. She hears him groan, senses his pelvic muscles contract, holding himself back before he finally pulls back and plunges deeply inside her.

Elizabeth feels like her head is going to explode. She has the impulse to scream but holds herself back. Tremors cascade down her torso. Spewing out secretions, all her pent up tension, she descends with him into a chasm of bliss.

7.

THE CROW OF ROOSTERS severs her from sleep. Elizabeth conjures an image of an orchestra of roosters — the eldest of the flock conducting the others to emit a succession of crows, spurring them on to outdo one another in shrillness and range. Turning onto her back, she looks over at the other bed. Richard is curled up on his side, in the fetal position, facing away from her. He must have returned to his own bed after she'd fallen asleep. Her limbs still resonate with the rush of last night's adrenalin. Relishing the chafe on her inner thighs, the lingering sensation of his thrusts, she breaks into a smile, thinks back to how he'd dared her to let herself go; but at the same time, she shakes her head to stop herself from gloating too much. *Perhaps my vulnerability brought out the animal in him.* As her vulnerability comes to mind, a wave of guilt washes over her. Her vulnerability, after all, is at her daughter's expense.

A light knock on the door provokes a *"Buenas dias!"* from the other bed. Rolling onto his stomach, Richard props his chin onto his pillow, appearing to stare at the wall.

"How'd you sleep?"

"Well, good morning, Miss Sexy." Turning to face her, he grins before puckering his lips, throwing her an imaginary kiss.

His words and gestures are like a tonic. She feels her pelvis contracting. Sitting up, she grabs her pillow, hurls it at him.

"What the fuck? What was that for?"

"You know," she points her chin in his direction, shoots him a look of admonishment. "You want me to become addicted to you?"

"Yeah! Let's get addicted to one another." Sitting up, he leans over to grab his shirt and pulls it over his head, before stretching his body across the bed to search the floor for his under shorts.

Elizabeth follows Richard's mannerisms with her eyes. She decides that she likes the earnestness with which he dresses and she senses that he appreciates that her comment about getting addicted to him wasn't made in jest at all, but was intended to distance herself from him after last night's lovemaking "What's going to happen when we get back to La Paz and have to team up with the others on the project?"

"Then the real fun will begin. No better sex than illicit sex." Turning around and seeing Elizabeth still sitting in bed with the bedcovers tucked under her arms, he says, "You'd better get a move on. We want to make it to San José before dark. And besides, the cave paintings are beckoning." He crosses the room and leans over to kiss her before picking up the wash basin and throwing a towel over his shoulder. "I'll bring you back some water." Tucking the basin beneath his arm, he opens the door, turns, and winks at her before shutting it behind him.

Dressing, Elizabeth catches a streak of light penetrating the cleft between the curtains. Footsteps resound on the other side of the door. Recognizing the click of Teresa's heels on the tiled veranda, Elizabeth hastily throws back the bedcovers. There, right smack in the middle of the fitted sheet is the ubiquitous stain, the evidence that she's leaving for Teresa to eradicate, wash away. She decides to make the beds, with the hope that Teresa won't strip the sheets until later, after they're gone. Pulling the sheet tight, Elizabeth conjures up the image of Richard hovering over her, how their eyes had locked before he'd entered her. Her body gives off an involuntary shiver; she smiles to herself.

Just as Elizabeth is tucking the last fold into the mattress, she hears a clunk on the bottom of the door. She hurries to open it for Richard. His characteristic stride has been supplanted by shorter, springier steps to prevent any spillage of water from the basin. Setting it down on the little wooden table, he bows magnanimously and says, "There you go, ma'am."

"Hey, thanks."

"No problemo. I'm going to go out and join *el Señor* on the veranda."

"Did you wash?"

"Yes. Antonio helped me with the hand pump. See you in a bit."

She retrieves her make-up case from her knapsack and sets it on the corner of the table. Leaning over the washbasin, she cups water into her hands and splashes it onto her face. Its cold freshness triggers a tingling up and down her spine. Unbuttoning her blouse, she dips the corner of her towel into the water, rubs some soap into it and applies it to her underarms. Washing the soap out of the towel, she rinses herself before applying deodorant. Rummaging for her hand mirror, she sits down on the bed to inspect her face a piece at a time, looks for the lines that, over the past few days, have etched themselves beneath her eyes, and for the encompassing shadows that have given her a haunted appearance. But the furrows have softened, the dark circles have almost disappeared. Her lips appear fuller, more sensual; they seem to convey more colour than normal.

Her thoughts go back to Richard struggling, last night, with the curtains, after spotting *el Señor*'s silhouetted profile through the window. No doubt the Mexican will notice something different about her. Why do women always feel so exposed? Men don't radiate like women do. *Is it because of our ability to get pregnant, give birth, nourish another human being with our own bodies?*

There he is, rocking back and forth in one of the wrought

iron rocking chairs, his mother seated beside him, while Teresa and Dorothea scurry to and from the kitchen with plates, cutlery, cups, and steaming platters of tortillas, scrambled eggs and bacon.

"*Buenas dias, Señora*. How did you sleep?" Rising, *el Señor* gestures towards the rocking chair across from them.

Elizabeth resists the urge to avert her eyes. That would only confirm his belief that his display of disapproval yesterday, over dinner, regarding his guests' ill-defined relationship had not been misplaced.

"*Muy bien, gracias*. The air here is so fresh. And it's so quiet, except for the roosters, of course."

"Oh yes, our roosters. But thanks to our roosters you will savour our fresh eggs this morning for *desayunos*.

"I smell bacon. Do you butcher your own livestock?"

"*Si.*"

"Come, let's sit down," says Dorothea, wiping her hands on her apron.

Richard and Antonio enter the dining area just as Elizabeth, *el Señor* and *abuela* take their places at the table.

Teresa circumnavigates the table with a large kettle of hot water. Following *el Señor*'s example, Elizabeth spoons instant coffee into her mug when she notices a quizzical expression erupt on Teresa's face. "What's that strange noise?" she asks.

Elizabeth excuses herself from the table and dashes across the patio to the guesthouse. Hastily flipping open the cover of her cell phone, she pushes the talk button and gasps out, "Hello?"

"Hi, Liz?" Bernard's voice brings her back to the modern woes of the twenty-first century, to his office on the eighteenth floor of a building in Calgary's downtown maze of skyscrapers. "I have some good news."

Elizabeth sucks in her breath and sits down on the bed.

"With the aid of satellite recognizance, they think they've located the hostages and their kidnappers."

"Are they still in Afghanistan? When did you learn this?"

"They wouldn't reveal the location. But I assume it's in Afghanistan. Just now, I got a call from Ottawa. They're not positive, so we shouldn't get our hopes up. It's not unusual for insurgents to move around, to stay ahead of NATO forces."

"But the good news is that the Canadian authorities are keeping us informed," Elizabeth says, toning down the anxiety she feels must be noticeable in her voice.

"That's right. How are you?"

Oh, God, what a question. On account of Bernard's call, though, somehow, she feels less guilty, less vulnerable. "I'm fine. And you?"

"You know me. Work is my panacea. What's that beep?"

"Probably my cell. Can you hear me?"

Bernard's voice fades in and out.

"I'll call you tomorrow." Her "tomorrow" echoes back into her ear. Static overcomes the line. She pulls the phone away from her ear and pushes the end button.

By the time she gets back to the table, the others have finished. Richard is the only one still seated at the table.

"I'm going to throw a water bottle into my knapsack. *El Señor* wants to get going right away. Do you need anything out of the room?"

Elizabeth shakes her head, moves her eggs and frijoles with her fork around on her plate before reaching for a tortilla. She watches him retreat from the veranda and thinks back to her conversation with Bernard and his "news" about satellite recognizance having possibly detected the whereabouts of the kidnappers and hostages. Looking up from her plate, she glances at the *Last Supper,* zeroes in on Jesus in the centre. Her parents, devout Catholics, had raised her to pray in times of crisis or when suffering from anxiety, as before an exam. Her studies and scientific training had culminated in her becoming a doubting Thomas. She scans the painting, wonders which of the disciples is the apostle Thomas.

"Ready?" Richard leans against the jamb of the veranda doorway.

"Yes. We shouldn't keep *el Señor* waiting any longer. I'm sure he has tons of work to do around here." Elizabeth takes her plate into the kitchen. She sees that the rest of the breakfast dishes are soaking in soapy water in the sink, slides her plate in with the rest and quickly immerses her hands to wash them.

Picking up her knapsack from beneath the table, she follows Richard down the steps and past their parked jeep to a penned enclosure of goats where *el Señor,* together with Antonio, is reinforcing a fence post into the ground.

"*Listo?*" *el Señor* asks.

"*Si. Disculpe me,*" Elizabeth apologizes. "I had a telephone call from family."

El Señor nods at her before turning to Antonio and giving him instructions on completing the task of fence mending. He then addresses Richard and Elizabeth with "*vamonos,*" and for emphasis gestures with his chin that they should follow him.

"Was that Bernard on the phone?" Richard asks.

Even though the inclining path is still wide enough to allow them to walk side by side, Elizabeth stops. *El Señor* is ahead of them, cutting a swath with his machete, clearing the trail of overgrown cacti, but she feels compelled to distance herself even further from him. Overcome by a feeling of despondency, she doesn't want to expose her vulnerability to *el Señor*. "Yeah. I have to recharge the battery tonight. The phone died just as I was asking him how he was. Thank God for Teresa. She has the hearing of a canine."

Richard slows his pace but projects his voice, and gestures with his hand for her to catch up. "Well? What did he have to say?"

Elizabeth resumes her steady tread up the mountain but stops again to look back and survey the valley within which the Carcamo ranch is nestled. "With the aid of satellite recognizance, the NATO forces think they've located the hostages and their kidnappers. They're not sure, but at least they haven't forgotten about her." Elizabeth's voice falters. She's overcome by light-headedness, quickly scans her surroundings, spots a boulder off the trail, and cumbersomely makes her way to it.

"I'll run up and tell *el Señor* that we'll be along in a moment."

She's still alive. There's still hope. For the past few days she's felt so guilty. She's been afraid to appreciate this place, Richard, the Carcamo family's hospitality. She's harboured this strange idea that she must tread carefully, not expect anything; that a higher power, like a satellite suspended into space and programmed to decipher every living thing's breath and movement, is scrutinizing her every thought, judging her, determining whether the final, determinative calamity — death — is warranted, whether she is worthy of having her daughter's life spared.

She eyes a couple of frigates, wings extended, harnessing the ascendancy of an updraft of air. Their black-feathered bodies shimmer in the sunlight. With heads thrust forward, they appear to have abandoned all vestiges of predatory instinct; to have embraced, with wild abandonment, trust, unity with the elements. A lump forms in her throat. She feels like screaming at the top of her lungs, letting loose her grief, like the women in black head coverings that she's seen on newscasts from the Middle East, openly emoting over the loss of a loved one.

She catches the sound of Richard's clothing grazing the prickly vegetation on his retreat, back down the pathway. Heaving a deep breath, she salutes the frigates with a nod of her head, straightens her shoulders and falls in line behind him. The path steepens and becomes rockier. She notices that *el Señor* has tucked his machete into a leather holder attached to his belt.

"Are your shoes, *Señor*, made in Baja California?" asks Richard. His tone seems contrived, as though intent upon diverting Elizabeth's thoughts away from the macabre, to settle them on the more mundane.

"*Si,*" *el Señor* nods, obligingly stops, and balances himself on one foot, like a flamingo. He raises his other foot to expose the heavy, corrugated rubber sole. "These are *teguas* — the official *zapatos* for us *vaqueros. Mira.*" He grasps his machete and points the end towards the thick, rough leather. "These thick pieces of cowhide are stitched together and onto pieces of old tires. The skin is so thick that cacti thorns cannot penetrate into the foot."

Elizabeth also resorts to assuming a flamingo stance in order to remove a piece of cactus that has become embedded in the sole of her hiking boot. Richard offers her his shoulder, while *el Señor* removes the cactus with his gloved hand.

"Is it possible to have some *teguas* made?" asks Richard.

"My wife makes them for myself and my sons. So far their wives haven't taken up the craft but they will have to soon because Dorothea's eyesight is failing. I could ask whether one of the other ranch wives would be willing to make you a pair. But will you be back this way after today?"

"No. We won't be back. I thought maybe in La Paz I could order a pair."

El Señor shakes his head, looks up at the sun, presumably to check the time, and resumes his ascent up the path. "We're not far now," he declares between laboured breaths of air.

The trail bends, develops into a switchback. Vegetation becomes sparse. A solitary ocotillo bush appears to be growing right out of a boulder. The path abruptly ends and obscured behind the foliage, a rock face, adorned with faded colours of red, black, and white paint, comes into view. *El Señor* stops, points at the cave and seats himself on the boulder, in the shade of the ocotillo.

"Elizabeth can you get my camera from the bottom pouch on my pack?" Richard asks, turning around to accommodate her retrieval of his camera. Handing it to him, she approaches the crag and methodically surveys its flanks.

A solitary human figure is surrounded by geometric figures

— chevrons — a deer and a turkey vulture painted entirely black, its wings crudely depicted by two horizontal lines, with shorter vertical lines extending downwards. The human figure is painted a bluish-gray colour, along a prominent rock fissure. The head is disproportionably larger than its body. Elizabeth is transported back to the classroom, and in her mind she summons up her lecture on the traveller or shaman, traversing the axis mundi, or axis of the world, beyond temporal consciousness to the outer and under worlds. By positioning the human figure along a crack, the painters intended to convey that the shaman communes with animal spirits, represented by the deer, painted entirely red, also along a fissure. "V" shapes, chevrons, believed to depict female vulvas, some red, others black, figure prominently throughout the mural. Women, by virtue of their childbearing capacity, were believed to have special powers not possessed by males. The symbolic depiction of vulvas endowed the traveller with supernatural capabilities, solidified his shamanic status.

Elizabeth ventures inside the cave. The temperature inside the cavern is palpably lower than outside. She runs her fingers along the ceiling and the wall of the grotto, adjacent to the opening. The texture is smooth. Carbon from a fire appears to have coagulated with animal fat and accumulated on the ceiling. She has the impulse to begin digging with her hands in the soft soil underfoot in search of artifacts — homemade utensils, bones from animals, remnants of clothing or skins used as blankets. Lighting her flashlight, she sweeps its beam back and forth across the ground, checking for any past disturbances. They don't have the time to conduct a proper dig. Better to leave it undisturbed. The beam of her flashlight reveals the spot where fires were ignited. Remnants of charcoal have darkened the ground. She retrieves a plastic bag and her pocket-knife, scrapes some of the carbon off the ceiling and seals it, ensuring that no air is trapped inside.

She pulls her sunglasses from her head back onto her nose

to counteract the harshness of daylight that she encounters upon exiting the cave. Nonetheless, a wave of nausea hits her, and propels her thoughts back to when she exited the *banos* of the *palapa* restaurant at Tecolote Beach. Snapping the top of her water bottle, Elizabeth takes a long drink and breathes in deeply.

"How do you suppose they painted so high up?" Richard asks, wiping his brow with his shirt sleeve.

"They must have built platforms out of some kind of building materials."

"Boulders. Hemp, maybe. Didn't see any hemp plants on our way here, but maybe vegetation was less sparse back then."

"I took some scrapings of the carbon deposits on the interior cave ceiling. We can send it off for carbon analysis to have it dated."

"Right on. Anything else interesting inside?" Richard asks.

"I didn't think that I should go digging around in there too much. The most obvious sign of the cave's habitation are charcoal remains in the fire pit."

"How deep is the cave?"

"I didn't venture too far inside. Do you want to join me?"

"We'd better let *Señor* know that we're going to be a little while here."

While Richard retreats back to the ocotillo bush and the boulder, Elizabeth examines the human figure on the cave exterior more closely. The rock upon which it is painted is superimposed upon rougher more porous stone, and is smoother, less susceptible to erosion by the natural elements. The most prominent rock fissure extends into a shape resembling an arrowhead.

"Interesting that the human figure is the only form facing directly east," says Richard. "While the deer faces north, and the vulture northwest."

"So you think that the direction that the figures are facing is significant?"

Richard nods. "Obviously east signifies the rising sun, new life, birth. But I was also thinking the painters might have considered the effect direct sunlight would have on the paint. Vulture's the most faded. Human figure the least. The deer's ears and antlers are more distinct than the rest of its body, but that could be intentional. In *Cueva Flecha*, human figures are wearing deer antler headdresses. They might have applied a second coat of paint for those parts of the body."

Retrieving his flashlight out of his knapsack, Richard suggests that they move inside the cave. Sweeping the ray of his light along the interior walls, he grabs hold of Elizabeth's hand and pulls her into the narrowing cavity. "Do you hear that?"

"What?"

"Water running."

Faintly, but unmistakably, she hears the trickle of water. Forced to lower their heads as the cavity's dimensions close in on them, Elizabeth feels her quadriceps contract as the cave floor develops a slight incline. The sound of water grows in intensity, resounding into an echo. She detects a muddy scent infused with a metallic odour. The flashlight beam illuminates the cavity narrowing into a hole, barely wide enough for a human body. "Are you ready to crawl on your belly?" Richard's last word, "belly," resonates against the walls.

Elizabeth has done her fair share of spelunking but isn't prepared for this. It's not inconceivable that the water source lies outside the cave, that this narrow cavity extends to a declivity. Without proper rock climbing equipment one could find oneself stranded on a rock precipice.

"Maybe you should go ahead and if something happens, at least I can get help," Elizabeth suggests.

Detaching the straps from his flashlight, he attaches it onto his head. "Doubt I can get through with my knapsack." He pulls it off his back and hands it to her. "This is amazing! A shelter like this with a natural spring would have been an oasis during the drier winter months. Hang on, give me my water bottle. I'd like to take a sample from the spring and have it analyzed."

"I'll continue to direct my flashlight toward you so that you have more light."

It's a tight squeeze but Richard manages to push himself through the cavity. After emitting a few more grunts, his feet disappear and Elizabeth's beam illuminates nothing but a void.

8.

"WHAT LUCK that the tide is pulling back."

"Don't walk so fast!" Having inherited her father's shorter stature, Patricia is forced to take two steps to keep up with her mother's every other stride.

"I'm a prairie chicken. I don't feel safe walking on this sea bed. Who knows how long before the waves come roaring back."

The ridged gray sand feels soothingly cool on the soles of Elizabeth's feet. The ache that had developed in her left knee from constantly applying the clutch to negotiate the craggy coastline to the small town of Percé is beginning to dissipate. A hollow, rushing sound resonates from the withdrawing tide, conjuring up an image of water cascading down a mountain stream.

The receding tide allows Elizabeth and Patricia to walk right up to Percé Rock and the hole that eons of churning sea water have carved out at its base. Watching Patricia tilt her head backwards towards the concave ceiling of the eroded arch, Elizabeth can't but help shake her head in dismay. Perhaps it's the sacred beauty of places like this that accounts for her daughter's decision to embrace a military career. Over the past few days, since they'd moved on from the bustling ambience of Vieux-Montréal, and headed north, along the south shore of the St. Lawrence, she'd begun to appreciate why her daughter was drawn to strife-ridden regions of the world. Fraught with political turmoil, the developing world is, nonetheless and probably as a consequence, flush with some of the last remaining untamed frontiers on earth.

Recalling her own feelings of invincibility at Patricia's age, the pervasive assuagement, in the early 1970s, of reckless impulses through drug experimentation, Elizabeth has to admit to herself that there is some truth to Patricia's accusation that she has a tendency to bury her head in the sand. Back then, her generation was tuning out, whereas now it's become cool to tune in.

"It was the French explorer, Jacques Cartier who named this place "Percé" — in honour of this pierced rock," Elizabeth says, turning toward her daughter.

"I know that. We studied the explorers in Social Studies."

"But you likely didn't learn that for the Mic Mac Indians, who inhabited this region for over 2,000 years before that, this northeastern point of the Gaspé Peninsula represented the edge of the world. In the Mic Mac language, the word "gaspe" means "land's end.""

Patricia nods, but doesn't say anything in response. She is distancing herself from Elizabeth, preparing herself for their separation. Elizabeth feels a pang of regret over having to relinquish her role as her daughter's teacher, mentor, and guide.

"Have you thought about how the military has its own culture, different from civilian life?"

Patricia stops, looks back towards the Rock. "I thought we agreed not to talk about this anymore."

"Let's keep walking. I don't want to spoil our day." Elizabeth gestures with her hand toward the shoreline and slows her pace. Inhaling deeply, she relishes the sharpness of the salt-infused sea air. Oxygen. Brain food. She knows she should let it go but she can't. "I respect your decision. I know I can't change your mind."

The gentleness of her tone causes Patricia to nod her head, but mother and daughter refrain from making eye contact with one another. Elizabeth has a habit of instigating a discussion, particularly one that could become heated, by saying the opposite of what she really intends to say.

"But as your mother I think I should bring to your attention that if you ever decide to leave the military, you might find it difficult to find your place again amongst civilians."

"Mother, if dad left the practice of law, or you quit being a prof, you'd have a tough time fitting in someplace else too."

"But military life is more regimented than civilian life, even the practice of law. You know how disciplined your father is, getting up at the same time every day, pulling into his downtown parking stall at exactly 8:30 every morning. But in the military, they train you to take orders, no questions asked, to cultivate an allegiance to other soldiers far above any duty that a lawyer is conditioned to owe other members of their profession. A lawyer's first duty is to the client, but legal professional ethics at least recognize that lawyers also owe a duty to themselves. I'm not sure that the military honours that."

"And that has to be a good thing, particularly on the battle-field. If a fellow soldier is hit, I have to take him out of harm's way. That's part of the military code of ethics."

Elizabeth visualizes Patricia in military gear, prone on the ground, an automatic weapon propped against sandbags, on the crest of a hill overlooking a desolate desert landscape, another soldier lying on his stomach beside her. "I'm just concerned about the military attitude that it's us against them; them being the rest of society. You have no idea how the American public treated Vietnam veterans when they returned home. They were vilified for serving their country. Since *Dziadzio's* freedom-fighting days things have changed. People have become very cynical about war and the military. Veterans are no longer treated like heroes. They're treated like losers."

"So you think I'm a loser! You're calling me a loser!"

"No!" Elizabeth reaches for Patricia's shoulder but she pulls away, shakes her head, and bolts toward the shore.

The sight of Elizabeth pursuing Patricia catches the attention of people on the beach promenade. *Why does she have to make a scene? I don't want my daughter to be a loser. That's not what I meant.*

"Sorry, Patricia." Elizabeth is out of breath.

"People don't like lawyers, or politicians or even university professors either." Patricia's hands are tightly clenched, seemingly readied to strike out if Elizabeth makes a move to approach her. "Everybody these days is being criticized, not just the military. How many times, Mama, have people said that you're in an ivory tower, isolated from the real world of business and free enterprise?"

People, meaning your father. Elizabeth has the urge to counter that he'd leveled that blow in the heat of an argument but tries a different tact instead. "True enough, but I still have to make decisions and, on an everyday basis, chart my own path. No one dictates how I teach or what I research and submit for publication. In the army they tell you what to do, how, and when."

She stops herself from adding that people join the army because it's the easy way out. They don't have to make any decisions about their life. Decisions are made for them. She doesn't want to remind Patricia how her grandmother would complain that *Dziadzio* couldn't make a decision if his life depended on it. Patricia likely had tuned out when they argued, retreated into the family room to watch television.

"Sometimes those decisions are bad ones and you have to obey, even it kills you," Elizabeth adds, a lump growing in her throat. She hadn't intended on causing Patricia so much distress. Bernard had always railed about her never letting anything drop.

Back on shore, they fall in line with the less adventurous tourists who've dismissed the auspiciousness of the low tide, in favour of observing Percé Rock from a distance.

If not for the pasty white droppings of hundreds of shrieking gulls and gannets, circumnavigating over its scraggy summit, Percé Rock, now shrouded in mist, could be mistaken for a gigantic sea monster. A sudden gust of acrid sea breeze seems to emanate from the mouth of the monster landmark and wafts over the town, which they have just reached.

Elizabeth and Patricia stroll quietly behind a motley cluster of painters standing or sitting on collapsible chairs in front of their easels. Each work in progress conveys a different interpretation of the outcrop. Patricia strikes up a conversation in French with a twenty-something painter from Montréal, whose rendition of the Rock is more abstract, depicting the monster-like impression that Elizabeth has just imagined.

"What time of year is it that you can see the sun set through the hole?" Patricia asks the young painter.

"*Je ne sais pas*. How do you know about it?"

"I saw a photograph of it in a brochure that we picked up at our hotel."

"I would like to paint that."

As suddenly as she'd stopped to chat with the artist, Patricia moves on, picks up the thread of their earlier conversation. "No one does anything for life anymore, mother."

The harsh tone with which Patricia enunciates the word, "mother" causes Elizabeth to cringe. Who was it anyway that said that motherhood was sacred? They must have been a delusional optimist because, depending on the context in which it's used, "mother" has so many contradictory connotations.

"People change careers every ten years. That's why the military is so aggressively recruiting. People retire early or become entrepreneurs ... or artists. You worry too much, Mama. I just know that this is the right thing for me to do at the moment."

Elizabeth can tell from how her daughter's nose crinkles up, that behind the dark lenses of her aviator sunglasses, Patricia is squinting her eyes.

"And yes, I'll gladly even go to Afghanistan if they send me there. I'm not afraid. Oh, look, Mama, there's a huge cloud building behind Percé Rock. We'd better check into our hotel. A storm is coming."

9.

A T LAND'S END, the powerful Pacific Ocean clashes with the much tamer Sea of Cortez. The tidal force of the two colliding bodies of water foments an ear-deafening din, and, over eons of time, has sculpted the cluster of sea-locked rock faces into the image of hooded monks. Known as "The Arch" — on account of one of the outcrops bearing a hole — Elizabeth had found it intriguing when reading about Baja's Land's End that the rock clusters are also collectively referred to as "The Friars." From the vantage point of a wrought iron table at "The Office" — a two-story *palapa* restaurant, strategically ensconced on the beach, across from The Arch — she watches flocks of marine birds, predominantly gulls, converge on the outcrops. By raising her hand over her brow to create a visor, Elizabeth can make out the splotches of bird droppings that have amassed over the rocks. She chuckles to herself over The Friars' hooded cassocks being so sullied by guano. Perhaps the missionaries who'd accompanied the Spanish conquistadores should have thought twice about renaming Land's End as "The Friars."

To the west of The Friars, where the water is more Pacific green than turquoise, Richard emerges with long, protracted strides. He hesitates and appears to struggle in gaining a foothold every time a wave thrusts him forward against the shore. It's late afternoon and from the beach, his glistening body has become eclipsed into a silhouette. Richard had warned her about the undertow at Cabo san Lucas being much stronger than at the beaches on the Gulf side, near San José. Elizabeth regards him as he ambles from the water's edge to their table. After his swim, the muscles in Richard's arms and legs seem to have swelled, evoking flashbacks of the gentle firmness with which he'd cradled her in his arms, before laying her down onto the bed. Thinking back to last night, in their hotel room, when she'd suddenly become seized by pangs of self-consciousness over having lost her trim figure, she inwardly smiles over Richard's response to her unburdening of herself. "Elizabeth, I'm making love to your person, your intellect and spirit." And then he'd added assuredly, "I'm not interested in twenty-year-olds." She picks up his towel from his chair and hands it to him. "How was the swim?"

"Great!" Richard grins. "You should have come in for another dip. Water's always warmer near dusk."

"The place is beginning to thin out."

Looking westward toward the descending sun, Richard suppresses a smile, before remarking, "Perfect timing. We'll race the sun to our hotel."

Picking up on Elizabeth's quizzical glance he explains that he likes to leave the beach just before sunset. "To test my timing. Get back to the hotel before the last rays of sun sink into the ocean. The sunset really starts after that, you know."

"I bet you've done that before."

"Yeah, I have."

Elizabeth notices his Adam's apple flounce. She has the urge to ask with whom, to finally uncover the identity of the mystery woman who she presumes is accountable for his confounding, repressed smile. *On second thought, though, I'd better not*, she thinks. The last time she confronted someone on a beach — Patricia — she'd had to run after her to apologize for having defied the rule that she not bring up her military career while on vacation.

On their drive east, along the winding coastline of the capes towards San José del Cabo, Richard looks up every few minutes, and throws a glance though the rear view mirror.

"Are we winning?" From the side view mirror, Elizabeth can still make out The Friars. She's captivated by what she can only describe as an optical illusion. The highway's higher elevation in relation to the beach gives the impression that the submerged rocky outcrops are level with the roadway. She wonders whether, like at Percé, it's possible from a certain angle, at a particular time of year, to catch the sun set through The Arch.

"Can still make out the flaming top rim of the sphere. But I think I might have lost my touch. Crazy, I know. The idea's to savour every second of beauty."

Between Cabo San Lucas and the tourist zone of San José del Cabo, the beach is a series of coves, separated by the same gray-coloured outcrops as The Friars, but with much smaller proportions. Just a handful of straggling beachcombers remain on the seashore. In the tropics, once the last rays of sun drop into the ocean, light doesn't linger. With the highway veering north up the peninsula, the sun no longer looms behind them. The darkening waters of the Sea of Cortez have lost their azure hue. The incessant succession of whitecaps rolling into shore yields the marine scape a slightly menacing aspect.

Richard gears down upon leaving behind the hotel zone. Ascending a slight rise in the pavement, the street lights of San José come into view. Scores of pedestrians, sporting newly acquired, reddish-tinged tans, suddenly emerge on both sides of the boulevard. Some of them loiter at the makeshift, wooden planked stalls of street vendors, peddling the same fare as on the beach in front of The Office. Just a few hours earlier, during siesta, on their way to Cabo, the stalls had stood empty.

Elizabeth could have used a siesta too, after yesterday's bone-jarring drive back down the boulder-laden stream bed from the Carcamo ranch, but Richard had insisted upon showing her The Friars at Land's End. She peers over at the scratches on Richard's arm, just below the elbow. The cavity through which Richard had squeezed himself yesterday had narrowed to the point that he'd had to wedge his lower arm into the hole to get a water sample of the underground spring. Pulling the water bottle back, through the cavity, without spilling its contents proved to be a little tricky and Richard had sustained a few nasty cuts to his arm in the process. Shifting her focus back to eye level, Elizabeth notices a sudden dimming of sunlight. "We can't even see what's happened to the sun," she laments.

"Sorry to disappoint. A heavy band of cloud must have rolled in just as the sun was setting over the horizon. *Mañana* we'll catch the set."

Their hotel is on a narrow street in the central part of town. After their cursory exchange of words about the risks of getting addicted to one another, neither Elizabeth nor Richard had broached the subject of how their relationship had deepened until Richard had pulled up in front of the hotel. Leaning over abruptly, Richard opened the glove compartment to retrieve a package of cigarettes that he'd stowed inside, before turning to her, and asking, "So, we're going to get a room together, right?"

Elizabeth's thought processes had immediately accelerated into high gear. Imagining Isabela, the secretary, showing Guzman their hotel bill — proof that they'd only been charged for one room — Elizabeth had nearly broken out laughing at the ludicrousness of such a possibility, before replying with her characteristic, "sure."

Having opted for a street-side view over a room overlooking the courtyard, Elizabeth with her hair secured, turban-style inside a towel, and sporting a short terrycloth robe, takes a seat on one of the two rattan chairs on their tiny balcony and catches the clatter of metal doors being elevated over storefronts and their echo up and down the street. The laughter of children coalesces with the hollow sound of rubber balls bouncing along the sidewalks and against the seamless line of adobe walls.

"How was the shower?"

Elizabeth jumps, turns her head abruptly to catch Richard standing within the balcony door jamb, a bottle of tequila in one hand, a can of coke in the other.

"You scared me," Elizabeth says, her hand smoothing back her hair.

"Sorry about that. What's gotten you so rattled?"

"I don't know. I should check my cell phone for messages."

Richard lays his hand on her shoulder. "Let me get it. You plugged it in by the bed after we checked in last night?"

She nods.

"Here." He hands her the refreshments. "I'll bring a couple of glasses and run down the hall to get some ice."

Despite Richard's solicitousness, the thought of her mother taking a bath before bed every night unleashes a wave of guilt. While showering, Elizabeth had visualized in her mind's eye the water running down the graded tiled floor into the drain, recalled her mother's habit of taking a bath every night before bed. Almost sheepishly Krystyna admitted that she imagined the day's worries being washed from her body, collecting in the bath water, then draining away.

Her parents would be agonizing over Patricia and if the battery hadn't run out of juice yesterday while speaking with Bernard, she would have asked him to call them on her behalf. After all these years, Bernard and her parents had remained cordial with one another, but her parents continued to resent her decision to leave her marriage.

Her parents' generation of post-war European refugees had valued marriage as a foundation upon which to forge a solid, economic partnership, and only secondarily as an emotional bond; accordingly Elizabeth had been confronted with a lot of resistance over her decision to leave Bernard. A secure kind of guy with a good profession, Bernard, like Stanislaw, was fiercely loyal. Patricia had inherited the same steadfastness. Bending her neck, removing the towel from her head, Elizabeth runs her fingers through her hair to untangle the knots. In Patricia's case, nature had obviously won out over nurture. She hadn't had much of a choice but to gravitate towards an institution that rewards that type of old world style dedication.

"Went down to the restaurant for a few wedges of lime. Single or a double?"

"I need a double."

"You should call your parents again. At the very least you can tell them about the satellite reconnaissance. Little bit of good news." Richard sits down on the other chair and sighs. "I feel tired. My ribs are still sore from squeezing myself through that cave. The swim limbered me up, though, so hopefully I won't be in agony tomorrow."

"*Salud.*" Elizabeth clinks her glass against his.

Echoing the toast, Richard takes a long swill of his drink before asking, "So, what d' you think of Land's End?"

"Incredible. You know, when Patricia and I toured Quebec we went up to Percé, where there's a similar rock outcrop jutting out at the end of the Gaspé Peninsula. At low tide, though, one can walk right up to the rock. It's also referred to as Land's End."

"Aboriginals no doubt coined it that."

Nodding, she explains that the Mic Mac Indians of Quebec believed that Percé Rock delineated the end of their universe.

"There's a Land's End in England, too. On a peninsula, at Cornwall. Legends of King Arthur speak about a submerged country, called Lyonnesse, which broke off from the British Isles and sank. And across the channel, the Bretons of Brittany had similar legends in reference to the same submerged landmass. But the Bretons called it the old sunken city of Ys, that's "y," "s." Legend has it that it sank because of its inhabitants' greed and wickedness."

"So these myths aren't exclusively Aboriginal."

"No. Interesting thing is, we now know that the continents were all connected at some time, then broke apart, and drifted into their present positions. The concept of continental drift entails all land masses drifting over tectonic plates that float over top of the volcanic mantle. Deep down inside the earth, everything is still moving all the time."

"And there's the myth of Atlantis, the small continent about which the ancient Greeks spoke, lying in the depths of the Atlantic Ocean. Some scholars believe that Atlantis was submerged during the floods after the last ice age, about 12,000 years ago," Elizabeth adds, swallowing the last of her drink.

"Heard that. Will you have another one?"

"This is hitting me pretty hard. I need to eat something. And you need to take a shower."

Scooping a handful of ice cubes into his glass, Richard pours himself another drink. "Think I'll take this with me into *el baño*. In the restaurant, downstairs, there's a lobster special tonight. What do you say?"

10.

THREE SCHOOLGIRLS in navy and white uniforms, their long dark tresses pulled back into ponytails, saunter along the narrow street of San José del Cabo, in the opposite direction from the sea. From their balcony, Elizabeth and Richard have only a tiny, narrow view of the seascape, but it's enough to tell Elizabeth that it's another cloudless morning; although, judging by the rhythmic, almost slow motion swaying crowns of palm trees on the beach, it's a little windier than yesterday. The high pitched sound of corn brooms being swept across tile is accompanied, as in an orchestra, by the creaking wheels of taco and hot dog push carts, along with the occasional crow of a rooster and the rumble of car engines with porous mufflers.

Elizabeth's reverie upon this symphony is severed abruptly by the backfiring of an engine. Jumping back from the edge of the balcony, she's jolted into recalling her dream. She was embracing Patricia, a Patricia with a very pale face, and almost indistinguishable facial features. Her face appeared as though it had been shaped out of clay and the sculptor hadn't yet chiseled enough definition to make Patricia look like herself. Elizabeth recalls feeling confused, panicky, doubting whether it was really her daughter. It had been her green-grey eyes, reflecting so much pain, which had definitively tipped the balance towards convincing Elizabeth that it was really Patricia and not someone else.

Strange that she hadn't woken up immediately after the dream. A stream of tears runs out of her eyes and down her face. She doesn't wipe the tears, but remains rooted to the spot she's standing in, back from the balustrade that she's been leaning over, absorbing the early morning sights and sounds of San José, until the backfiring engine rudely disconcerts her.

The last time she'd talked to her mother, Krystyna had sounded more distraught than Stanislaw. Like always, Krystyna had asserted that she'd sensed something was wrong for weeks. And as for her father, once a soldier, always a soldier. After Elizabeth had updated him with the news about the reconnaissance satellite having spotted the insurgents, he kept insisting that the military, after all, is supported by the state and will justify the public expenditure, to secure the release of Patricia and her fellow officers, even when it's a lost cause.

She imagines the heated discussion that must have ensued, after her telephone call. She sees every room, nook, and cranny in the forty-four-year-old bungalow in which Elizabeth spent the first half of her life. How she couldn't wait to move out. Her father had regarded her decision to rent a one-bedroom apartment across the river from the university as a personal affront. No amount of convincing that it was time for her to go out on her own could appease his dismay over her determination to liberate herself from the stifling confines of her childhood home.

"Good girls don't live on their own before they get married," Stanislaw had admonished. "And why get a student loan when you can live with us for free?"

"Nothing in life is free," she'd wanted to say, but held her tongue instead.

Richard is still sleeping peacefully, not even emitting a snore. She picks up her watch from the bedside table. It's just a quarter to eight in the morning. She feels restless, decides to dress and go for a walk, but upon exiting the bathroom,

Elizabeth sees Richard sitting up in bed with a broad smile pasted on his face.

"It must have been a good dream," she says.

"Dream? Don't recall any dream. Usually takes about a week before I begin feeling at home again down here. Must have been that excursion we took to Cabo yesterday. And *los langostinos*. Man, that was good! Are you on your way out?"

"Actually, yes, I've been awake for a while and thought it was my turn to get us a couple of javas."

"Hey, that'd be nice." He lies back down and turns over on his side to face her and the door. "Wake me up when the coffee arrives. Don't forget. Two sugars and lots of cream."

Shutting the door behind her, Elizabeth spies a male figure abruptly turn the corner of the hallway that leads downstairs toward the lobby and courtyard. Her heartbeat accelerates. She's overcome by a sense of dread, an uneasiness. An image flashes in her mind of this person having stood at their door, listening to their conversation. She considers retreating, telling Richard about her suspicions, but convinces herself that her imagination is running away with her. He's probably just a common thief, scoping out the place, and didn't expect to encounter anyone at this early hour.

Even so, she hangs back in the courtyard to survey the pool deck and patio. A lone pool attendant, net in hand, languorously sweeps his instrument through the slightly rippling waters of the kidney-shaped pool. Turning, she cuts through the lobby and out onto the street. Heading uphill away from the plaza, past *la catedral* in search of a cappuccino bar, her nostrils pick up a whiff of brewed coffee and, sure enough, when she peers down a narrow street to her left at the next intersection, she sees two round tables with chairs on the sidewalk in front of a café. The unmistakable high-pitched sound of milk being scalded in a container momentarily drowns out the soft melodic riff of Spanish guitar emanating from a sound system. A solitary male patron, a newspaper obscuring his face, sits at a table in the corner by the window. Approaching the counter, she notices that the man is eyeing her from behind the edge of his newspaper. The uneasy feeling of trepidation that took hold of her in the hotel corridor returns. Sucking in her breath, Elizabeth orders a regular coffee and a café latte to go, all the while focusing upon the shelf above the head of the waitress that displays an array of bagged fair-trade coffee beans.

She considers, on her way out, approaching the male patron, with the pretext that perhaps they've met somewhere before. That way, she could get a good look at his face and perhaps glean some impression of him — whether he is the same person of whom she caught a glimpse in the hotel corridor.

Thanking the waitress, she turns to discover that the man has left. Again she's left with only a receding fragment of his figure through the edge of the storefront window.

Encumbered by the two coffees she now must tote back with her to her hotel room, she looks over her shoulder every few paces on her downward trek through the narrow streets. She has the uncanny feeling that this person, whom she sensed was American or Canadian, and not Mexican, is somehow connected to Patricia and her ordeal overseas. Her daughter had been very secretive about her assignments with the armed forces. Elizabeth had never pressed her into disclosing anything about her work, accepting that any information she had access to was strictly classified. She'd never contemplated until now that her daughter might have information indispensable to the enemy maintaining and expanding its insurgent operations.

She reaches the hotel and takes the elevator to their room. Setting one of the coffees onto the floor, she looks behind her to ensure that no one is lurking about before she retrieves her room key from her front pocket and opens the door.

"Hey, thanks," says Richard, sitting up in bed and nodding with gratitude. "It smells great."

"I'm going to go down to the courtyard for some fruit and a pastry. Did you want anything?"

The look that Richard throws her tells her that her speech is laced with a nervous edginess that wasn't there before she left, but he appears to simply chalk it up to her unremitting moodiness. Shifting his gaze away from her, he removes the plastic lid from his coffee. "No, thanks, I'll get something a little later."

She takes her coffee with her, deciding to drink it in the courtyard, away from the reproachful study of Richard's ever-watchful eyes. She's grateful for his attentiveness, knowing that without it her anxiety would likely spiral into a depression, but she also has a hunch that he might classify her latest conundrum as sheer paranoia. And she isn't entirely sure that he might be wrong.

11.

THE BEACH THAT ELIZABETH HAD SPIED that morning from her balcony, between the terra cotta rooftops of San José's adobe dwellings, is long and wide. Interspersed with dilapidated wooden shelters, fishermen have convened, as if for a religious ritual, within the concave, palm-fronded umbrage of a *palapa*. Richard urges her to watch the ceremonial dissection of a hundred-pound marlin.

The skipper runs the sharp edges of the knife blades against one another. The clean sound of the metal reminds Elizabeth of when her mother used to sharpen the knives of the household before hunkering down to cut a pound or two of beef for goulash.

"How do they reel in a fish that size?" she asks.

"With a harness strapped to the waist. It can take up to an hour to subdue such a monster."

"Have you ever tried it?"

"Many years ago."

"Did you catch anything?"

Nodding, he adds, "Overfishing has made it rare, now, to catch that prized hundred-pounder. They have to start imposing and enforcing conservation. The Sea of Cortez is known as a fish trap, particularly during the sweltering summer months when its temperature rises over thirty degrees centigrade. All forms of marine life migrate from the cooler Pacific waters, only to risk the lines of deep sea fishermen who gravitate from all corners of the globe to hunt hundred-pound marlin like this one, and tuna and dorado."

The Mexican deftly splices the belly of the fish and reaches inside the cavity with his other hand to scoop out its entrails. He throws the guts onto the sand a few meters away from where they're standing. Marine fowl — predominantly seagulls, but also a couple of brazen pelicans — descend upon the discards. A lone skinny dog tentatively approaches, half-heartedly barks at the birds, and then sniffs at the spot that in a matter of seconds is stripped clean, with only a lingering dark red stain remaining, attracting scores of flies.

"We should think about venturing up the west cape tomorrow, to Todos Santos."

"What's there?"

"The infamous Hotel California, the *catedral*, a few colonial buildings."

"Why infamous?"

"It's the name of the Eagle's famous album and, over the years, a few gringos have bought it and tried to make a go of it. No one's managed to hold onto it for very long. Mexican graft tends to wear them down and eventually it falls into disrepair again. But apart from the hotel, it's a very charming village. On our way, I'd like to stop at the palm beach just south of there. There's another fisherman's beach from where the Mexicans launch their *pangas* but it's not as scenic as the palm beach."

"Our holiday is almost over."

"Yes, Monday's fast approaching. You haven't spoken about your daughter since yesterday. Don't hold in your anxiety, Elizabeth. Let it out. Flow is important."

Elizabeth looks out to sea, notices a barge navigating the turquoise blue waters of the Gulf. Its sheer size gives the impression that it's hardly moving. No wonder time seems to pass so slowly at the beach and then, once one looks up again at the horizon, a passing vessel suddenly disappears, plunges into obscurity, swallowed up by the horizon and the void of the earth's curvature.

"I've been wondering what type of information she might have that made her a target for the Taliban."

"I wouldn't go there. The insurgents likely are holding her for the singular objective of putting pressure on NATO forces to abandon their mission."

"But she's in intelligence," Elizabeth counters, shaking her head. She's reticent about disclosing her encounter with the spy outside their room and in the café. How would the man have known that she was going to go into that café, unless he'd indeed overheard their conversation through the door and knew that there was nothing else open at that early hour? "What do you know about geosequestration?"

"Not much, other than that it's a method of sequestering carbon dioxide emissions in the ground. Why?"

Shrugging, she answers, "I was just wondering whether there's more to the NATO Afghani mission than meets the eye, than what they're telling us. I read somewhere that while the Taliban were still in power, before 9/11, Cheney and the heavyweights from Unocal were negotiating for the right to construct a pipeline through Afghanistan — presumably to transport oil or gas or both from the Persian Gulf to the Indian subcontinent."

"So what does geosequestration have to do with that?"

"Maybe the pipeline was never intended for oil or gas but for liquefied carbon dioxide. India produces a hell of a lot of CO_2 because of its coal-fired generating plants. A lot of service jobs have recently been outsourced to India so it's in the best interests of corporations to keep the Indian professionals wired with power. But I have a hunch that sooner or later international protocols will put pressure on India to responsibly dispose of their rising carbon emissions. Afghanistan presents lots of options for sequestering liquefied CO_2 in its barren, arid, and unpopulated mountains. Really, the Indians can't afford to power their electrical grid with oil and gas. Coal is the name of the game down there, but it's the worst emitter of greenhouse gases."

"And you're thinking that Patricia had access to this information?"

"She mentioned something once, before she was stationed over there. She struck me as depressed. You see, when she signed up, she was adamant that she would be playing a role in the betterment of the average Afghani's life, particularly the women and children, but just before she left, she no longer had the same enthusiasm. She talked a lot about the Intergovernmental Panel on Climate Change, and how geopolitically things were going to change now that it's garden-variety knowledge that the greenhouse effect is caused by our insatiable desire to consume energy."

"Makes sense, I have to hand you that. It was one thing when factory workers lost their jobs to sweat shops in Mexico and Asia, but another when the middle classes started feeling the pinch, with accounting and other clerical positions going to India. Bad news for democracy. You lose your middle class, you might as well say *adios* to freedom and democracy. I never considered, though, the ecological cost of Indian professionals supplanting our white-collar workforce."

"Sooner or later the insurance industry will put their foot down and demand that something is done about climate change. All this erratic weather is costing them too much money."

"You wouldn't know it here, though. Just listen to that gentle surf. It's positively hypnotizing." Richard takes Elizabeth's hand and pulls her gently up off the dune upon which they've perched themselves. "One last dip in the sea. There's no swimming on the Pacific side. It's too wild over there for a frolic in the sea."

Elizabeth unclasps her wristwatch and throws it on her towel. She follows Richard to the water's edge and into the rising tide of surf, which at this closer range resonates more sharply in tone with each rushing ebb and flow. The seabed drops off abruptly. With the next wave, Elizabeth loses her foothold, is forced to extend her arms and to give herself up to the buoyancy of the sea. Richard is beside her and, like her, alternates between treading water and breast-strokes on the undulating water. Their eyes lock for a moment; between waves Elizabeth senses his desire for her, feels it to the core of her being. She spreads her legs and kicks them to counteract the inundating effect of the next wave, the last and most forceful one in a series. It lifts her up and folds in on itself behind her, before shedding its sharpened angle, leveling out and sweeping onto shore.

12.

"*B*UENAS DIAS, DOCTORA,*" Guzman calls out from the passenger seat of one of two jeeps, parked side by side in front of the Humanities building on the university campus.

Extending her hand through the window, Elizabeth reciprocates Guzman's greeting and sucks in her breath. With his eyes obscured beneath dark sunglasses, she can't decipher his mood or outlook.

"*Como estas?* Any news about your daughter?"

"Only that the NATO forces' reconnaissance surveillance might have located the kidnappers' cell. But that was almost a week ago, and since then I haven't had any news."

She notices Guzman's nose crinkle up as though he's caught a whiff of something unpleasant. Changing the subject, he introduces her to the drivers, Mario and Roberto. Engaged in the task of securing the team's canvas-bundled supplies onto the vehicle's rooftop rack with heavy rope, they nod toward Elizabeth and in succession greet her with the customary, "*Mucho gusto.*"

"Did you have a good trip down through the capes and to *La Concepcion?*"

"*Si*. We discovered an underground spring in the cave."

"*Muy bien*. Did you take any samples of the water?"

"*Doctoro* Wellington took it to the lab this morning, along with some scrapings of carbon from the roof of the cave."

Nodding, Guzman points across the parking lot toward a pushcart coffee vendor. "*Doctora*, help yourself to a coffee over there." Checking his wristwatch, he adds, "We have another fifteen minutes or so before we leave."

"*Gracias*," she mumbles to herself and feeling her heart race, she walks in the direction indicated to line up behind a group of students at the coffee stand. She tries to stem the wild knocking of her heart by concentrating on the female coffee vendor's efficient hand movements — taking patrons' money, counting out change, pouring coffee, pointing to cream and sugar set out at the far corner of the pushcart.

Suddenly Elizabeth feels the skin crawl on the back of her neck. Turning around she notices a man with sunglasses, in khaki trousers and a white shirt line up behind her. Deciding against coffee, she asks for an apple juice instead. The can of juice that the woman retrieves from the ice box is perspiring from the coldness of the cooler and soothes Elizabeth's sweaty palm. Her other hand, though, shakes as she gives the woman a ten-peso note. She stiffens the muscles in her forearm while keeping it outstretched to receive her change.

Standing aside to retrieve a straw from the dispenser at the end of the stand, she watches the man ask for a coffee. His Spanish is impeccable and he never once glances sideways at her, even though it would be virtually impossible for him not to realize that her eyes are fixated upon him. He asks the vendor for a lid and does not add anything to the coffee. Swallowing hard, Elizabeth follows him. "*Por favor, Señor*. Do I know you from somewhere?"

He stops suddenly, and turns around. His facial expression feigns incomprehension. Answering in Spanish, he asks, "Have we met somewhere? I don't think so. You must be mistaken," then turns away and heads toward a building across from the Humanities building.

With her heart still pounding, she makes a mental note of his description — tall, slim build, receding hairline emphasizing a broad forehead, olive complexion, well-manicured moustache, nondescript lips and nose. Surveying her surroundings, she spots an alcove, a *jardin* of sorts with a park bench, at the side of the building into which the stranger receded. She can collect herself there, before returning to the caravan.

Snapping back the metal opener of the can of juice, she drinks it back, cursing to herself about her aborted encounter with this stranger, who she's sure is the same person she spotted in the hotel corridor and in the café in San José. She also can't get it out of her mind that this person, who is obviously following her, is connected somehow to Patricia and the Afghani mission. She hadn't sensed anyone following her in Todos Santos or in La Paz last night, but on second thought, what about the restaurant she and Richard had dined at on the Malecón? In Mexico, Sunday night is the busiest night of the week for restaurants, and El Feliz Camaron had been predictably packed with patrons — a perfect spot for a mole to remain undetected while conducting surveillance.

But are NATO's plans to develop geosequestration such a big deal? Everyone is already resigned to CO_2 emissions causing climate change, and the public would be just as happy to continue burning fossil fuels to maintain their standard of living. There must be something else — some highly sensitive classified information that Patricia has become privy to — that they're afraid she might have divulged prior to her deployment.

Elizabeth throws the empty can into an overflowing garbage bin and races across the parking lot to the waiting vehicles.

"Where have you been?" Richard demands. "Everyone's waiting for you."

Between gritted teeth, she replies, "I just needed a moment to collect myself. Which jeep are we assigned to?"

"We're not together. You're in Guzman's vehicle."

Nodding, she opens the back door and slides in. "*Pardone me*. I had trouble finding a *baño*."

"Well, you certainly planned things out well for yourself,"

Maynard remarks, having become sandwiched in the middle, between Elizabeth and Bartek.

"Oh, hi. What?"

"I would think, since you've delayed everyone, that you should be relegated to taking the bum middle seat."

"*Hola.*" Bartek reaches across and shakes her hand. "Relax, Maynard. It's a long trip. We'll switch places many times before we get to San Ignacio."

13.

TAKING HIM IN SURREPTITIOUSLY through her side vision, Elizabeth can't believe that she failed to notice earlier just how handsome Bartek is. His dark hair is streaked with striking bands of silver grey, and it has a natural, windswept look. Elizabeth has always been attracted to men with moustaches, and his is thick, but impeccably trimmed, outlining his upper lip, which sensuously contrasts with a thinner lower lip. It's his eyes, though, which are most telling — evoking passion and a deep sensitivity, with a palpable glint of pain.

They pass the exit for the airport and the traffic thins out. The shimmering waters of the sea follow them on their right until they come upon a roadside checkpoint.

"It's the Department of Agriculture," Guzman announces, turning his body sideways so that his voice projects into the back seat. "From La Paz south, our climate is more semi-tropical. North of here, near Ciudad de la Constitución, there are many commercial farms dependent upon irrigation. The Department prohibits the export of any produce south of here, to protect the crops north of here."

The official, attired in a khaki uniform, recognizes Professor Guzman and waves them on. The road becomes a straightaway and, in the distance, the ribbon of asphalt climbs over a hill and disappears.

"Well," Guzman pipes up, turning his body to make eye contact with the rear passengers. "To make the time go faster, why don't we get better acquainted by each of us telling something about ourselves. *Doctoro* Tomeszewski. Why don't we start with you?"

Elizabeth feels nervous all of a sudden. She realizes that it is Bartek's anxiety that has caught hold of her. Sighing a couple of times, he breaks into his heavily-accented English by disclosing that in the eighties he was actively engaged in Poland's Solidarity movement. "My wife and I ran an underground printing press out of our apartment. We printed censored news about what the Jaruzelski government was doing to Solidarity members; and to the public, in general. Twice our apartment was searched. Ransacked. On the third occasion they arrested me."

"Did they find the printing press and papers?" asks Maynard.

"No." Bartek shakes his head, nervously shifts his hands from a prayer-like pose into clenched fists, and finally drops them into his lap. "Both times we'd just finished a press run and had moved the equipment and publications into the garage of a neighbour."

"So you were tipped off by someone that the *milicia* were onto you?" Elizabeth asks.

"No. We routinely moved everything out of our apartment after a press run. It was standard procedure ... to minimize the risk of getting caught."

"And were you convicted of an offence after you were arrested?" asks Brigham.

"No. I was detained for almost three weeks but they never even interrogated me. They didn't have the evidence that they needed. My wife, who was also a professor at the Jagiellonian University, was called to the police station for questioning while I was in jail. But, in the end, they had to release me. After that, Malgorzata and I went to Italy. We were very surprised that the authorities issued us passports. We went on a tour to visit the Vatican, and then claimed refugee status. We were in a refugee camp, occupied mostly by Poles, for eighteen months.

And then the Berlin Wall came down and we abandoned our claim with Canada Immigration."

"Yes," Elizabeth interjects. She recalls her own astonishment when catching the news on television, the footage of young East Berliners climbing on top of the wall, over to the other side, waving flags, cheering, and dismantling the rock and wire with their bare hands. She offers in a muted voice, as though thinking out loud, "No one predicted that the wall would come down."

"No," Bartek shakes his head. "But we knew with Wojtyla as Pope, it was only a matter of time before the Soviet occupation of Eastern Europe would collapse."

"What was the jail like?" asks Maynard.

Bartek shakes his head before answering. "Terrible. I was arrested in February. It was very cold. There were many prisoners crammed in each cell. And many of the people were sick. My biggest worry was not to get sick. Of course, I worried about how long I would be in there, and every time the cell door opened I almost had a heart attack that they would be calling me for questioning. But my biggest worry was to stay healthy."

Pausing, he looks down at his hands. The knuckles of his hands, which he's clenched into fists, are starkly white. Elizabeth has the urge to reach over to release his hands from their tight grip. As though reading her thoughts, he unclenches them, and lays them flat onto his thighs.

"Food was not a problem for me because my wife and mother took turns bringing something every day. I often shared what I had with some of the other prisoners who didn't have family in the vicinity. Sometimes the family didn't even know where the arrested person was being held."

Elizabeth's heart begins knocking rapidly. She feels very hot, all of a sudden. Reaching down towards the floor, she retrieves her knapsack, unties the drawstring, and pulls out her water bottle. Food. What about food for Patricia? She feels compelled to interject, interrupt Bartek, spill her guts, protest that his story is past history; he is safe and sound, while her daughter's life hangs by a thread.

She catches Guzman peering at her through the periphery of his sunglasses. "*Profesoro* Brigham, hopefully you can lighten the mood a little. Tell us something about yourself."

"Gee, I don't know. Compared to Bartek, here, I've lived a pretty sheltered life. I'm a Vancouverite. Born and raised. I have a brother and sister, older and younger. I guess I'm the proverbial middle-child. I was the one who got into trouble on the playground, at school, challenging authority. I played bass guitar with a rock band in high school, and after graduating spent a year travelling around the country, performing gigs in bars, staying up late, partying hard. My parents lost hope that I would ever settle down to study and were surprised when I decided to go to grad school."

"Your parents are professionals?" asks Elizabeth.

"My father was an engineer. He's retired now. My mother was a nurse, but stayed home once I arrived on the scene. She went back to work part-time after my younger sister started school. That's about it. I guess I've lived a charmed life. Your turn, *Señora*." In jest, he turns and makes a fist, holding it towards Elizabeth's mouth as though it were a microphone.

"I was born and raised in Edmonton. After graduating with my Master's in Anthropology from the University of Alberta, I moved to Calgary where I completed my doctorate. That's also where I met my husband, Bernard, who's a partner of one of the largest law firms in the city. He specializes in oil and gas law. My daughter, Patricia, is overseas right now with the Canadian Armed Forces."

"In Afghanistan?" Bartek asks. His eyebrows lift in astonishment.

Elizabeth nods.

"And why did you choose anthropology as a field of study?" Guzman interjects.

"Actually, it all started with monkeys. I remember seeing a movie when I was very young, with a young actor, a little boy, who had a pet monkey, and I wanted one too. The little boy's father was an organ grinder and the monkey sat on his shoulder when he wasn't performing acrobatic tricks for the street audience." Laughing nervously, she wonders whether she's making a fool of herself. "Whenever we visited the Storyland Valley Zoo, in Edmonton, I was totally enthralled. My parents had to pull me away from the monkey cage. When I was a little older, I read books about the field trips of Margaret Mead, and Jane Goodall's work with chimpanzees. And then Diane Fossey's work with the great apes. I was intrigued. One of my professors at the University of Alberta, Denford was his name, taught me physical anthropology. He'd worked in the field for two years with lemurs on the Island of Madagascar. I remember when he would scratch his head during a lecture, he'd move his hand like this."

To demonstrate, Elizabeth curves her wrist inward and bends her forearm into an awkward position to reach the back of her head. "I was amazed that he'd actually adopted some of the lemurs' gestures after spending years watching them in the wild. Anyways, Denford cautioned me about aspiring to do field work. He suggested that I consider specializing in cultural anthropology instead, as the work that Mead and Goodall did is still considered the domain of male anthropologists."

"And are you glad that you listened to him?" asks Bartek.

"Yes, before I decided to study science, I wanted to be a nun — a missionary." She glances over at Bartek, whom, she has a hunch, likely understands her better than the others in this regard. "I've always wondered what we're doing here. In a spiritual sense. The study of anthropology, for me, hasn't answered any questions about our purpose here on this earth, in life. But I believe that our evolution as a species is somehow linked to our quest for the answer to how we could have evolved from such lower forms of life, yet feel such a strong connection with something higher. As scientists, we've relegated our connection to a deity to something that is in our heads. But still we seek that connection. Maybe it has something to do with our mortality. We have a difficult time accepting it. We don't relate anymore to our physical environment like we once did. But I believe that we're slowly moving back in that direction."

"Yes, I believe that you are right," says Bartek. "We had to become secularized before we could become spiritual again. Spiritual leaders are no longer regulating our lives. That ended when the Berlin Wall came down. It's a natural philosophical and social progression. A result of the dialectic and materialist philosophy. *Doctoro* Guzman. Your turn."

"*Gracias*, Bartlomiej. Like *Profesora* Thiessen, I wanted to become an anthropologist since I was a child. It wasn't monkeys that inspired me, though. It was the pyramids of Teotihuacan, south of D.F., that made me want to study the cultures of the Aztecs and Toltecs. I felt ashamed that the Spaniards were so savage towards *los indios*. My family is directly descended from Spain."

"What percentage of Mexicans are of mixed blood?" asks Elizabeth.

"Approximately ninety percent. For example, the majority of Baja Californians are descendants of Spanish soldiers and Indian women. Still today, unfortunately, Mexican society is very class stratified. Those who claim to be direct descendants of the Spaniards consider themselves superior to the mixed bloods. And *los indios* are considered to be on the lowest rung of the hierarchy."

"And your family enjoys certain privileges from being directly descended from Spaniards." Maynard says this matter-of-factly, rather than as a question.

"*Si*," Guzman nods. "My children enjoy certain privileges that I and my sisters and brother, and parents before us enjoyed. So I am not as optimistic as Bartlomiej and the *Profesora* that modern man is on the brink of a spiritual renaissance. That he is searching for some spiritual connection to his physical environment. Since the 1980s, peasants have been pouring into Mexico City, settling in drug-infested, crime-ridden barrios. They leave the countryside behind and find themselves living in a much worse environment. Our infrastructure is crumbling from the booming population, and, of course, criminals do not pay taxes. One doesn't *live* in Mexico City. One *survives*. When someone leaves their house in the morning, they don't know whether they will return. Every day, people are abducted for body parts."

"So, you took a position at the university in La Paz to get out of there." Brigham asserts.

"*Si.*"

The irrigated farms, about which Guzman spoke earlier, come into view. Their geometrically-patterned fields are a mélange of green hues and a welcome respite from the monotony of the desert landscape. Various farm vehicles cross the highway, and Mario decelerates to 50 kilometers per hour.

Elizabeth reads the large sign announcing their arrival at Ciudad de la Constitución, with a population of 80,000 inhabitants. "Are we going to be stopping here?"

"Yes, for a short coffee break," Guzman replies.

14.

"SO, ROBERTO, what have you got playing on the CD-player this morning?" Winking at Mario, Guzman props his elbows onto the table and rests his chin onto his folded hands. Like at the Carcamo ranch, the tables are covered with plastic tablecloths, but instead of a red and white checkered pattern, the restaurant has opted for a flowered design, in muted earthy tones that blend with the pastel green walls and beige crown mouldings.

"The latest top hits from *los Estados Unidos,*" Roberto unabashedly replies. "My brother visited last week and brought us five new CDs. I asked *los profesores* if they would mind."

Guzman laughs and leans back into the backrest of his chair. "I think I'd better travel in your jeep to Loreto to give *los profesores'* ears a rest. *Doctoro* Wellington, would you mind changing places with me until lunch?"

Shooting a furtive glance in Elizabeth's direction, Richard nonchalantly replies, "Not at all."

Elizabeth has a hunch that Maynard will claim the front seat and that she'll be relegated to the middle rear position, sandwiched between Richard and Bartek. She now feels torn about having become intimate with Richard. Their trip together down the east cape, to Los Cabos and back up the Pacific side, in so many ways, had been a blessing. She thinks back to Richard's attentiveness, how he'd fallen into the habit of asking her what she was feeling, and gently nudged her to express her anxieties about Patricia. A warm sensation, like the comfort of a blanket, overwhelms her, but in the next moment Elizabeth chastises herself. *How can I feel so good about what Richard and I shared when Patricia is being terrorized, treated like a pawn in a game of politics!*

Elizabeth pushes her sunglasses away from herself into the middle of the table and looks over at the next table at Bartek. His razor-sharp instincts, an indispensable attribute cultivated through his survival of communism and the imposition of martial law, will undoubtedly alert him to something peculiar having developed between her and Richard. She considers treating Richard stone-heartedly. He might react a little perplexed, but later, in San Ignacio, when they catch a few moments alone together, she can explain her intentions. Forever careful to avoid mixing business with pleasure, she consoles herself with the thought that had she not encountered Richard on Tecolote Beach that afternoon, she would have had to face this nightmare alone. The cold-shoulder treatment, though, might only cement any premonitions that Bartek might harbour about her and Richard. Best to just go with the flow.

After the waitress has taken everyone's order for coffee and *quesadillas*, Guzman launches into a narrative about the trip by mule from the village of San Francisco to the cave site. Elizabeth is only half-listening. She takes in the mundane interior decor of the restaurant. The ubiquitous Baja map hangs between the bar and *baños*. Like the others she's studied in hotel lobbies and restaurants, it's acquired a faded blue tint. The adobe walls are otherwise bare. The rhythmic whirring sound of the overhead ceiling fan prompts Guzman to project his voice, which in turn rouses the proprietor behind the bar to look up from time to time from the tedious chore of drying freshly-washed glasses, carried in on a tray from the kitchen by a young boy.

A group of office workers claims the table next to theirs. "*La cuenta, por favor*," Guzman calls out to the waitress. Draining his coffee mug, he winks at Roberto. "And Mario, no party music in my absence, eh."

"I prefer *mariachi* music, *Doctoro*" Mario counters, "But ten kilometers out of La Constitución, the static drowns out the reception."

The male scientists line up at the door to the *hombre*'s washroom, while Elizabeth remains seated at the table. Not having much of an appetite, she decides to wrap up the rest of her *quesadilla* in a napkin and tuck the package into one of the pockets of her knapsack. Again, she thinks about what Bartek had said about food in the Polish prison. She opens the main compartment of her pack and retrieves her cell phone. No messages. She wonders what kind of reception she can expect further north. If the radio doesn't play ten kilometers up the road, it's unlikely that cell phone reception is any better.

The fertile fields of Ciudad Constitución retreat in the rear view mirror. As they head back toward the Gulf coast, the road becomes more winding, steeper, and the desert takes on a different personality. The moonscape of dust-laden cacti and grey, taupe-coloured soil has receded, and the earth has taken on a red tinge.

On their left, a range of imposing rock faces rises out of the desert. The sun has not yet ascended to its highest point and the contours in the rock still cast inward shadows. A flock of frigates hovers above the cliffs, indicating an upward draft of air. The valley teams with turkey vultures, perched, as is their habit, on the phallic point of cardon cacti. Their jet black wings are relaxed by their sides. Their ugly profiles, embellished by blood-red feathers, are directed toward the highway, as though to warn travellers that, despite the surrounding stark beauty, death rules supreme in the desert.

A harbour, hemmed in by mountains comes into view. Maroon-coloured outcrops punctuate the churning, heaving sapphire-emerald water, and form a barricade against the fluctuating tide of the Gulf.

"Most people consider the Bahía de Concepción to be the high point of this road, but I prefer this," remarks Richard.

"It is very beautiful," Bartek agrees, slowly enunciating his words. "What is it called?"

"Puerto Esconidido." Richard leans forward to speak more directly to Bartek. "Hidden Port. It's a hurricane hold."

A half dozen anchored sailboats drift in the much calmer waters of the harbor. Elizabeth senses, even within the interior of the vehicle, the dearth of wind in the surrounding desert landscape, at odds with the more volatile marine environment beyond the confines of the bay. "It's cold looking, even though it's hot," observes Elizabeth.

"It's because of the higher elevation," suggests Bartek.

"It's also a very deep harbour," Richard adds. "The water, although greenish-blue, is of a deeper hue, due to its depth."

Just as quickly as the bay came into view, they pass it, and the desert alters its profile once again. Here the landscape is littered with smooth, rounded boulders and smaller rocks, some bearing graffiti. The cacti are more varied and appear greener, suggesting higher humidity. The sea comes into view only sporadically — whenever they come out of an *arroyo*.

"This would be a good place to sequester carbon dioxide emissions underground," Maynard suggests, turning his body sideways.

It's the first time that Elizabeth has this vantage point from which to view Maynard's profile. He has a lean, starved look to him, not unlike Bartek's. But whereas Bartek's complexion is slightly Mediterranean in tone, Brigham has a ruddy complexion. His skin still bears some trace of having been very freckled during childhood. "What do you know about geosequestration?" she asks.

"It's still in its infancy stages of being developed. There's no question that it can escape and kill, not unlike coal methane; so that's why empty, uninhabited places like this are a perfect spot to sequester CO_2 underground," Maynard explains.

"But what about earthquakes?" asks Bartek. "This is one of the most actively seismic regions on earth. If it wasn't for the San Andreas Fault, the Baja peninsula wouldn't even exist."

"Absolutely, the subsurface has to be seismically surveyed for geosynclical features to determine whether there are any underground cavities or tunnels in which to bury the gas. But," Maynard retorts, "this is a cheap place to monitor sites. Labour's cheap."

"But what about water?" counters Bartek. "Underground springs could become diverted and contaminated."

"They can seismically survey for that too. There's not much water here, from what I understand."

"What about Afghanistan?" asks Elizabeth. "Do you think they're considering sequestering CO_2 there?"

"I think it's a possibility," Bartek cuts in. "I didn't mention that I also have a degree in geology. Any desert area is an ideal environment for geosequestration. It's much easier to work in such an environment, and there is little risk of suffocating people or livestock."

"The opium crop might suffer," Maynard offers, chortling.

"Do you think the war might be about that?" asks Elizabeth.

Richard, until now, has sat quietly listening to this exchange. "Wouldn't put it past our government. There's the conundrum of what to do with India's CO_2 emissions. American corporations have been outsourcing a ton of their accounting and clerical work to Indians who need to be connected. Their electrical power is almost exclusively generated by coal-fired power plants — heavy emitters. Why not run a pipeline through Pakistan and into less densely populated Afghanistan?"

Elizabeth notices Maynard's ears turning bright red. Her heart skips a beat when she thinks about the man in the queue at the beverage pushcart this morning. How would he have known that she would be meeting with this group in the parking lot of the Humanities Building? Maybe he'd been tipped off. But still, she can't get it out of her mind that she doesn't know anything. Is the information about NATO forces furthering the cause of geosequestration as a means of reducing greenhouse gases so very classified? Did it warrant sicking a mole after her?

"Bartek, do you think that if sequestering CO_2 emissions underground is the real reason that NATO has been dispatched to Afghanistan, that such a motive would be classified information?" Elizabeth asks, clenching her teeth to remain calm, and not betray the edginess to her question.

"Well," he pauses by stroking his moustache with his right hand. "It isn't public knowledge, so it's probably classified."

"And do you think that, if Richard is correct that the U.S. government is behind this, that they would try to keep it a secret?"

"I learned something very valuable in my involvement with the Solidarity movement. People tend to overestimate the competence of government. Government, I find, is quite often very juvenile," Bartek responds thoughtfully.

"Mickey Mouse," interjects Richard.

"Yes," Bartek laughs. "That is a very good way to describe it. Mickey Mouse. The government is, in the end, made up of people. The Russians have the best description for bureaucrats — *apparatchiki*. Which implies that all government officials are only parts of the apparatus."

"The left hand doesn't know what the right hand is doing," offers Richard.

"Yes," Bartek agrees. "Without coordination of effort, nothing gets done and often chaos results."

"Piecemeal." Richard leans forward to catch Bartek's eye. "Everything is done in a piecemeal fashion, a downside of division of labour. It's fine on the assembly line but once you get into administering a project, or waging a war for some so-called higher cause, the focus becomes overshadowed by the individual tasks or assignments of each bureaucrat."

"Yes," Bartek agrees. "Exactly. Piecemeal. There's a saying in Polish — without legs or arms."

15.

"SEE THE BELL TOWER of the church?" Richard points over Maynard's shoulder to the right. "Couple of earthquakes and tropical storms destroyed the original mission. What you see was reconstructed in 1959. One of the original bells, brought over from Spain, dates from the 1700s. The original effigy of the Virgin of Loreto is inside the church. It was brought over from Mexico City by Padre Salvatierra."

Bartek flips through the index of a skinny publication on the history of Baja California. Elizabeth can't stop herself from reading over his shoulder. A compulsive reader, she can't tear her eyes away from the text. "So, this was the first mission established in the Californias — by Salvatierra," Bartek sums up, looking up and catching Elizabeth's eye. "And Salvatierra was later succeeded by Padre Junipero Serra, who established seventeen other missions north and south of here. They were both Jesuits, but after being expelled by Spain from the region, the Franciscans took over and later the Dominicans."

Maynard turns around and, upon realizing that Bartek is summarizing the text in the book, says, "And I thought I'd missed out on some reading assignment! What else does it say about Loreto?"

"After Padre Salvatierra landed here, the Cochimi Indians attacked with rocks and arrows. The Jesuits arrived with soldiers and they opened fire with harquebuses and a mortar. The surviving *indios* were rounded up, enslaved, and converted. It is written here that the Jesuits gave the Indians gruel to eat and that the copper kettle in which the gruel was cooked is on display in the Museum of the Missions, here in Loreto."

"How's that for political correctness?" Richard interjects. "What year was that rag that you're reading published?"

Bartek flips back to the second page and leans forward, squinting to decipher the publication date. "1979."

"Might as well be 1949!" Richard shakes his head.

"Look out!" screams Maynard.

"*Ay Caramba! Dios mio!*" exclaims Mario. Slamming on the brakes, he yanks the steering wheel to the right.

As though viewing a movie in slow motion, Elizabeth sees the last longhorn in a herd of five lift its rear legs. As it lopes out of the way, it narrowly misses getting dinged by the left front fender of the jeep.

"Whew!" Mario expels a deep breath and leans his forehead against the steering wheel.

"That was a close one!" Richard exclaims. "*Gracias* Mario. You have superb reactions *amigo*." Leaning forward, he gives the driver a pat on the shoulder. "That's why it's not a good idea to drive after dark on these roads. These longhorns come out of nowhere, and when you're clipping along at 80 kilometres, how can you stop?"

"But during the day, *las vacas* don't usually cross the highway," Mario states. Craning his neck to eye the passengers, he asks, "Is everyone alright?"

"Yes, we are fine," replies Bartek.

"*Doctora?*" Mario lifts his head slightly so that his eyes are positioned in the middle of the rearview mirror.

"*Si, gracias.*"

The other jeep has stopped alongside the highway, on the narrow shoulder. Pulling up behind it, Mario gives the thumbs up to Roberto, and the little caravan carries on up the highway towards San Ignacio.

The close call with the longhorn brings to mind a moose that she and Patricia had narrowly missed hitting on the Gaspé Peninsula highway on their way to Percé. It, too, had come out of nowhere, emerging from a grove of trees flanked by two high ridges overlooking the sea. She recalls Patricia breaking into nervous laughter after their rented sedan had stalled from Elizabeth's automatic reaction in braking and gearing down.

Restarting the motor, Elizabeth had looked over at Patricia and was surprised to see tears in her eyes. "It's not too late to change your mind, you know."

Shaking her head, Patricia pulled down the visor to check for any mascara streaks in the mirror, before countering, "Mother, I'm not going to change my mind."

Then what's made you so emotional? Elizabeth had wanted to say, but held her tongue instead.

Elizabeth can't help but think that all the anti-American sentiment that Patricia had grown up with had somehow backfired. After the Second World War, nationalism had become identified as a dangerous propaganda tool. And yet, over the past decades, with a view toward aspiring to its own unique identity, as Canada strived to distinguish itself from its powerful southern neighbour, it might have unwittingly spawned a nationalistic attitude that is arrogant and intolerant of other ways of life and cultures. How many times had Patricia railed about the Taliban, how Afghani women and children are oppressed, and deserve a life as good as one in Canada? Regardless of the analogies that Elizabeth had tried to draw between what the Americans professed to be doing in Iraq for the Iraqis, and how the Canadian government was justifying its military involvement in Afghanistan, Patricia refused to see any similarity between the two country's respective propaganda machines.

"We're not the U. S. of A., mother. We're not a melting pot, we're a multi-cultural society, committed to furthering democracy in other parts of the world," Patricia had insisted.

Melting pot, multicultural society. What's the fucking difference? If it hadn't been for the occasional glimpse of Mario's eyes in the rearview mirror and Bartek seated on one side of her, and Richard on the other, Elizabeth would have shook her head in dismay.

She recalls editing an essay assigned by Patricia's grade ten social studies teacher on the topic of Canada's multicultural heritage. She hadn't given much thought, at the time, to the concepts that her daughter was regurgitating out of her textbook. She'd had her own curriculum to synthesize and spoon-feed to her undergraduate students, and had been gratified when Patricia had scored a ninety percent on the assignment. She realizes now, particularly while sandwiched in the backseat between Richard and Bartek, neither of whom would be swayed by such cretinous political propaganda, that she should have engaged Patricia in a deeper discussion on the topic.

Looking back at their near encounter with the moose on the highway and how Patricia had erupted into tears, Elizabeth questions the authenticity of her daughter's professed commitment to improving the lives of Afghani women and children. Patricia's tears might have intimated conflicted emotions — feeling torn between what she really wanted for herself and her future, and what she thought was expected of her. Perhaps, on some level, Patricia had simply wanted to challenge, even defy, the value system within which she'd been raised by Elizabeth and Bernard, if only to find out, on her own, what she really believes in and who she really is.

"Ah, the oasis finally looms on the horizon."

Richard's remark spurs Elizabeth to extricate herself from her reverie and to take note of the approaching palm grove, flanking the Town of San Ignacio on its northern edge.

The turnoff takes them past a trailer court from which a broad concrete walkway extends. Modern street lights line the boulevard. Hundreds of date palms spring from the banks of a shallow, but swift flowing river. It's a wide valley, teeming with birds and insects.

They park opposite the mission, in front of the *zócalo*, obscured through the lacework superimposition of the overhanging branches of two gigantic willow trees. Reminiscent of the Québécois settlements that dot the southern shore of the St. Lawrence, *la catedral* dwarfs the one-story adobe dwellings constructed within its perimeter. Elizabeth and Patricia had marvelled at the overbearing gothic churches, predictably positioned at the highest point of every Québécois town, looming like a beacon on the horizon.

Guzman exits the first jeep, approaches them, and turns and points diagonally off the square. "Our hotel is down that narrow street. I thought we could tour the mission first."

"As a group? Or can we just go off on our own?" asks Richard.

"Whatever you would like."

Richard heads off to the left, through a wooden gate that opens onto an adjoining garden. Rather than join the others gathering at the base of the broad stone steps of the *catedral*, Elizabeth decides to follow him. The surrounding stone wall is remarkably well preserved. She imagines the Indians labouring for a bowl of gruel, six days a week, beneath the unrelenting heat of the sun, stacking these stones one on top of another, according to the specifications of the Jesuit missionaries. What must they have thought about this garden? She has no doubt that the missionaries had actually requisitioned grass seed from Spain.

Inlaid rocks provide a pathway across the verdant lawn towards three wooden doorways, hewn an eye's even distance apart into the rectangular wall of the one-story rectory. Elizabeth hesitates before choosing the middle door. It opens with a sonorous creek. Lowering her head to enter, she recalls having encountered such low thresholds in Europe — a testimony to people having been much shorter than they are currently.

A second door lies within the first, constructed of wood and glass. Through the glass pane, she observes a small study lined with bookshelves which are stacked with leather and cloth bound books. A heavy, dark, colonial-style desk and a chair are positioned in the centre of the room. A faded, crème-caramel coloured manuscript, inkwell, and quill inspire the vision of a Jesuit priest bent over, recording the mission's daily yield of dates, corn, eggs, and other provisions.

"Great study, eh?"

"Oh!" Elizabeth jumps and turns around, nearly knocking Richard back against the inverted threshold. "You scared me!"

"Sorry about that. Didn't mean to startle you."

"It's okay. What's behind the other doors?"

"Come on. Let's take a look."

The other two doors open into small bedrooms, much more sparsely furnished than the study. Except for a crucifix, the walls are unadorned. The beds are shorter than by today's standard. A kneeler and bedside table are the only other furnishings.

"Should we join the others inside the church?" Elizabeth asks, worrying that their absence will be noted.

"You go ahead." He points his chin back, towards the direction of the gate. "I've been here many times."

Who with? She wants to ask. She has noticed that when reminiscing about past incursions into the Baja desert, Richard's voice takes on a wistful, faraway tone. "What are you going to do instead?" she asks.

"There's a really cool *tienda* on the corner, over there." Pointing across the lawn, he adds, "I think I'll get myself a *refresco*."

Nodding, Elizabeth retraces her steps along the stone pathway and up the steps into the main building. As soon as she opens the heavy wooden doors, the coolness of the interior hits her and the lingering scent of incense fills her nostrils. An echo resounds from two of her colleagues speaking in lower tones.

Nonetheless, their voices carry. It's Maynard and Bartek peering up at the raised pulpit, above the altar, engaged in a lively, if muted, discussion. Made of ornately carved hardwood, the pulpit is adorned on its apex by a statue of the Virgin of the Ascension. It's a tiny statue, colourfully painted. Mary's arms are bent at the elbow, directed upwards, and her head is raised towards the heavens.

Genuflecting upon passing in front of the altar, Elizabeth backs up into the front pew. Loath to drop the kneeler onto the tile floor, she sits down instead. Crossing herself, she bows her head. Elizabeth has much to pray for, but she's distracted by the unrelenting echo. She notices that Raul and Guzman are seated to the side and appear to be praying. Bidding herself to concentrate, she opts for rote recitation of Our Fathers and Hail Marys. She asks God to spare her daughter, and to give her strength. *Please, dear God, may she make it home safely.* She repeats the phrase over and over.

16.

L A CASA DE SAN FRANCISCO doubles as a restaurant and
tourist information centre. Starched white tablecloths
drape the half dozen colonial style wooden tables, each
romantically illuminated by candlelight. Two men, dressed in
black trousers and white shirts, stand awkwardly behind the bar.
One of the waiters approaches them, nods, mumbles "*buenas
noches*," and extends his arm in invitation for the group to
enter the dining room. As though in anticipation of their arrival, one of the tables is set for eight people. The waiter adds
another place setting and a chair from the adjacent table.

As the area specializes in excursions to *las pinturas rupestres*,
the restaurant's walls and ceiling have been embellished into a
seamless fresco replete with replicas of the birds, deer, arrows
and symbolic geometric figures depicted in the cave murals.
The traveller is also depicted, although unobtrusively, in one
of the corners of the room.

Elizabeth seats herself at the added place setting and Bartek
takes the chair beside her. Richard seats himself across from
them. Guzman, Raul, Mario and Roberto occupy the opposite
end of the table, while Maynard and Pierre join Elizabeth,
Richard and Bartek at their end, forming the English-speaking
contingent of the team.

"So you almost slaughtered a cow on the highway this afternoon?" says Pierre, reaching into his breast pocket for his
cigarettes and offering one to Richard and Elizabeth.

"Thanks. Yes." Richard leans over to catch Pierre's proffered light. "We were lucky."

"You guys were in the backseat," Maynard quips. "It wasn't much fun being in the front, I can tell you."

"So Roberto must have noticed the herd of longhorns through his rearview mirror?" Bartek suggests.

"I think he saw the herd before Mario did. All of a sudden he slowed down and said '*Dios mio*.' When I saw his eyes focused in the mirror, I turned around and saw Mario swerve just in time. You have been here before, Richard, *non*?"

"A few times, yes."

"Has it changed much over the years?"

"Last time I was here, five years ago, there was no boulevard running from the trailer court to town. Just a narrow asphalt road ran through the palm grove into town."

"It is quite impressive," says Bartek.

"Just another example of Mexican machismo and corruption. Whoever got the contract for a project of that magnitude was probably able to retire for life. You also have to wonder who it was who came up with the idea that by constructing the boulevard, the town would attract tourists and flourish. How ridiculous! They don't even have a decent bloody toilet to take a crap in, but they have a resort promenade!"

Bartek's eyes narrow and a deep line develops across the bridge of his nose. Elizabeth has to stop herself from breaking out laughing. His expression reveals utter exasperation at Richard's outpouring of frustration. She jogs her memory for another instance when Richard has let loose such pent up anger, and then recalls, on their drive to the Carcamo ranch, his diatribe about the unsustainability of urban sprawl in Southern California due to limited water resources. Bernard, too, had been prone to such outbursts. Sometimes for days she'd sense the tension build up inside him. Relentlessly asking him what was wrong, he'd invariably respond with "nothing," until, as they were turning in for the night, she'd finally confront him and his anxiety over a client's lawsuit would finally surface, but not before projecting his frustrations on her. By the time they'd separated, she'd had her fill of Bernard railing about how she couldn't leave things alone and always had to stir things up.

Elizabeth waits until the waiter has circumnavigated the table with two bottles of wine, before raising her glass and proposing a toast to their first evening together.

"*Salud!*" the team members declare in unison.

"Mmm, *pas mal*." Setting down his glass, the Frenchman leans across the table and counters with, "But the Baja, from what I've seen of it, is beautiful. And there are many trailers in the park. What is this Mexican machismo?" he asks Richard.

"Lofty dreams that turn to dust," Richard takes one final drag off his cigarette before extinguishing it. "It's a chauvinistic mindset or attitude. I find that a lot of the men down here are full of bravado and have an inflated opinion of themselves and what they can accomplish. Have you ever noticed all the buildings with rebar jutting out of the concrete? They start something but don't finish it. They don't think it through and run out of money."

"Or grease someone's palm for the funds to finish it," interjects Maynard.

"But they did finish the boulevard," Elizabeth counters. She intentionally resists looking over at Bartek, who might interpret her interruption as more than a collegial interjection and is gratified by their waiter having chosen this moment to bring out baskets of tortilla chips with salsa.

"This restaurant wasn't here either. It's quite the place," Richard concedes, a tinge of sheepishness permeating his tone.

"So, I take it one can arrange an excursion up to the cave site by mule through the proprietor?" Elizabeth poses her question bluntly, intending to inculcate a spirit of civility and collegiality amongst the group. A veteran at directing conversational traffic in the classroom, she's come to realize that few of her male colleagues consider the instructional component of their academic positions to have much value. The priority of her male academic colleagues is to compete for the accolades and recognition garnered through the publication of papers.

"Appears so, yes," Richard replies "I recall only being able to do that through a restaurant in Guerrero Negro."

"And that is north of the Sierra de San Francisco, *non?*" Pierre asks.

"That's right. Great place to watch the Pacific grey whales this time of year." Richard throws Elizabeth a cursory glance, intended, she presumes, as an acknowledgement that a modification in his tone was in order.

"And at San Carlos, I understand," Bartek adds.

"Magdalena Bay, which is one of several lagoons that the Mexican government, as far back as the seventies, decreed as conservation zones to protect the grey whales mating and breeding grounds." Richard digs into the tortilla chips and salsa and then lifts the basket, inviting the others to follow suit.

"And have you seen them?" Brigham asks.

"At San Carlos, yes. But that was a few years back, and then, it was like the longhorns on the road this afternoon. You get into a *panga* with a Mexican skipper and before you have a chance to digest your coffee and know what's going on, a pod of whales is swarming around you and then you realize, holy cow, pardon the pun, one big slap of the tail and you're in the water."

"No life jackets?" adds Maynard.

"*Nada.*" Richard shakes his head.

The conversation becomes suspended by the waiter completing his rounds with the main courses.

"What is that?" Bartek asks, pointing delicately with his fork in Elizabeth's direction.

"Chicken in mole sauce. It's a mixture of various peppers, almonds, and chocolate."

"So that's what gives it such a dark colour?"

"Yes. And a slightly bitter taste. Almost like coffee."

"Chocolate without the sugar."

"Yes. Would you like a taste?" Elizabeth senses Richard's body stiffen. Is she punishing him for his outburst?

"*Si, por favor.*"

Carving a piece of white meat off the breast, she sets it along the rim of her plate. Bartek picks it up with his fork and dips it into the dark brown sauce. He chews very slowly, appearing to savour the taste, before breaking into a smile. "Mmm. It's — how do you say it in Spanish? — *Muy rico.*"

"*Si. Muy rico.*"

"So you have tried this dish before?"

"Yes, in San José del Cabo."

"So you visited the capes after your fact-finding mission with Dr. Wellington?" The emphatic manner in which Bartek enunciates Richard's name tells her that it's not merely her imagination that Bartek has sensed something beyond mere friendship having developed between her and Richard.

"Yes." She hunches over her plate so as not to have to make eye contact with Richard.

"You mentioned that your daughter is stationed in Afghanistan."

A wave of nausea overcomes her. Willing herself to appear unperturbed by his question, she sets down her knife and fork and leans back into the backrest of her chair. "Yes."

"Is she able to contact you by cell phone?"

"No. My ex-husband is passing on news of her to me."

"Do you think you will have reception in the high sierras?"

Shaking her head, she replies, "I doubt it, but I'll be calling Bernard tonight before we leave civilization."

"Are you worried about your daughter being posted there?"

"No. She is in intelligence and is not sent into combat."

Breaking into a smile, he asks, "You don't appear to me

like a person who would be in favour of your child pursuing a military career."

"I wasn't. We had plenty of arguments about it. Patricia was absolutely adamant that by joining the military she was engaging in a humanitarian effort. I tried to dissuade her from these, what can I call them?"

"Illusions."

"Yes. Illusions. But she thought I was being cynical."

"My involvement with the Solidarity Movement in Poland was an illusion too. But such is the idealism of youth. You have raised a good person and you should be proud of that."

Unable to continue to keep up appearances, Elizabeth excuses herself from the table. Cursing herself for being so generous with her feelings, she catches the eye of the waiter who points her in the direction of the *baños*.

I should have changed the subject, or at least stopped myself from mentioning how Patricia and I argued over her recruitment, she thinks. She can't imagine she'll be able to keep the truth from Bartek for much longer. He'll likely give it a rest for the time being but she knows there's little doubt that he'll bring up the subject again. The thought of calling Bernard after dinner makes her want to scream. *Fuck! Why did we have to start talking about this?* And Richard, upon seeing her exit the *catedral* ahead of the group, had insisted that they see one another in his room, after everyone else has turned in for the night. *He'll likely have something to say about Bartek. He doesn't own me, for Christ's sake. Surely he must realize that now that we're rubbing shoulders with everyone else in the group, our liaison has to end.*

She applies a coat of lipstick, which she's destined to consume with the rest of her *pollo mole* anyway, but as she leaves the sanctity of the bathroom she feels somehow armed, ready to once again face the inquisitive intellects of her colleagues in the dining room.

17.

"WHAT'S WITH YOU and the Polish geologist?" Richard asks, turning over and propping his head onto the palm of his hand.

"He's not a geologist. He studied geology before going into anthropology."

"Aren't we being defensive?"

She shifts her body from its prone position and sits up. She has the urge to flee back to her own room, but after her telephone conversation with Bernard, spending the night alone would mean tossing and turning, fighting all night to overcome one of her insomniac episodes.

Not since their separation had Bernard sounded so distraught, so agitated. He'd hardly made sense, spouting off about yesterday's partnership meeting, his partners having decided, on account of Bernard potentially posing a security risk, that he should be relieved of handling a file for an oil company involved in a joint venture drilling project in Kazakhstan. When she asked whether the client's operations included sequestering carbon dioxide underground, Bernard had blown up. "How the fuck should I know!"

"I just knew you'd get all out of joint over my sitting beside Bartek. He's a colleague, just like you. You and I just happened to get intimate because of what's been going on with Patricia."

"Is that the only reason?" His eyes narrow, accentuating the fine wrinkles clustering around them. She feels a pang of regret at having stated the obvious. "I didn't mean it like that. Look, if we hadn't met on the beach that afternoon, it's highly unlikely we'd be together right now. What's happened, happened. I have no regrets, you know that." Running her fingers along the small of his back, she adds, "I've been pretty vulnerable and needy since Patricia was taken hostage. I haven't been myself. And I don't know if I'd even be here if it wasn't for you."

"But we went over that," Richard said, his fingers lightly tracing the line of her collar bone "You'd be doing the same up there. Worrying. And what's with that Guzman? Man, I was embarrassed for you."

As though on cue, as soon as the dinner plates had been whisked away, a flamenco guitarist had casually strolled into the restaurant. Guzman promptly ordered a round of brandy and after downing two snifters, invited Elizabeth to join him on the dance floor. During the second song, he'd held her so close that she could feel his heart beating against her breasts.

"I know. He took advantage of me. He's a predator."

"You say that so glibly. He knows what you're going through. How can you be so unemotional about it?"

"All men are predatory."

"But we're talking about professional ethics here."

"Old habits die hard. He was just having a bit of fun. He drank too much, which unleashed his limbic system. That old mammalian part of our brains that's responsible for hard-ons."

"Man." Richard gives off a shiver, turns onto his back and pulls the covers up to his chin. "Just a few hundred kilometres up the peninsula and you can feel the desert chill this time of year. Don't want to think about what it's like higher up, in the sierras. Wait a minute. Did I hear you correctly? All men are predatory?"

"Come on, you know the theory. We've evolved physiologically according to the preference of the opposite sex. Women were naturally selected to have the hourglass shape, while you guys have narrow hips and broad shoulders. Applied psychologically, women select the most predatory males, while men prefer the nurturing type of woman."

"Yeah, yeah, yeah. But our limbic system has been displaced by the part of our brains that is responsible for reasoning and socio-political behaviour."

"I don't know. Maybe women should govern. I think we're more socio-politically inclined than men. Male predatory instincts guaranteed our survival. But they're pretty tough to shed in only a few thousand years."

"War. That's what's kept us predatory."

"Do you think he's a misogynist?"

"Who? Guzman?"

Nodding, Elizabeth lies back down. As she drapes her body along the length of his, she pulls the covers over her shoulders.

Richard shifts his head a bit to share his pillow with her. "Well. Mexico has mandatory military service. The military is misogynist. I've done a bit of reading on that." He turns his head toward her and waits until she follows suit, captures her attention with his eyes. "The Vietnam War precipitated a lot of analysis on what caused so much mental illness among the vets. A lot of those guys, even the ones who weren't maimed, never married."

"I didn't know that," Elizabeth concedes. She pulls her arm from beneath the cover and grasps Richard's hand.

"Loving a woman, having a family, is diametrically opposed to training someone to kill another person. On sight. Simply because they're behind enemy lines. I read that in the marines they condition recruits to kill by using deprecatory language in reference to women. Remember that scene in *An Officer and a Gentleman* when the marines are in training, doing maneuvers and singing?"

Elizabeth jogs her memory, recalls the scene of the regiment, training, marching in song. "That's a great film."

"Yes, but…" Richard nods his head for emphasis. "The songs they sing in real life are nothing like in Hollywood movies. They're full of swear words, calling women cunts, sluts, and whores. The intent is to stamp out all sensitivity, all tender feelings that a young man might harbour for a woman, even for his mother."

"What if they have children and wives?"

"They draft eighteen-year-olds."

Elizabeth gives off a shiver. Patricia had been recruited at school, and only later revealed that the recruiter had pumped her for all kinds of information about her grades, whether she enjoyed school and planned to further her education. Elizabeth recalls having felt very dismayed. She'd always assumed that Patricia had taken it for granted that she and her father would pay for her university. The recruiter had spoken about the Canadian Forces Base in Kingston, and how Queen's University had a "dynamite" (Patricia had used that adjective) International Relations program, tailored for the military's best and brightest recruits. When Elizabeth had discussed the recruiter's tactics with Bernard he'd compared the military's tactics to the brainwashing that the Moonies had applied in the seventies to conscript wayward adolescents to join the ranks of the Unification Church. *How could I have allowed her to throw her life away?* Elizabeth laments. *Maybe Bernard was right. Maybe I didn't do enough to dissuade her from enlisting.*

"The Nazis used pornography to suppress occupied countries during the Second World War. They inundated the place with pornography. The message was that women, even the enemy's women, were theirs. They wanted the men in occupied countries to know that."

"So what's happening with my daughter?"

Richard pulls himself away from her, like one does when observing a painting in a museum, to gain a better perspective, and then shakes his head. "Don't know. These fundamentalists are a strange breed. Osama bin Laden has his wives live near their training camps. I understand he's a good husband and father. I don't think your daughter's being abused." He hesitates before blurting out, "She may be safer with the Taliban."

Elizabeth shoots him a look of bewilderment.

"I don't know about the Canadian military in Afghanistan. I only know that in Iraq, female soldiers have it bad."

"How so?"

"Before I came down here, I heard about two female soldiers who died of dehydration." He pauses before continuing. His Adam's apple jumps as he swallows. "It had been a long, hot day. They should have been drinking lots of water. But there were no lights on the way to the latrines. They were so afraid of getting jumped on the way to the latrines, they stayed in their barracks."

"This made the news?"

"No. I picked it up on a website."

"Why didn't you tell me this earlier?"

"Look, the Canadian army isn't the American military."

"What else did you pick up on this website?"

Richard shakes his head. "You don't want to hear this."

"Yes, I do."

"The theory is that in Vietnam the military was able to control the sexual urges of the troops by paying Vietnamese women to prostitute themselves, but in Iraq that's not possible so they've recruited way more women to serve in combat roles."

"You can't be serious."

He nods. His eyes dart back and forth, as though he is having second thoughts about having divulged this latest revelation about women in combat roles.

"What else?"

"I don't want to say any more. You're already distraught."

"No, please, tell me."

Richard hesitates. "There's a woman who's currently sitting in jail after going AWOL. She refused to withdraw a complaint about being sexually assaulted. They convicted her of desertion."

Elizabeth suddenly can't get enough air. She begins hyper-ventilating.

"Are you alright?"

She shakes her head, lies down, turns over on her side, and assumes a fetal position.

Richard lies down beside her, spoons her against his body, rocks her back and forth until she falls asleep.

18.

P ARTING THE CURTAINS, Elizabeth looks out onto the back of the hotel where the jeeps are parked. None of the adjacent houses are illuminated yet. The faintest glow of the rising sun is reflected in wisps of cloud, superimposed upon a sky slowly shedding its blackness, embracing an intensifying navy blue hue.

The chill of the desert morning washes over her. Her naked body gives off a shiver. It's still warm beneath the covers but she decides against crawling back in beside Richard. As quietly as possible, she pulls on her sweater, underwear, and jeans.

"What're you doing?"

"I don't want the others to see me," she whispers. "Go back to sleep."

With three quick movements, he's out of bed, pulling his T-shirt over his head, and his undershorts over his buttocks. Waiting until she finishes lacing up her running shoes, he takes her in his arms, holds her close for a few moments. "Was last night really our last time together?"

"Let's not talk about this now. I have to go."

A loud bang, as though something has dropped on the floor in the room next door, prompts Elizabeth to disengage herself from his embrace. Placing her forefinger against her lips, she listens for any other sound before opening the door and poking her head out. She raises her hand in parting and closes the door quietly behind her.

She catches a whiff of fried bacon wafting from the kitchen as she walks across the seemingly deserted courtyard. Pulling her key out of her front pocket, she quickly inserts it into the lock of her door, but is suddenly startled by the screech of one of the parrots caged within the courtyard's tropical foliage. Just as she is about to open the door to her room, she catches the shadow of another person in the courtyard. She has the feeling that it's the mole. *What the fuck is this!* She can't believe he's followed her here, to San Ignacio.

Clutching her room key, she steps back out into the courtyard. A small woman with bronze skin and graying hair pulled back into a bun, stands at the opposite end of the *jardin* with a garden hose, methodically shifting its nozzle from one clay pot to another.

"*Buenas dias.*" Elizabeth struggles to control her voice from sounding agitated.

Nodding, the woman mumbles back her greeting.

"*Por favor, señora.* Did you see a man pass through the courtyard a moment ago?"

"*Si.*"

"Did you notice in which direction he went?"

The woman points toward the back of the motel.

"*Gracias.*" Elizabeth hurries back across the courtyard, toward the gate that leads to the back of the motel. Skirting the side of the building, she sees an all-terrain vehicle pull out of the parking lot and accelerate down the dirt road. She takes note of the fact that the rear licence plate is a white one, with a "DF" inscription. Through the rising dust, she's unable to make out the number.

Retracing her steps back into the courtyard, she's surprised to bump into Maynard Brigham.

"Everything all right?" he asks.

Is it her imagination or does she detect a trace of sarcasm in his question? "Yes, fine."

"You seem out of breath."

"It's nothing. What time is breakfast, do you know?"

Checking his wristwatch, Maynard replies, "Not for another half hour. Did you want to grab a *café con leche*?"

"Sure."

"So did you get a hold of your ex-husband last night?"

"Yes." Elizabeth is taken aback by his question, until she realizes that he likely overheard her conversation with Bartek over dinner.

"Everything all right with your daughter?"

Prickles run up and down her spine. There's something spiteful in his tone. "Yes," she replies quickly, hoping to avoid further questions.

Maynard claims the first table in the dining room, adjacent to the tropical bird cages in the courtyard. Elizabeth studies the cages and wonders which parrot screeched out its warning.

"Your father, he's retired?" Elizabeth asks, as he politely pulls out a chair for her.

"Yes, he is."

"What type of engineer is he?"

"Pipeline engineer. Why do you ask?"

"I found it interesting that you know so much about geo-sequestration."

Maynard smiles. "Leo, my father, did his Master's degree in chemical engineering. His thesis examined the possibility of sequestering carbon dioxide underground."

"When was that?"

"In the 1970s. Late '70s."

"So they've been considering this palliative remedy for a while?" Elizabeth cannot hide the sarcasm in her voice.

"Palliative remedy! You make it sound so nefarious."

"It is nefarious, don't you think? Shouldn't we be pursuing less greedy options, such as conservation, wind, and solar power?"

"And your father?" Maynard arrogantly raises his chin challengingly towards her. "What did he do for a living?"

Elizabeth cringes at his question. Again, she has the uncanny feeling that he knows more about her than he's letting on. "He was a lab tech at one of the refineries in Edmonton."

"Ah, yes. Refinery row. And now they're expanding the industrial heartland of central Alberta northwest, I understand."

"I didn't know that. *Gracias*." Nodding at the waitress, Elizabeth reaches for the sugar bowl and heaps a spoonful of sugar into her cup.

"What part of Edmonton do you come from?"

"You know the city?"

"My uncle, my mother's brother, lived there. He, too, was an engineer. For Esso."

"Northwest. My father didn't want to raise us in the eastern part of the city near all the industry, so he put up with the commute for over thirty years."

"Yes, thank god for the prevailing west winds. But I understand it doesn't make much difference now. With climate change, Edmonton has become a lot windier; and once they finish constructing the upgraders, north of the city, whenever a north wind blows, the entire city will become engulfed by toxic fumes."

"Unless they capture the emissions at the source," Elizabeth adds, sipping at her coffee.

"Precisely."

"It's an expensive proposition."

"No doubt."

Maynard shoots her a look of bewilderment and, under ordinary circumstances, Elizabeth would back off, change the subject, but she's too agitated. "But not for India." Or Kazakhstan, she wants to add, but bites her tongue.

"I wouldn't know." His mouth is obscured by his cup. Licking some of the foam that clings to his lips, Maynard appears to be straining his lips, counteracting a reaction to smile, gloat. His eyes, though, belie his answer. They convey a shiftiness, as though he's hiding something.

Elizabeth gropes for another question that might edge her closer to the truth, and what he has to do with the man who's been following her. It suddenly hits her that Richard was assigned the last room in the row let out to the group. A stranger had occupied the room next door. Was it the mole? Had he fled after dropping something on the floor? She conjures an image of a handgun and shudders. Whatever it was that he dropped was heavy. "Have you ever been to the Baja before?" she asks, determined to uncover anything that might be suspicious.

"Just to Los Cabos. A couple of years ago over Christmas."

"When did you arrive here?"

"For this assignment?"

He waits for her to nod before answering. "On the Tuesday. And you?"

"The following evening. On Wednesday. Where did you stay in La Paz?"

"I didn't. I stayed in San José. I drove up on the Monday morning."

"At the Tropicana?"

"Why? Is that where you and Wellington holed up for the weekend?"

She feels herself blush. That he knows that she and Richard had travelled to the capes is a no brainer. She'd mentioned to Bartek that she'd first sampled *pollo mole* in San José. "Yes. We quite liked the beach nearby. And it's so central, just off the *zócalo*."

"Yes, I know what you mean. That's where I stayed with my girlfriend two years ago."

"And are the two of you still together?"

Sliding his coffee cup into the centre of the table, he shakes his head. "No. It didn't work out. She's now married to my best friend."

"Oh ... I'm sorry," Elizabeth says in a genuinely apologetic tone.

Maynard shrugs. "Now that I've stayed at the Tropicana again, I've wiped out the memory of our being there together. I can move on. The slate is clean."

Elizabeth envisages erasing words off a whiteboard as she's done hundreds of times in front of the classroom. Instead of wiping away words, though, Maynard has spoken about erasing memories, some undoubtedly steeped in tender moments, others overflowing with laughter and joy. But betrayal can debilitate. He must have been serious about her or he wouldn't have felt compelled to suppress his girlfriend's memory, the wound that she and his friend had inflicted. Her own parents had felt betrayed after the war, relegated to immigrating as refugees — displaced persons — unable to return to their homeland after it had been overrun by Stalin's military machine. Stanislaw had never lost hope that Poland and the other satellite countries would one day regain their independence. Her mother, though, like Maynard, had wiped the slate clean and rarely spoke about the past. Whenever Elizabeth had suffered rejection or disappointment over a severed friendship, Krystyna always counseled her to look ahead, to embrace the future and put the past behind her.

"Thanks, Maynard, for inviting me for coffee." With a heavy heart, Elizabeth rises from the table. "I need to pack my things before breakfast." She knows that this is a lame excuse for not lending him more of her ear but she feels too overwhelmed by her own worries and simply cannot fathom ever wiping the slate clean.

19.

V ARIANT HUES OF GREEN overwhelm the eye. The San Francisco mountain range reminds Elizabeth of a gigantic green terrace. Thousands of coniferous saplings, stunted in their growth, cling precariously by their roots to the rugged, rocky slopes.

The villagers are goat herdsmen. The soft tinkling of bells rises and falls with the goats' sure-footed clamber across the inclining terrain. The settlement is littered with old rusted cars, many of which have had their tires stripped. The tires have been painted blue and white and arranged for use as a playground for the village children. A group of *niños* clambers up a pyramid of blue painted tires; two others jump from one tire to the next, submerged vertically in an evenly spaced row.

The flickering sunlight off the chrome of retreating jeep bumpers, disappearing out of sight over the crest of the hill, creates a pang of apprehension in Elizabeth's chest. It's as though the last remnants of civilization have vanished with their departure. Any contact, albeit limited, that she had with the outside world has departed in a cloud of dust.

Even with the chauffeurs' departure, their numbers have expanded by two. Dr. Guzman introduces the team to the oldest of their four guides, José Morelo. A broad-chested man with a full head of dark hair, his brown eyes convey a deep sensitivity with a tinge of mischievousness. Shaking the hand of each team member, he stands back beside his three sons — Felipe, Antonio, and Pablo.

"Please call me José. *Mucho gusto y bienvenidos a La Sierra de San Francisco.*"

A discussion ensues between Guzman and Morelo about the photographer, Carolina Madero, due to arrive in a few days' time from Mexico City. It's agreed that one of the guides will return to the village to accompany her back to the base camp.

Elizabeth's brain goes into high gear. "*Doctoro* Guzman, *por favor*. Can I make one last call on the land line here in the village? And would it be possible for me to leave the number with my ex-husband in Calgary?"

Guzman turns to José and explains the situation. She's grateful that the others have convened at the other end of the small ranch to survey the mule team that will convey them and their supplies to their base camp.

José asks Elizabeth to follow him. Magenta bougainvillaea drapes the front of the Morelo ranch house. A flock of chickens root along the ground, spread their wings momentarily, and scurry out of their way. The door to the *casa* is open. A woman stands over the kitchen sink, peeling tomatoes. Mariachi music pours out of the transistor radio propped on the window sill. The reception is heavily punctuated with static. José directs Elizabeth to the telephone in the living room, a typically dark room, with just one window facing west.

When the voice message system kicks in on Bernard's direct line, she leaves a message with the Morelo's telephone number. She peers through the window at the mountain range. A pair of frigates soars above the highest peak. The birds' circular surveillance of the landscape for prey, as methodically executed as a choreographed dance movement, brings to mind the satellite images of Patricia with her captors — a bird's eye view, discernible predominantly due to movement. She imagines that her captors move their victims every few days, in the dead of night. The grainy snapshot captured in a split second of light, beamed from the stratosphere, is treated like a mere experiment, an exercise in testing reconnaissance technology.

The voices from the kitchen become muted. She turns to face José. "*Gracias.*"

"*De nada,*" José replies. "*Doctora* Thiessen, *mi esposa*, Dolores."

"*Mucho gusto.*"

La Señora hastily wipes her hands on her apron, and extends her right one for Elizabeth to shake.

Embracing his wife, José explains that if, in their absence, she receives a phone call from Canada, she should write down the person's name and convey the information to the base camp, through one of the other guides in the village. Turning to Elizabeth, he says, "There is nothing else you can do. It rests now in God's hands. *Vámonos.*"

A group of preschoolers awkwardly fall in line behind them as they cross the dusty yard to the mule pen. The children hang back and lean against the gray, splintered boards of the animal enclosure to watch the saddling ritual.

"I have just the burro for you. Very gentle and obedient. You can ride behind me for the first leg of the journey." José lifts the metal clasp to open the gate.

There are fifteen mules in total, four of which evidently serve exclusively as pack animals. The quartet has been segregated from the rest of the herd, and upon their backs Antonio and Pablo strap bundles of provisions and camping equipment.

José jostles his way into the centre of the fray, nudging the rear ends of the mules. He asks everyone to give him five minutes of their attention. "*Los burros* will be hydrating themselves along the way from the mountain streams. Do not drink any stream water. As you can see." He points to Antonio securing two large blue bottles of water onto the back of one of the pack animals. "We have water for drinking. Please fill your individual bottles. There is a satchel attached to your saddles that you can carry your water in. Each of you must carry your own duffle bags. If you can't manage to securely harness it onto the ends of your saddle, just ask for help. The terrain we'll be traversing is very steep and we don't want anything falling over a cliff and becoming irretrievably lost."

"Here, let me help you with your duffle bag," Bartek smiles widely at Elizabeth as he strides over to her.

"Thank you, Bartek, but I should try and do it myself."

"No, it's okay. My mule is ready to go." He smiles at her before asking, "Is everything all right with your daughter?"

Elizabeth pauses before answering. "No. You've been sensing that all is not well." Sighing deeply, she no longer holds herself back. "She was kidnapped by the Taliban almost two weeks ago. And last night I learned that my ex-husband has been relieved of handling a file on behalf of an oil company doing business in Kazakhstan."

"I've been sensing that you're under a lot of strain." From behind his sunglasses, Elizabeth detects a sympathetic crinkling of his eyes. "You left the Morelo's phone number with your ex?"

"Yes."

"That is all you can do."

"Yes."

He pulls her close to his side and rubs his hand up and down her arm, before releasing her. Turning away, Elizabeth blinks her eyes hard a few times to keep herself from crying. One tear manages to escape. She claws at it as it traces its way down her cheek. The glare of the sun seems to be conspiring against her. It's too bright all of a sudden. She longs for darkness, to become invisible, non-existent.

"Everything cool over here?" Richard ambles over to them, but stops in his tracks upon seeing Elizabeth wipe the tear from her face.

Recovering her composure, Elizabeth replies, "Yes, everything's okay, Bartek was just helping me with my duffle bag."

"Did you want to ride in front of me?"

"José has offered to let me ride directly behind him. I guess he must have sensed that I'm a little nervous. Apparently they've relegated the gentlest and most obedient mule for the female member of the team." She pats the grey and white mottled buttock of her burro.

"It looks like we're ready to go," says Bartek. "See you later."

"See you. And thanks." Turning to Richard, she says, "I had to tell him. He's been asking about my daughter."

"Soon everyone will know."

"Is that so wrong?" She realizes as she studies his face, particularly his mouth, which he's sometimes in the habit of leaving open after speaking, that no relationship is exempt from covetousness and control. Or is it mere habit? Richard has become accustomed to being the only one in the know. It has set him apart from the others, yielded him an exclusivity, a distinctiveness.

"No."

"Don't be jealous of my friendship with Bartek."

"I'm not," Richard retorts, turning on his heels and walking away.

20.

AS SEÑOR MORELO HAD PREDICTED, the first stream they encounter serves as a resting post for the mules. The burros lap up the water as though it might be their last chance at a drink.

Antonio disperses white handkerchiefs and shows the team how to beat the heat. Dipping the rectangular cotton cloth in the stream, he wipes his face and neck, re-immerses it in the water, wrings it out, clutches it by its two ends, and turns it a couple of times before tying it around his forehead. "Further along, the path becomes much steeper. Sweat in the eyes can prove a hazard when reigning in an animal that decides to stray."

Everyone remounts their burros and the caravan continues its descent into the canyon of the cave painters. Elizabeth has become as docile as her burro, who she's secretly christened *"Seguridad"* — security. Allowing her body to be jostled gently by the rhythmic swaying flanks of her mule, she rests her eyes upon the horizon. Layer upon layer of rock castles, like a rolled out bolt of blue cloth, one mountain range seamlessly gives rise to another jagged furrow of heaved up terrain.

Elizabeth watches José prod the flanks of his mule with his boot heels. She imitates the clicking of his tongue, urging her burro forward along the steepening trail. Even though she doesn't suffer from vertigo, she purposely desists from looking downwards. Up ahead she glimpses the silver thread of a stream dissecting a narrow wedge at the base of the canyon. A small avalanche of rocks tumbles down the ridge, towards the stream bed. Echoes of plunging stone ricochet against scree. The burros are well trained and hardly flinch at the giving way of rock. From time to time one of the burros exhales a loud snort. Their hides glisten with sweat and exude a sweet, musky scent.

Seguridad suddenly bellows vociferously, stops in its tracks, refuses to budge. *"Adelante, burro,"* she urges, kicking its haunches and jostling her bum forward in the saddle. A rattle, followed by hissing sound, cuts the dry mountain air. The mule brays again, belligerently stomps its hooves. Elizabeth instinctively wrenches the reins. The burro yanks its head forward, resists her impulse to restrain it from stomping the serpent to death.

Antonio, who's directly behind her, dismounts and runs up to them brandishing a machete. He grabs the reins with one hand, and in one fell swoop with the other, decapitates the snake.

Cowering with her back edged along the canyon wall, Elizabeth cements her gaze upon the decapitated serpent, its body still writhing spasmodically, emitting its final tremors.

"Tranquilo, burrito." Antonio strokes Seguridad's mane and nods toward Elizabeth before offering her back the reins. "This is not a good spot to rest." Gesturing with his chin towards the steep precipice, he kicks the coiled snake's body off the cliff. Her hands shake as she takes the reins from him. He cups his hands together and gestures with his head for her to allow him to help her step back into the stirrup.

"Gracias."

"De nada. No te preocupes. It could have happened to anyone."

José waits until his son is back in the saddle, heel butts the sides of his burro and kick starts the caravan back into motion.

Overcome by an overwhelming craving to drink something, Elizabeth swallows hard a few times to stimulate her salivary glands. The path they're traversing is so precipitous, that any attempt on her part to retrieve her water bottle from her satchel would almost certainly court another disaster.

"Don't look down. Keep your eyes ahead of you," Antonio commands, as they round the side of the mountain and the pathway winds onto a plateau.

José's mule picks up a little speed. Seguridad follows suit. To thwart the jarring effect of her mule's canter on her spine, Elizabeth sits tall in the saddle, straightens her back. Seguridad has already forgotten about the snake. There is no lingering, incapacitating trauma. In comparison to lower forms of life, humans are at a distinct disadvantage. Memory is a two-edged sword. Danger is indelibly etched on the human brain's gray matter as a precaution against its recurrence, but the broader, more expansive range of possible emotions somehow militates against speedy recovery. If Patricia survives her ordeal, she'll undoubtedly become the latest casualty of post-traumatic stress disorder. Her own father never recovered from the horrible indignities suffered at the hands of the Nazis in Mauthausen concentration camp. He'd been a pill popper for as long as she could remember — sleeping pills and tranquilizers, the latter having been lauded the panacea for chronic depression before antidepressant medication was concocted in the same pharmaceutical laboratories that had been given the privilege of experimenting on death camp inmates.

The sun is now behind them, composing angled shadows of the caravan. At this time of day, their shadows are ludicrously shrunken. She has the urge to wave, to see how short her arm appears in shadow form.

The burros do a beeline for the stream on the floor of a wide valley. Here they're enveloped in shade. A cool breeze wafts through the canyon, condenses the sweat on their bodies. Someone, it sounds like Pierre, complains that he feels cold.

"Boy, you're sure having a time of it," remarks Richard, gulping back water out of his bottle as he approaches Elizabeth.

"I was terrified I was going to fall backward, down the ridge."

Guzman ambles over towards them. "*Todo bien?* Sometimes, *los serpientes* can be tricky."

Sweating profusely, he wipes his brow and neck with his handkerchief. "Mules will stomp a snake or other predator to death, you know. That is why *los vaqueros* often keep burros in the same pen with the horses. For protection. How are your buttocks?"

Elizabeth is taken aback by his question. Instead of looking into his eyes, her focus is upon Guzman's mouth. The harder her heart pounds, the larger his lips appear. She imagines, with a shudder, him kissing her, the slobbering wetness enveloping her mouth.

"Not to worry, *Doctoro*, I can give her a massage tonight," Richard says, placing his hand on Elizabeth's shoulder.

Guzman laughs and grabs onto his own backside. "I could use one too."

Elizabeth feels like striking Guzman over the head. She's astounded at her impulse. She conjures the image of the rattlesnake's forked tongue protruding out of its jaw, but Guzman's head, instead of the serpent's is decapitated with Antonio's machete.

"It's not far now," Guzman says. "We should make it before sunset. Oh, *mira*, some snacks to help us get through the last leg of our journey."

She follows Guzman's focus towards Felipe making his rounds with a paper bag.

She shakes her head at Felipe's proffering of a granola bar.

"You must eat something, *Doctora*," Felipe insists. "After such a shock you are not hungry, but it is better to eat. We still have at least two more hours before supper. It is a specialty of our village, with dates from the oasis of San Ignacio and rolled in honey. Honey is good for you. It has chemicals that ward against depression."

"*Gracias.*" A chill washes over her and she begins to shake uncontrollably. Eyeing a large boulder overlooking the gorge, beyond the shadow of the summit, within a block of angled sunlight, she furtively extricates herself from the others. Like a salve, the day's heat radiates from the rock surface, and through her body. The chill evaporates, but she feels herself falling into a well of self-pity. Out of eleven riders, why did the rattler have to provoke her and Seguridad?

Elizabeth takes a bite out of her granola bar. The sweetness brings on a flood of tears. Salt trickles down her throat, making it difficult for her to swallow.

She hates feeling so needy. Her father had always frowned upon vulnerability. "Never let them see you sweat," he'd chastise. "Always hold your head high." She'd unwittingly passed on the same lessons to Patricia. *Does she have a chance to have a cry in a corner by herself, beyond the immediate, prying eyes of her captors? Is it even possible to cry with a blindfold bound across your eyes?* Elizabeth's eyes well up again. She blinks hard, suppresses her urge to weep.

Standing, she casts her eyes upon the craggy rim of the canyon and ponders her conversation last night with Richard, takes solace from his belief that the Muslim fundamentalists are a strange breed, that it's unlikely Patricia's captors will harm her. *But can I, should I, believe him? What about the Taliban forcing women to cover themselves with a burkha, prohibiting girls from attending school, sentencing married women accused of adultery to death by stoning?* Elizabeth thinks back to how, with so much passion and conviction, Patricia had defended her decision to better the lives of those women and she is overwrought with despair.

21.

ATHED IN GOLDEN TWILIGHT, hoodoo-like volcanic formations, coloured like salamanders in shades of grey and brown, with a splash of ochre, rise like phallic symbols from the sun-baked arroyo of San Pablo. The expedition pitches camp within the circular formation of the stone outcrops. The ring of boulders is reminiscent of a rampart, contiguous to a medieval fortress. A frigid desert breeze, its howl resonating within the canyon walls, whips through the *arroyo* — a signal that only minutes of sunlight remain. The team works frantically, as though to outpace the pending darkness. Duffle bags are inverted upside down and their contents are shaken onto the ground. The Morelos hand out tents and bedrolls, and designate spots for the pitching of tents.

Pablo collects fist-sized rocks to use as makeshift hammers for the pounding in of spikes. Distributing the rocks to the team members, he then picks up a piece of choy — desiccated cordon cactus — and hands it to Elizabeth. "There should be lots of this throughout the arroyo. Can you collect some?"

"*Bien.*" Elizabeth scans the ground for kindling. She can't imagine that the choy burns very efficiently, but, as Richard has counselled on more than one occasion, Mexico is full of surprises.

She observes that the vegetation in the arroyo appears to be in transition. With a warming climate, the cacti are flourishing, while the coniferous saplings appear threatened by the new competition. She recalls reading somewhere that this setback, during which adaptation occurs, might be temporary; that plants thrive when in competition with one another. Human beings also thrive when rivaling one another, but on a crowded planet with dwindling resources, the breakneck pace of competition is no longer sustainable. How different it must have been when the cave painters occupied this arroyo. The sheer remote ruggedness of the landscape would have guaranteed seclusion. It was altogether possible for a tribe to remain ignorant of other humans occupying another arroyo in an adjacent canyon.

Pablo directs Elizabeth to pile the choy beside a rock outcropping a few meters from her tent.

"After *la comida* your tent will be in the shade." He points behind them in the projected direction from where the sun's rays will be shining. Crouching onto his haunches he examines the netting and nylon. "It's important that there are no holes, to keep out scorpions and mosquitoes. The rainy season has passed. *Entonces* mosquitoes shouldn't be a problem, but there are many scorpions and their bite is very painful and will cause swelling."

Elizabeth assembles the bamboo poles and crawls inside the tent to position one of the poles at the rear. Pablo pulls the rope extending from the ceiling and secures it with a stake.

"Okay," he calls out when the stake is in place. "You can erect the other pole near the door."

"Do you need any help with your tent?"

"No," he replies, vigorously shaking his head. His brown eyes convey surprise, if not confusion, at her offer. "I share a tent with my father. We'll pitch it after the others have been set up. *Gracias.*" He nods, hands her a bedroll before pulling the zipper down on the door and along the floor. "Never leave the front flap unzipped. And just in case, in the morning when you dress, shake your clothes to make sure that a scorpion is not clinging to the fabric."

Pulling back the zipper, she crawls inside and unrolls her bedding. She sighs with relief at the semblance of privacy offered by the nylon walls of her new home. Lying down, she stretches her body, flexes the muscles of her buttocks to release the tension from her strained seated position on Seguridad's swaying back. She listens to the voices of the others. With the approach of nightfall, the sound of the stream is amplified and everyone speaks in muted tones.

My things. Springing into action, she crawls out of the tent, and returns to Seguridad to untie her duffle bag from the saddle and retrieve her water bottle from the satchel.

"All set up?"

"Hey!" She falls into the crook of Richard's arm and gives his side a quick squeeze. "We made it without anyone falling off a cliff."

"Somebody came awfully close, if I correctly recall." From the breast pocket of his jean jacket, Richard produces a mickey of tequila. Taking a hefty swig, he passes it to her.

"How many bottles did you bring?"

"A few."

Savouring the burning sensation of the liquor as it runs down her throat, she takes another drink before handing it back.

"You can keep this one if you want."

"Are you sure?"

Nodding, he screws the cap back on, takes her duffle bag, unties the end and stashes the bottle inside. "Every couple days they go back to the village for provisions and can bring me another bottle. Show me your tent." He heaves the bag over his shoulder.

Bartek emerges from the tent next to Elizabeth's, with a towel slung around his neck. "*Buenas tardes.*" Eyeing the Californian suspiciously, he turns his body sideways, creating a barrier between himself and Richard. "If you need anything or can't sleep at night, don't hesitate to wake me."

"That's very kind of you, Bartek."

Richard sets her duffle bag at the door of Elizabeth's tent. "See you later," he shrugs and walks away.

"See you. And thanks," Elizabeth calls after him. The way that Richard retreats to the other side of the encampment, his shoulders slightly hunched over, she can tell that he's feeling like the odd man out.

"How did you enjoy the trek down through the canyon?" Bartek asks.

"It was spectacular. I'm looking forward to seeing the cave murals tomorrow."

"Me too."

"Here let me help you." Bartek kneels down to unzip the zipper on her tent and shoves her duffle bag inside. "I was going to go down to the stream to wash. Would you like to join me?"

"Sure. Let me get my jacket and a towel." Crawling inside, she unties the drawstring on her duffle bag, retrieves the mickey, places it near her pillow, and digs for her towel and fleece tunic. She feels the cold metal of her flashlight and pulls that out too.

"Do we know where we're going?"

"I think we can just follow the sound of the stream."

They skirt the outer rim of the stone outcrops, in the opposite direction from where the animals have been left to graze. Crossing the arroyo at a diagonal, they encounter a segment of the terrain that is more compact, as though it's been tread upon before. The bustle of the encampment recedes, the stream's serenade grows in intensity.

"Oh, look." Bartek stops and points ahead of him at a mountain summit. "The moon is rising. Soon we'll have a bit of light."

As the vegetation thickens, they're forced to tread single file down a slightly inclining embankment. Elizabeth hands Bartek the flashlight and allows him to go ahead of her. Casting the beam up and down the bank, he finally settles upon a spot conducive to washing. Peeling off his sweat-shirt, he crouches down and splashes water under his arms and onto his chest and back. He quickly rubs his bar of soap between his palms to create a lather and applies it to his torso and armpits. He repeats the water splashing ritual to rinse himself off, and vigorously rubs himself with his towel, before throwing on his sweatshirt, followed by a fleece jacket.

"You're in great shape," Elizabeth remarks. "What do you do for exercise?"

"The bicycle. Up and down hills, just south of Krakow."

Crouching in the spot where Bartek has just performed his ablutions, Elizabeth's body produces an intense shiver. "I don't know about this."

"Don't agonize. Just do it."

She decides to leave her bra on and is careful not to get it wet. Her mind races while she applies soap to her underarms and neck. She recalls her father having mentioned once that when he was in the death camp, he religiously performed certain routine tasks, such as brushing his teeth, combing his hair. Somehow it helped him endure the stress and to maintain his dignity. It became an act of defiance against the Nazis' attitude that he, like the other inmates, was subhuman, didn't deserve to live.

He picks up her towel from the rock she'd laid it on and hands it to her. "Thank-you." Drying herself, she notices that out of respect he looks her in the eye and not at her semi-naked body. She has the urge to confide her suspicions that someone has been following her, but the sound of a bell preempts her. They retrace their steps back to camp for dinner.

Depositing their towels and soap on one of the stone outcrops, they join the rest of the team seated cross-legged in a semi-circle around the cooking fire, tended by Felipe and Pablo. The sweet marinated scent of meat grilled over a fire wafts over them. Elizabeth senses her stomach growl. *El Señor* stands beside a camp stove and stirs the contents of a pot with frijoles, while Antonio, by his side, methodically flips tortillas on a cast iron frying pan.

Guzman pops the corks out of two bottles of red wine, fills his own cup, and passes the bottles around. "After tonight, we'll have to be content with water until the next run for provisions down to the village. So drink up and enjoy."

Raul, seated next to her, hands Elizabeth a tin cup and, before pouring himself some wine, graciously offers her some.

"*Gracias.*"

"*De nada.*" He leans over and passes a cup and the bottle to Bartek. Waiting until Bartek empties the contents, he lifts his cup and toasts them with, "*Salud.*"

The faint shadows of the hoodoos flicker in the firelight, dance upon the canyon walls, and hem in the encampment. The first stars appear in the darkening sky while the moonlight wanes with its ascent and diminished circumference. Everyone eats in silence. The fire's embers burn red hot, casting eerie, pronounced definitions upon the diners' faces. Everyone's skin colour emits an unnaturally infrared glow. The flames lick the charred remains of the choy. They watch the embers shed their colour, and crumble into grey ash.

22.

*S*HE'S RUNNING DOWN THE HALLWAY *of a house, an unfa-miliar house. Tucked in the crook of her arm is a bundle of blood-soiled undergarments and bedding. Richard is playfully chasing after her. They're laughing. She hurries up the stairway, drops something on the stairs, tries to pick it up but leaves it lying there as Richard is close behind and she's anxious to get to the bathroom to throw the bloodied clothing in the bathtub, to run cold water. She concentrates very hard on which door opens onto the bathroom. She's intent upon Richard not seeing the bloody mess. She opens the right door, quickly closes it behind her, and locks it. Richard tries the door. Her heart is beating frantically.*

Awakening to the unmistakable cramping in her uterus, the sticky wetness between her legs, she throws back the bedcover, examines the hem of her flannel nightgown, and groans. She examines her sleeping bag and heaves a sigh of relief that she didn't stain it. She visualizes her nightgown hanging on a clothesline, strung between two ocotillo bushes in the arroyo. Like a flag lowered at half mast, out of respect for the death of a dignitary, her dirty laundry will serve as an announce-ment to all the men that she is a woman, and that the woman is indisposed.

Rummaging through her personal effects for the foil sealed toilettes which were included with her plastic cutlery on the plane, she urgently rips off a corner, wipes her face, before applying the scented paper sponge to the inside of her thighs, and the crease between her legs and vagina.

She recalls her dream in bits and pieces. A bloodied sheet. Richard giving chase. The meal bell announcing that *desayuno* is being served rings sonorously and echoes against the canyon walls. Her stomach growls with hunger.

Shaking her clothes and looking down to check whether any scorpions drop onto her sleeping bag, she again thinks of her dream. She stops her busyness and gauges what she's feeling. Guilt. She feels guilty over her growing fondness for Bartek. She'd sworn to never hook up with a Polish man. Better to have settled upon Bernard, with his stubborn Dutch background. And yet she feels a certain comfort in the midst of that confounding central European angst that defines Bartek and, to a lesser extent, her own father, even though Stanislaw would never dare show it. To expose oneself in the camps was to face annihilation. Thank God Patricia has the option of being merely a woman. She can't imagine that she'd suppress her vulnerability, project her military persona, and risk humiliating her captors. No. Elizabeth shakes her head, secures the flap on her tent. Patricia's too smart for that. Ultimately, their heated arguments over females engaged in combat was not for naught.

The Morelos, as usual, steer the ship, tending to the scientists by refilling coffee mugs, adding tortillas to baskets, and spoonfuls of salsa to the rims of plates. The eggs have yolks the colour of pumpkin. The salt pork is sparsely distributed owing to the lack of refrigeration. The sun creeps over the mountains. It's still early, and the birds persist in making their presence known by chirping and swooping down from ridges to prey upon insects and tiny lizards.

Guzman hands out sheets of paper summarizing the week's assignments. Elizabeth notices that she's paired up with Guzman. Somehow she's relieved. There is something bizarrely comforting about having to contend with the prejudices of the old boy's network. Familiarity breeds contempt and today she'd rather feel contemptuous than fall into deep guilt-ridden introspective thought.

"*Doctoro, por favor*, I must attend to some washing this morning before we head to the cave."

The way that Guzman scrutinizes her face, she can tell that he recognizes the symptoms — she always looks so pale this time of month, as though the blood-letting drains all the colour out of her face. "*Bien.* Perhaps Antonio or Pablo can accompany you to the mural. I hope you don't mind, *Doctora*, if I accompany the rest of the group to the cave site?"

"No, of course not. I'll speak with Pablo and be along in half an hour."

Grabbing her blood-stained nightgown, and her plastic case with bar of soap, she retraces the steps that she and Bartek had tread the previous evening. Crouching down along the stream's edge, she turns her head and glimpses behind her before unfolding her nightgown and immersing it in the water. She watches the fabric bleed red streaks, the current dispersing it, carrying it downstream. Only a pinkish stain remains that she manages to knead out of the flannel with her soap. A final rinse completes the chore, and she stands to wring out the water before setting down the sodden garment on a rock and dampening the corner of her towel. Again, she turns her head to ensure that she's still alone before stripping from the waist down and wiping off the remnants of dried blood from her inner thighs.

On the way back to camp she's suddenly struck by the thought of Patricia getting her period while held captive. Likely the sheer terror of her situation would keep it at bay. The body has a tendency to shut down as a form of adaptation. Like going into shock after an accident, the pain of an injury isn't felt, emotionally a person goes numb, unless the person is a mother. Nature miraculously allows for that too. When she'd found out that Patricia had been taken hostage, her protective maternal instincts had kicked in. Since then what has she been doing? Suppressing them. But emotions can't be buried. Eventually they surface, sometimes in the form of paralyzing anxiety.

Guzman must have given Pablo the heads up about escorting her to the cave overhang. Casually leaning against a boulder, the youngest of the Morelo clan abandons his post and falls in beside her. Elizabeth hadn't realized how quickly she's been walking, as though someone is chasing her. She slows her pace and asks about hanging up her laundry.

"*Si*, we've strung up a clothesline. *Vene*. I'll show you where it is."

It's just where she imagined — between the two ocotillo bushes. Pablo gestures for her to pass him the nightgown.

"*Gracias.*"

"*De nada.*" He unfolds the nightgown in segments so as not to soil any of its edges and clips it with clothespins to the line. Turning back towards her, he grins at the realization that she's been watching him. "Are you ready to join the others or do you have to return to your tent?"

"No, I think I have everything I need."

"*Bien. Vámonos.*" Pablo tucks the plastic bag with clothespins in a recess of a boulder and slings his knapsack on his back. Pointing in the opposite direction from where they've just come, they set out, with him in the lead up an inclining path.

The sky is clear and the early rays of sun bathe the surrounding ridges in golden, mauve light. Looking down, Elizabeth notices snippets of cacti littering the path. *Señor* Morelo must have cleared it with a machete. Recalling *Señor* Carcamo having had to extract a chunk of cacti out of the sole of her boot, she's careful to avoid stepping on the thorny clippings.

Pablo suddenly stops. "*Escucha.*" Cocking his head to the left, he indicates from which direction the hissing sound is emanating.

Elizabeth freezes up. Neither of them moves a limb. Pablo points ahead of him to the large thick reptilian body slithering across the trail. He pushes his hand back to warn against immediate movement and then nods before resuming his lead up to the cave site.

23.

THE GREAT MURAL is five-hundred feet long and thirty feet high. Extending across the recessed rock overhang, the pictographs are sheltered from the elements, except in late afternoon when the angle of the sun illuminates the mural, a segment at a time. The four human figures are larger than life-size. Their arms appear raised in ritualistic celebration, and they are coloured black, white, and red; two of them half black, half red. Superimposed on these figures, *los primitivos* painted bighorn sheep, deer, bobcats, and vultures, their outstretched wings depicted as on the exterior face of the cave on the Carcamo ranch — two horizontal black lines and a dozen vertical lines running perpendicularly. Many of the figures appear to be deliberately obscured by other paintings. The overpainting of animals and smaller human figures yields it a dynamic, kinetic impression.

Each member of the group absorbs the mural in his own way. Only the silence is uniform. Bartek paces back and forth from one end of the overhang to the other, stopping every now and then to breach the distance between himself and a motif. Pierre and Maynard sit in the centre on two boulders, taking notes. Raul methodically makes his way from the left side of the mural to the right, backing up from time to time to gain a distant perspective on a motif.

Guzman shadows Richard, whose camera is pressed against his face as he as he positions himself in line with the morning light that has crept over the summit and is beginning to generate heat. The female photographer isn't due to arrive for a few days and Richard offered to take photos in her stead. "Did you capture the human figure with the headdress? The one painted red and white?" Guzman demands, panting heavily on Richard's heels.

"I'm getting it all, *Señor Profesore*," Richard exhales irritatedly.

Elizabeth claims a boulder at the right end of the mural, assuming the role, for the time being, of an observer, rather than participant.

"Do the eyes of the *monos* follow you, as you move back and forth in front of the mural?" she asks Bartek, whose pacing has brought him to her end of the overhang.

"What do you mean?" he asks, two creases forming on his forehead, along the bridge of his nose.

Elizabeth laughs. "I was just thinking of Rembrandt's *The Night Watch*. Do you know it?"

Bartek shakes his head. "I know of it. I've never seen it."

"The eyes of the brigadiers follow a person when they pace back and forth in front of the painting." She has the urge to add "like you," but stops herself. Leaning against the rock boulder upon which she's seated, Bartek crosses one ankle over another. "*Los monos* don't have eyes."

"They so meticulously painted every finger and toe on the shamans' hands and feet, but never thought of giving their faces any distinct features."

"The shamans saw with their hearts and their souls."

"They released themselves to a higher power."

Nodding, Bartek hesitates before saying, "Just as you should."

Giving myself up to a higher power. How fucking Polish, she wants to scream, but she holds herself back and nods. When push comes to shove, people are comforted by what they know, even when it's painfully familiar. She's grateful for

Bartek's companionship and his inclusion on the team. "What do you make of the different colours?"

Bartek stands away from the boulder and assumes a lecture-style stance. "I read somewhere that the bicoloured figures depict male and female synonymy." He struggles with this last word, enunciating each syllable painstakingly. "Red is a male colour, symbolizing spirituality; black is female."

Just like over there. She visualizes Patricia's head covered with a black hijab, framing her face, her grey-green hooded eyes. She shakes her head.

"Why do you shake your head?"

"I was just thinking of my daughter."

"The colour black?"

"Yes." She feels a cramp erupt in her uterus, and stops herself from wincing. She's thankful for the discomfort. It's more palpable than emotional angst, the pain of not knowing what is happening with Patricia.

"The shaman might have been considered androgynous. Capable of not only travelling the *axis mundi*, but also assuming the forms of both sexes, which is symbolized in the bi-coloured *monos*"

Elizabeth sidles off the boulder, reaches for her packsack, retrieves her water bottle and takes a long drink. Another cramp erupts in her uterus. She should be lying down in her tent, out of the sun, away from everyone, but that would only give way to more thinking, agonizing. "But the unicoloured figures might represent male and female. There are many more red figures in the mural than bi-coloured or black. Hunters."

"Yes. There's beauty in simplicity. Perhaps we shouldn't analyze too much. The mural is a celebration of the hunt, superimposed upon the painting of the giant *monos* which symbolize the four stages in shamanic initiation — suffering, dismemberment, death and rebirth."

"Like the crucifixion."

"Yes. But getting back to androgyny. Your comment about

the eyes of the figures in Rembrandt's painting following an observer is interesting because Da Vinci's *Mona Lisa* also has that reputation."

"Yes, it does."

"And many art critics believe that the *Mona Lisa* is a self-portrait."

"So, Da Vinci explored his female side through his painting. Like the shamans, to attain a higher level of consciousness," Elizabeth suggests.

Bartek nods.

And Patricia is exploring her male side by risking her neck in Afghanistan. Why hadn't I seen that earlier, before she left? Elizabeth has the urge again to shake her head, but is distracted by *Señor* Morelo venturing towards them.

Morelo stops and leans on his walking stick. "So what do you think of our *cueva pintada*?" Tilting his straw hat, he brushes the sweat off his forehead with his hand.

"*Muy guapo. Muy interesante*," replies Bartek. "What do you think it represents?"

"It's a pagan celebration of young boys coming of age. When they were initiated into the hunt."

"What happened to the painters?" asks Elizabeth.

"No one knows. The Jesuits questioned *los indios* about *las pinturas* and were told that they belonged to a race of people that came from the north."

"From Asia," Bartek interjects. "Ten thousand years ago, when there was an ice age, a tribe crossed the Bering Strait to Alaska, and then migrated south, and eventually crossed the Gulf in canoes to the mainland."

"Yes," agrees Morelo. "I have heard of such an idea. From some of our tallest mountains it is possible to see the mainland. Once they travelled there and discovered a less hostile land, they moved their families across the sea."

"Why do you think the figures are so tall?" Elizabeth asks.

"The painters were themselves very tall people. It's believed that some of them were over three meters tall. They are still referred to by Baja Californians as '*los gigantes*'."

"And what is this little gathering about?" Guzman asks as he joins them, crossing his arms and resting them onto his slightly protruding stomach.

"We were just asking *Señor* Morelo about *las pinturas rup-estres*." Bartek takes a step back to enlarge the circle they've spontaneously formed, so as to include Guzman.

"*Señor* Morelo has been a guide on so many *expediciones* that we will never match his expertise in *las pinturas*," Guzman adds.

Morelo nods obligingly towards Guzman, removes a handkerchief from his jean pocket, tilts his hat, and runs the cloth over his forehead.

"By the way *Señor*, have any of the tourists ever done any digging around the site?" Guzman's tone is as piercing as his look. "There are two holes at the far west end of the site. And they appear to have been recently excavated."

"Not that I can remember, *Doctoro*." Morelo lowers his eyes, shakes his head. Switching his walking stick to his left hand, he shifts his weight onto that side. "You know that there is nothing to stop anyone from coming up here without a guide." Turning to Elizabeth and Bartek, he adds, "The government prohibits it but no one enforces the law."

Guzman nods vigorously. "That is the problem. After we are finished here, I intend to petition the governor to do something about that."

Elizabeth extricates herself from the group and walks to the opposite end of the cliff overhang to see for herself the two holes about which Guzman has questioned Morelo. As she strides past the mural, she has the sensation that the motifs are in motion. She imagines the tribesmen dancing ritualistically in front of the cave overhang, their reverence for the mural intensifying their hypnotic, ecstatic state.

Nearing the western edge of the overhang, she slows her pace, casts her eyes downwards, searching for any disturbances in the earth. She deciphers two spots, about a meter in diameter, where the earth is of a lighter hue, the excavation having accelerated the rate of evaporation succeeding the rainy season, four months earlier. Standing over the two covered up holes, she senses that the disturbance wasn't the work of a tourist or the Morelos, but of someone else. She looks up at the cliff and feels exposed, as though someone might be watching her, not in person, but through a surveillance device that could have been mounted surreptitiously by the same people who followed her in San José and later in San Ignacio. Her body gives off a shiver. She has the urge to flee, to retreat out of the tiny camera lens' perspective.

"What are you looking at?" asks Richard, striding energetically towards her, the strap of his camera case slung across his chest.

"The ground's been disturbed here. Look."

"Yes, I know. Guzman's been cursing about it all morning. No, up there. What were you looking at?" He points up, toward the ridge.

"I thought I saw a lizard up there. You're done taking photos for the day?"

"Yes. I don't know why Guzman couldn't wait a couple of days. But since I brought my equipment along, I volunteered to do a series of shots. Glad I did. When a person has to focus so intently upon something like this, it gives you a unique perspective."

"What did you see? A hunt?"

Shaking his head, Richard sucks in his breath, as though a sudden rush of oxygen to his brain will help organize his thoughts. "More than that. I see a lot of movement. The fissures running through the rock give the impression of the figures moving in slow motion, something like in the early black and white films, when the picture frame flickered up and down. When I shifted my focus quickly away from a figure painted along a rock fissure, I could swear the figure, and everything surrounding it, moved. But I don't get the impression the human figures are hunting the animals. It's like some sort of trance-like transformation is taking place. Like a story is being told. Like something out of the Bible."

Elizabeth feels a surge of envy rise up in her. *If only I could experience the same kind of enthusiasm. Instead I've been imagining, in this remotest of landscapes, being the subject of surveillance. Haunted from all conversation, by images of Patricia.*

"What is it?"

"Nothing."

"Maybe there'll be some news when the Mexican photographer arrives with Felipe and Antonio. They left this morning to go back to the village to meet her."

"I didn't know that."

"No?"

"No."

"What's happening with you? You dropping off the radar?" Richard takes Elizabeth in his arms, rubs the back of her neck, releases her, and peers into her eyes. "Just concentrate on your work here. Don't think too much."

24.

THEY WORK IN PAIRS AND TRIOS, the mural having been divided into three sections, designated to the left, central and right panels. After a last-minute shuffle, Elizabeth is paired up with Raul to study the right panel. A small human figure, painted red, between two groups of deer, separates the central panel from the right one. The deer in the right panel total fifteen, superimposed upon eleven human figures. The ungulates' heads point in the opposite direction from those in the central panel, giving the impression that there are two separate hunts depicted, side by side.

"This one deer, Raul, is really a sheep. He has horns instead of antlers. And his two hind legs are not hoofed but look like human feet."

"It's a metamorphosis. *Mira.*" Picking up a stick from the ground, he points at two bi-coloured *monos* hovering over the sheep's backside and to the upper torsos of two other human figures painted on its back. "*Aqui.*" He circles the motifs painted over the sheep's back. "Two more human heads. Look at how the antlers of the deer, upon which the sheep is superimposed, look like human hands."

"And the bicoloured *monos* are emerging from the antlers. They look like twins, except that they're painted in reverse to one another."

"*Si.*" Raul throws her a quizzical glance but hesitates only momentarily in resuming his exposition. "This rock fissure is the most prominent, extending across the nose of the sheep and touching its front hooves. The sheep, unlike the deer, has four front legs. There must be some significance in this," Raul observes. "The other two front hooves have digits, but in a different way from the rear ones."

"Assuming for a moment that this panel depicts male puberty rites, I'd venture a guess that the sheep symbolizes the shaman. He's traveling the *axis mundi* to solicit spiritual intervention for the initiation. That's why so many *monos* are depicted on its back. The shaman is carrying the initiates to the spirit world."

"And back."

"You know, south of Calgary, in the Crowsnest Pass and Waterton National Park, there are many vision quest sites, on ridges in the Rocky Mountains. The two most famous sites are on Chief Mountain and Crowsnest Mountain. An elder assigns an initiate a vision quest site, where the young man sits alone, for three days, exposed to the elements, without food or water."

"How are these sites selected?"

"The two mountains are considered sacred. Chief Mountain is the first in the High Rock Range and Crowsnest Mountain, the last. For First Nations people, Chief Mountain is the home of thunder — the precursor to spring rain, while Crowsnest Mountain is the sanctuary of the raven, which is symbolic of metamorphosis. Both mountains are geologic oddities, known as klippe. Seismic activity resulted in Precambrian rock sitting on top of younger Mesozoic layers. It is imperative that a vision quest site has a particular type of rock — black basalt, solidified lava — found on the upper ridges of both mountains. Maybe, as with the black human figures, the black basalt is believed to symbolize female powers."

"Or perhaps the black basalt is considered to have metamorphic powers, which the initiate can draw upon during his vision quest."

"Yes, that, too, is a possibility. The initiate can't leave until his animal totem, often a predator endemic to that landscape — a bear, cougar, bobcat, wolverine — appears to him. It's believed that humans are born with an animal spirit and, during the vision quest, the initiate, hopefully, connects with that animal. The animal will protect the initiate throughout his life, particularly when he joined in the buffalo hunt."

Raul nods. "The initiate during the vision quest was transformed into the animal spirit."

"Yes."

"Are there are any *pinturas rupestres* in your part of the world?" Raul asks.

"Yes, but nothing as elaborate as this. At least not that we've discovered."

Turning back to the panel, Raul points again to the deer with the antlers that look like hands. "This may be another shaman. The initiation of the bi-coloured *monos*, emerging from the antlers, is almost complete. That's why they are painted differently from the others."

"Red — the colour of blood — symbolizes new life, the completion of the initiation. But where would the primitive people have come up with an idea like the *axis mundi*? And that the shaman traveled it to the outer and underworld?" Elizabeth asks thoughtfully.

Raul points with his stick toward the sky. "We don't think about the sky like *los primitivos* did. We live by the day, unless we live in a city with a lot of artificial lights. Predators, like bobcats, are more active at night. The tribe, particularly after a hunt, would have had to be vigilant about safeguarding their cache of deer meat. They didn't have the same understanding about the solar system as we do, didn't know that the earth is round, that it revolves around the sun in a twenty-four hour sequence. That it was the natural order of things. They didn't understand about the stars and other celestial bodies. *Pero,* the night sky was part of the daily rhythms of their existence and they made sense of it by believing that it was the outer world and underworld, to where the shaman could travel to gain special powers for his tribe."

"And the rock fissures? Why do they symbolize the *axis mundi?*"

"This is an earthquake-prone zone, but also very arid. Water is scarce. After an earthquake, they might have witnessed shifts in the layers of bedrock when groundwater appeared in new areas, seeping through rock fissures. In many cultures, water is the symbol of life. Maybe by painting a shaman along a rock fissure they were depicting a rebirth. To become a shaman, a tribesman had to die before being reborn."

"They didn't understand what caused earthquakes," Elizabeth nods. "They believed them to be the work of a higher power. As a new source of water, rock fissures came to symbolize conduits of spirituality."

"*Si, exactamente.*" Raul smiles. Like Guzman, he's fair-skinned, with a thin moustache. His well-defined chin, large dark eyes and typical hawkish Roman nose give him an unmistakable Latino appearance.

"It's a real pleasure working with you, Raul."

"The pleasure is all on my side, *Doctora.*"

"Please call me Elizabeth."

"*Bien.* Elizabeth."

A quizzical expression erupts on Raul's face. She gets the feeling that he's considering asking her something. Probably about her daughter. "Let's make some notes before we forget something."

"*Si.* Good idea." He extends his arm toward a nearby boulder with a flattened surface but only wide enough for one person, and seats himself, with his legs crossed, on the ground.

"I guess I've been relegated to the secretarial position?"

"It comes with the chair." Raul smiles up at her.

"You'll want to read what I've written and add your own notes later."

"*Bien.*" Leaning back against the base of the boulder, he nods and pulls his hat over his forehead, blocking out the sun that is now directly overhead. "Wake me up when they ring the bell *por la comida.*"

"Yes, I'm getting a little hungry myself."

Like a painter studying a subject, she glances every now and then at the mural, while making notes. Sensing that Raul is looking at her, she peers down and indeed, sees him observing her. "*Que tal?*"

"I was just thinking." He sits up and tilts back the rim of his hat. "It must be very difficult for you here, when your daughter is in so much danger."

So, he knows now too. Someone must have told him. "Yes. I feel very guilty."

"You shouldn't. It is her life. Her path. It is difficult when a child's path is so painful. I have two children, a son and a daughter. *La niña* is married, with a daughter of her own. Her husband is a good man and they are happy. But my son," he shakes his head, "...is lost. He is now studying in a third faculty at *la universidad*, and he still doesn't know where he is going, or what he wants in his life. He lives at home and doesn't have many friends. He had a *novia*, but she broke it off with him, and ever since he has been depressed."

Elizabeth's heart sinks. *If only that was Patricia's problem.*

Picking up on her thoughts, Raul continues. "*Yo sé.* What I'm saying is not much consolation. Your worries about your daughter are so much more serious, but I just wanted to share my thoughts with you. To sympathize a little."

"*Gracias.*" Elizabeth stands up and lays her notebook and pen down on the flat surface of the boulder. Retrieving some toilet paper from her knapsack, she turns and surveys the terrain beyond the cave site. "I'll be back in a few minutes."

The air feels slightly cooler away from the cave overhang. She notices, too, that the vegetation is sparser and less green. Descending into an arroyo, the soft soil of the embankment gives way beneath her boot-clad feet, forcing her to jump down. She lands on a thin crust of clay. It emits a hollow, crunch sound. Sun-baked, after the summer and autumn flash-floods, the coulee beds are littered with rock and other vegetative debris, washed away by the torrents of water from the ridges and screes, higher up. A perfect spot to bury her mess. Her presence, though, coupled with the still air within the coulee, attracts scores of pesky flies. Crouching down, she waves her hands in front of her and curses at the bugs.

Emerging from the arroyo she spots Maynard standing beside the boulder. He appears to be speaking with Raul. The surveillance camera that she'd imagined being planted in a crevice on the ridge comes to mind. *Did Maynard plant it?* Chastising herself for being paranoid, she attributes her delusions to her vulnerable, anxiety-ridden state. *What could they possibly learn about the Afghani mission in this barren place?*

"Hey, how's it going?" Maynard calls out to her.

"Good."

"It looks like Raul here is enjoying a bit of a siesta."

"Oh, he's not getting off that lightly. After I'm done taking a few notes, he has the job of editing them."

"I hear the Mexican photographer is due to arrive soon, and that there'll be a replenished supply of wine from that restaurant in San Ignacio. Maybe there'll be some news about your daughter."

Elizabeth peers at Maynard's face, tries to decipher what he means by this last comment, whether it's meant as a jab, or is simply a case of verbal diarrhea. She doesn't sense any malice on his part, but the inappropriateness of his remark is validated by the manner in which Raul, who's since abandoned his semi-prostrate position against the boulder, raises his eyebrows.

"If I know my ex-husband, he wouldn't leave a message with the Morelos unless something earth-shattering developed."

The ring of the dinner bell spares Maynard from having to reply to her last remark.

25.

"*DOCTORA, POR FAVOR.* I'm switching your assignment back to the central panel. I hope you don't mind. I could use your expertise and *Doctoro* Guttierez has informed me that you have made a lot of progress on the right panel."

"*Muchas gracias, Doctoro.*" Nodding, she manages to feign a smile. After witnessing how he'd driven Richard to take as many photos as possible, she expects that working with Guzman will present its challenges, but she can't help but feel flattered by her sudden elevation within the male-dominated pecking order of the team.

"*De nada.*"

"Did you want to take a stroll over to the stream with me to wash?" asks Bartek.

"Sure. Let me get a towel."

"It's okay. You can use a corner of mine."

"What were you working on this morning?"

"The central panel, but I understand you'll be replacing me. There are three of us. Pierre is staying on with you and Guzman, and I'll be pairing up with Raul." Bartek lays his towel on a rock beside the stream. Side by side they crouch at the edge of the stream. Massaging a bar of soap in the palm of his hands before handing it to her, he rinses them before throwing water onto his face.

Elizabeth copies his actions, and feels as though she's washing away her fears and anxieties. Unlike the Mexicans and Europeans on the team, the North Americans, she decides, feel awkward in her presence. Even Richard. They're at a loss for meaningful, empathetic words, but feel compelled, like Maynard, to say something for the simple sake of saying it.

"Go ahead. I can use the towel after you."

She picks up the towel from the rock, and immediately feels an intense shot of pain erupt on the thumb of her left hand. She throws the towel down onto the ground and eyes the scorpion emerge from beneath it. Her heart begins to throb erratically, and she feels hot and then cold.

"What's wrong?"

"I've been stung by a scorpion."

"Where?"

She raises her hand, shows him her swelled thumb, which has become very red. Her whole arm begins to throb.

He puts his arm around her shoulder, leads her to the stream, and gently sits her down. "How are you feeling?"

"Weak. Hot and cold, like I have the flu."

"Lie down. Stretch out your legs. Put your hand in the stream. The cold water will help." Bartek seats himself behind her head, with his legs apart and places her head in his lap so that his body shades her face from the sun. "I don't think you'll be working on the central panel this afternoon. Do you suffer any allergic reactions from insect bites?"

"Not that I know of." She's slurring her words, overcome by panic. She starts hyperventilating.

Bartek runs his fingers across Elizabeth's brow, wiping the beads of perspiration with his shirt sleeve. "The scorpions here in the Baja are not lethal, but their sting can cause a lot swelling and pain. You're lucky that it was your left hand and not your right. This is a lesson for me too. We must shake a towel before using it. The scorpion was probably hiding under the rock and was startled when I threw the towel onto it."

Elizabeth feels a jumpy restlessness in her lower extremities, her leg muscles begin to twitch. She's been trying to hold back her tears but is overcome by the urge to cry. Drowning in tears, her nose plugs up and she starts to weep. She moans, whimpers, and emits sounds that she'd never imagined releasing.

Bartek strokes her forehead, leans towards the stream, cups a bit of water in the palm of his hand and runs his wet fingers along her neck. "You must drink a lot of water. To flush out the venom." Grasping her upper arm, he motions that she should take it out of the stream. "How does your hand feel?"

"Numb." *Like my heart.*

"Your whole hand?"

"No, only the thumb. But my wrist feels like it's starting to swell." A lot of saliva has collected in her mouth. She swallows, develops a sudden urge to urinate but commands herself to hold it.

"I think we should get you back to camp." Bartek suggests. "Do you think you can manage the walk back?"

"Just give me a few more minutes."

"Okay." He places her hand back in the stream.

She closes her eyes and settles her shoulders into the clay that is punctuated with rock. Somehow, fortunately, her shoulders fit within gaps in the stone. She concentrates on breathing. The pain subsides a little. Her endorphins must be kicking in. She read somewhere that a person is capable of controlling pain by channeling energy to the distressed, ailing part of the body. She's practiced this cognitive pain therapy, which she calls mental healing, after spraining an ankle, or undergoing some dental work. It works best on the body's extremities but has proven challenging when trying to control a tooth or headache.

She lifts her hand out of the water and, with her shoulders and elbows, lifts herself into a seated position. The sun's intensity almost makes her pass out. She gestures for Bartek to pass her hat.

He scrambles to his feet and puts his arm around her waist. "Just wait a moment. You must get used to standing before we can walk back. Let me take a look." He takes her hand and examines her thumb. A red circle with dark blue patches encompasses the point of puncture. "It looks pretty nasty." He seems fascinated by the grotesqueness of the swelling and discolouration.

She still has to urinate but decides to hold it until they return to camp. With Bartek still steadying her, they shuffle up the path. She's sweating profusely, but is steady enough on her feet to walk unassisted. She disengages herself from his clasp, focuses on getting inside her tent, lying down. *The snake two days ago and now this. Don't start feeling sorry for yourself. Three. Patricia, the snake, and the scorpion. The bad karma has exhausted itself. And me.*

They reach her tent without encountering anyone. Bartek crouches, unzips the entrance, and pulls open the flap. "Do you need anything?"

"There's some toilet paper in there." She points with her chin towards her knapsack still slung over his shoulder. Can you give it to me?"

Rummaging through her pack, Bartek retrieves the roll and hands it to her. "I'll wait to make sure you make it back okay."

Nodding she turns towards the cacti forest, to the spot that she discovered after her arrival, sufficiently dense to hide her presence. She feels suddenly very thirsty, decides that she should ask Bartek to refill her water bottle before he heads off for *la comida*. She doesn't feel the least bit hungry. Tired, she feels tired and thirsty.

She has trouble pulling down her jeans. Her left hand throbs, and she compensates with her right one. At least the flies in the heat of the day are sparse. She doesn't have to change her sanitary napkin. The stress has probably stemmed her flow.

She heads back and climbs inside her tent, pulls her knapsack inside, drains her water bottle, and hands it to Bartek. "One more thing. Can you get me some more water?"

"Yes, of course."

"Thanks."

She sighs with relief at the sound of his retreat. She just wants to be alone. *So where's divine intervention? The blessings that I'm supposed to receive from having faith in a higher power? I shouldn't feel angry. It's not God's fault.* She has the urge to laugh, cynically. *So much for faith.*

The clatter of pots and pans, in the distance, distracts her, quells the impulse welling within her to cry and scream at the same time. She hears the murmur of voices, visualizes Guzman's face with a "what now?" expression. *Don't think about it. Just concentrate on your hand, on controlling the pain.* Her legs feel jumpy again. She no longer tries to hold back her tears.

"I'm back with the water," Bartek announces as he unzips the door and pokes his head through the opening. "Are you all right?"

Sitting up, she wipes the tears off her face and takes the bottle from his outstretched hand. "I feel so down."

"That is to be expected. Just rest. Should I bring you some food?"

She shakes her head.

"Guzman said not to worry about it. I'll come back later to see how you're doing."

"Okay."

Her mind races with images of the right panel, snatches of her conversation this morning with Raul, about his son and daughter, and how children have their own path in life. She wonders about scorpions in the Afghani desert, what type of building Patricia is being held in, and whether she is still alive. It suddenly dawns on her that Patricia hadn't sounded herself when they'd last spoken over the phone. She'd sounded nervous, as though she wanted to tell her something but couldn't. The line that she'd used to call her, probably for the exclusive use of intelligence personnel, could have been bugged. Would they have attributed Patricia's nervousness to having disclosed something earlier about her assignment to her mother?

Before leaving, Elizabeth had scoured the newspapers for any articles about the Canadian mission in Afghanistan. There had never been any inkling about NATO forces securing the region for geosequestration of CO_2.

And what about Bernard, a senior partner, being relieved as counsel for the Canadian oil company drilling in Kazakhstan? Has he, too, been placed under surveillance?

Her head whirls. She falls back onto her bedroll, battles her restlessness and the onslaught of her anxiety.

26.

"WHO'S THERE?" Elizabeth's abruptly awoken by the sound of the zipper being drawn open.

"It's me," Richard whispers back. Poking his head through the opening, Richard shines his flashlight at an angle from his chin to illuminate his face. The light gives him a spooky, cryptic appearance. He's grinning, although Elizabeth detects worry in his eyes.

She moves closer to the wall of the tent to make room for him, winces from the pain in her hand, which she's thoughtlessly leaned on.

"How are you?" he asks as he positions himself next to her, his arm protectively circling her shoulder, pulling her closer.

"I'm okay," Elizabeth murmurs, allowing herself to respond to his closeness, grateful not to be alone.

Richard struggles to remove his boots, plants them at the end of the sleeping bag and slides in closer to her, his body wrapping around hers. "How's your hand?"

"It still hurts but it's better."

"Fucking rotten luck!" he says, his face nuzzling her neck.

"I know." A lump forms in her throat. Her eyes begin to well up. *Don't start crying again*, she commands herself. She's all cried out. After Bartek left her with her water bottle, that's all she did — weep. She swallows hard. "You're not supposed to be here."

"Says who?"

"Says me."

"What do you mean? What did you expect me to do? Wait for second-hand information fed to me by Bartek?"

"Oh, come on. Richard. He's just a friend."

"Shh! We have to whisper. Better yet, let's not talk at all. I've been worried about you." Taking Elizabeth in his arms, Richard gently pushes his abdomen against hers and kisses her, his tongue probing urgently and without hesitation.

Elizabeth pulls her face away. "You've been drinking."

"Yeah, so what?

"Booze breath." *And a heavy dose of belligerence.* This is not what she wants, or needs.

As though he can read her thoughts, Richard lies back down beside her, taking care that her left hand is on her stomach before once again cradling her shoulder. Elizabeth feels her resistance melt away. Richard's kiss is familiar, an old friend that she's instinctively drawn to. She turns towards him, unbuttons his shirt, fingers the hair on his chest.

He lifts her nightgown, feels her panties, withdraws his hand and turns his head to face her. "That time of month?"

"On top of everything else."

He nestles his chin against hers, and sighs. "It's just good to be with you again."

The stillness of the night seems to conspire against any urge to engage in conversation. She allows herself to sink into Richard's gentle, but firm, embrace, until a sudden gust of wind pushes the nylon wall of the tent against her. The momentary flapping of the tent is followed by the hollow sucking sound of the wind flowing through the canyon. She wonders whether the weather is changing, she wishes that it would. The incessant sunny skies seem to make a mockery of her despondent feelings. She wishes that it would rain, that the skies would turn gray, like her mood, and unleash a torrent a rain, redolent of the tears she's shed over Patricia, over herself.

"Is it past midnight? Tomorrow, I have a feeling there might be some news from Bernard," Elizabeth states, willing her tears not to fall. The certainty she feels is like a stone in her stomach. Solid, heavy and unmoveable.

"I hope so." The glibness of Richard's reply has the desired effect: of impressing upon her that Richard doesn't want to talk about Patricia. "Tell me about this scorpion," he says, shifting his weight in order to face her on his side, his head propped up against his left hand, his eyes inquisitive.

"There's not much to tell. I picked up a towel from a rock along the stream where I'd gone with Bartek to wash up before lunch and got stung. I had a pretty severe reaction — hot and cold flushes. My thumb and wrist went numb. I couldn't stop crying."

"You were already under a lot of stress. Venom can push you over the edge."

I'm already over the edge, she thinks. *Shake it off,* she tells herself. "What about you? How are things going on the left panel?"

"Okay. Except that Maynard is fucking weird."

"Why do you say that?"

"Well, for one, he was going on about a girlfriend that he'd spent a holiday with on the capes. She jilted him for his best friend."

"He told me about it."

"When?"

"When we were in San Ignacio. After our last time together. After hearing that heavy object fall in the room next door, I ran into him in the courtyard and we had a coffee together."

"Boy, you're sure doing the rounds around here," Richard comments sardonically.

"The rounds? Richard! Bartek and Maynard are our colleagues," Elizabeth cannot disguise her irritation.

"Shh. We have to whisper. What else you guys talk about?" Richard asks, his voice accusing.

"Why do you think he's fucking weird?" Elizabeth asks, her anger palpable.

"Oh, I don't know, he's just really intense. Going on about geosequestration and how the Baja is a perfect place to sequester carbon dioxide underground. How the 'wetbacks' can monitor these underground storage facilities for cheap and we can stop global warming. I wanted to remind him that I was travelling in the same jeep when we talked about this."

Elizabeth tenses the muscles in her back, recalls the strange feeling that came over her when she investigated the two excavations about which Guzman had grilled *Señor* Morelo. "The 'wet-backs'?" she says, the ire in her voice unmistakable.

"What's made you so uptight all of a sudden?" Richard asks, clearly puzzled by her response.

"I cannot tolerate racism," Elizabeth counters. Then, in an almost conciliatory tone, she adds, "The venom makes my muscles twitch. I was just trying to counteract my legs going all jumpy."

"At least Maynard doesn't mind taking notes. Tell him what to write and he obliges. But he's not into it. Going on about his girlfriend, geosequestration, and how Afghanistan is about sequestering carbon dioxide. I kept trying to shift his focus back to the mural, but he's obsessed."

"What else did he say about Afghanistan?" Elizabeth's heart begins erratically knocking. She curses to herself over Richard having woken her up, getting her all riled up when she should be sleeping, healing from the scorpion bite.

Richard doesn't answer at first. "That you were an idiot for allowing your daughter to go over there."

"What did you tell him in response?" Elizabeth sucks in her breath.

"You didn't have any say about it. Your daughter's not a minor."

"And how did he respond?"

"He didn't. I gave him shit and told him to give it a rest.

Like you should." Disengaging his arm from beneath her head, he turns onto his side. "I'm going to go. You back at it in the morning?"

"Yes, I don't want to lie in this tent anymore, agonizing over everything. I've come to realize that it's a godsend that I'm out here, away from television, the mass media. It must be hell for Bernard."

Richard brushes his lips against hers and crawls towards the opening. Pulling his boots back on and the zipper up, he turns and tenderly urges, "Get some sleep. Sorry to have woken you."

"It's okay."

"Love you," he murmurs. "See you in the morning."

27.

THE CENTRAL PANEL measures twenty-one feet across and comprises fifty motifs — thirty-three deer, one coyote, a bobcat, a vulture, four giant human figures, and eighteen small human figures, one of which they believe to be female. Located within the apex of the rock overhang, the oversized human figures or *monos*, one bearing a height of nine feet, are the panel's dominant feature. Five of the deer also have gigantic proportions. The buzzard, red in colour, its front legs abutting a rock fissure, is superimposed on one of the giant deer. Extending diagonally to the bottom of the overhang, the crack runs horizontally, parallel to the ground until it loops upward, past the deer, and encompasses triangularly all other motifs in the panel. The smaller *monos*, including the one female, are painted beneath the feet of the giant *monos*, outside the margins of the triangle. The four stages of initiation are depicted as occurring beyond the dimension of the smaller human figures — symbolically in the tribe's outer or under worlds.

Pierre and Guzman measure the width of the panel and the four giant figures' dimensions with a tape measure. Elizabeth takes notes. It's a relief to be back at work. Her hand and wrist are still swollen but the pain has become bearable and today they are blessed with some cloud cover. She's beginning to feel anxious about the Morelo brothers' pending return, with Carolina Madero, from the village. Bernard, she's sure, has called and left a message. The snap of the rewound metal tape inside its dispenser startles Elizabeth and makes her jump.

"*Doctora*," Guzman calls out, peremptorily, his back still turned away from her, "What do you think about these four *monos*?"

Elizabeth flinches in reaction to the gruffness of Guzman's tone. "The one with the most elaborate headdress, superimposed on the deer, is the deer shaman, believed to be endowed with the greatest powers. That's why he's painted the tallest and is depicted above the others." She fleetingly shifts her focus to the two human figures to the right which are eight feet tall, and then to the one on the left with a less imposing height of just six feet before adding, "Deer were considered to be endowed with special female properties."

She knows that what she's saying is nothing new for Guzman. It's his way of studying the mural. He needs to have someone recite the theory and, through such recitation, he hopes to solicit discussion, further analysis, and clarification. She finds his tone to be jarring but can't fault him for not making allowances for her predicament and her latest encounter with the scorpion. "Deer were considered to be sexual for various reasons." Elizabeth speaks without affect or inflection. She's distracted. Their focus on the deer gives rise to thoughts of Patricia.

She intuits that Patricia's captors might regard their female hostage with acute interest, particularly in light of Patricia's posting in intelligence. While the double standards of fundamentalist Muslims in their treatment of women are sickening, they are also bewildering and telling. When a woman commits adultery and is condemned to death by stoning, the man's life is spared. Yet at the same time, women are elevated to a pedestal, prohibited from exposing any part of their body that might incite unwanted, forbidden sexual advances. Elizabeth harbours the hope that notwithstanding her gender, Patricia, by virtue of her position as an intelligence officer, has value for the insurgents. The irony of the situation, however, doesn't elude her. Might not Patricia's elevated rank pose a threat to her captor's convictions that women — apart from their servile role in maintaining the status quo — are worthless?

She has the urge to shake her head at current Western women's fashions — the low-riding waist bands of jeans exposing the navel and the rear bum crack, low-cut tops emphasizing cleavage. Whatever happened to women's liberation? All the wrong messages are being conveyed to the daughters of Western society's staunchest feminists. Women used to go braless in protest. Now breast implants and tight-fitting under-wire bras are all the rage, and women aspire to become nothing more than sexual objects. Islam is venting its consternation at that too, and perhaps Patricia's decision to join the armed forces was a form of rebellion against Western society's double, conflicting standards.

Guzman turns around, throws her a quizzical glance. She follows up on his cue. "The two-pronged antler is visually like the female pubic triangle. The sweet, musky odour of deer is reminiscent of estrous females. Deer hooves print vulva symbols. Their hind legs, viewed from the rear, are knock-kneed with the appearance of the female hourglass shape."

Pierre interjects with the theory that the sexes naturally selected one another to evolve into their present shapes. "Men preferred women with the hourglass shape — those with narrow waists and wider hips — which would reduce the risk of infant mortality and improve the chances of a newborn's ability to survive passage through the birth canal. The world over," he gestures with his hands in a circular motion, "men are typically a third larger than their female counterparts. Women, it appears, selectively chose men with broad shoulders and narrow hips. For women, it was also a function of survival. A man with upper body strength was better able to protect his family from predators and inclement weather."

"Have you taken note of the fact that the rock fissure is

triangularly shaped?" Guzman asks, directing his question to Elizabeth.

"*Si, Doctoro,* I've made a note of it," Elizabeth answers. It didn't dawn on her, though, that the triangular fissure must have been considered to have special female powers. She imagines the excitement of the painters when they traced the fissure, realized it runs triangularly. Fascinating how humans, even primitive humans, extrapolate, need to make sense of everything, to justify a belief, conviction.

"And what is the significance of female powers or energy being depicted symbolically in shaman initiation?" Guzman directs his question to both of them.

Elizabeth looks at Pierre. He shrugs and raises his hand toward her, indicating that he'd rather she answer. She clears her throat. "A man could get lost in female sexual energies. Sexual intercourse was considered a vehicle through which a male could become transformed or transported to another dimension. Like sleep, or even death. But we mustn't lose sight of the death/rebirth theme which deer are also believed to represent. Predominantly because of the regenerative properties of their antlers."

"But all the antlers are two-pronged," Guzman counters. "And that isn't always the case. The fact that the only vulture in the mural is superimposed on a deer outside of the pubic-shaped rock fissure supports the theory that the central theme of the panel is transformation by sexual intercourse. And not by death. Death, symbolized by the vulture, is depicted outside the shamanic initiation process. *Los indios,* when questioned by the missionaries, called the mural '*cuevas flechas.*' Consider where the arrows pierce the giant *monos.*"

Many of the arrows are depicted as piercing the groin areas of the shamans. Others, however, are aimed at the heart, stomach, mouth area and shoulders of the *monos.* Elizabeth points to the first giant human figure, painted red and outlined in white. As the first in the quadruple sequence, it represents suffering.

"See how the arrows penetrate almost every part of the body. Not just the groin area." She stops and throws a piercing look at Guzman. He can't see her eyes beneath her sunglasses, but she's managed, nonetheless, to make him feel uncomfortable. He tilts his hat back and scratches his head. "And the arrows are not consistently depicted over or under the red paint, which gives the impression of penetration into the flesh."

Pierre steps in and points to the first figure. "See how the part of the body associated with the heart is painted white, and outlined within a circle. None of the other *monos* are painted *comme ça*. Suffering, for *los primitivos*, might have been depicted by a heart painted outside the body. On the surface."

"But don't you think it represents dismemberment?" asks Guzman. "The heart is dismembered from the body." Even though his question is directed at Pierre, he grasps Elizabeth's shoulder, directs her toward the last *mono* on the right end of the central panel. Pierre follows on their heels.

"*Mira*. This is the only *mono* depicted as touching the rock fissure. See how his left foot is painted alongside the fissure." Guzman positions himself so close to her that she can sense the warmth of his breath. She steps back, prompting Pierre to move to the side.

Guzman turns and focuses his gaze on Elizabeth before gesturing once more to the mural. "This *mono* depicts shamanic travel. He is the traveller. The transformation is complete. See how his right hand touches the leg of the deer shaman, who, as you yourself said, was considered the most powerful of the shamans."

"*Sí*." Elizabeth suppresses a shudder. *Double standards. Why me? Why not Pierre?*

"The female figure in the panel is depicted beneath the traveller's right foot and is the only smaller human figure connected to the fissure." Picking up a stick from the ground, Guzman makes a circular motion and points to the red female motif, which is wearing a tripartite cloverleaf-shaped hat. "She symbolizes female power, indispensable to travelling the *axis mundi*. This shaman," he points to the traveller, "assists the deer shaman in experiencing the ecstatic process of death and rebirth."

Guzman grasps Elizabeth's elbow, leads her back to the first *mono*. "Have you noticed, *Doctora*, how the arrows are all portrayed as being hurled from below? Don't forget that the female realm was associated with the underworld and death. And death is merely a precursor to rebirth, a female phenomenon."

"What about this bobcat superimposed on the feet of the second shaman?" asks Pierre. "A bobcat dismembers its prey. That is why this *mono* represents dismemberment in the sequence."

"I think it's important to bear in mind," Elizabeth interjects, "that all four figures represent the shaman, but at different stages of initiation. It's like the Christian Stations of the Cross. Jesus is depicted at each station."

"*Si, exactmente*," agrees Guzman. "*Bien*, let's take a siesta. Good work *doctores*."

28.

"M OM! THE DOORBELL."
"Excuse me for a moment." Setting down her drink, Elizabeth squeezes between the shoulders of two of her colleagues, and jostles her way through a group of Patricia's friends, through the patio doors and into the house. With perfect weather, the guests have gathered outside. Eyeing the dining room table laden with appetizers, she reminds herself to invite the guests inside to sample the food.

Bernard, with his back turned, stands on the front doorstep. As Elizabeth unlatches the lock on the storm door, he turns. Their eyes meet and she detects irritation written all over his face. "Sorry, Bernard. Have you been standing out here for very long?"

"It's okay." He leans over to brush his lips against her cheek. "Here," he hands her a bottle of wine and a bouquet of irises.

"Thank you. You shouldn't have."

"Has anyone from the office arrived yet?"

"No, but you remember Phillip Bowes from the faculty and his wife, Rose?" Sliding his sunglasses onto his head, his eyes evoke a momentary cerebral timeout, as though he's scanning his memory for a visual picture of the colleagues she's mentioned. She hasn't seen Bernard for over a year, not since last summer, before Patricia returned to Kingston for her final year of studies and training.

He's aged. His thick hair has almost completely grayed, and beneath his eyebrows, which have managed to maintain their blondness, the skin around his eyelids has begun to sag. Slim, of medium height and build, despite his workouts on the squash court, she notices, too, that he's developing, along the jawbone, middle-age jowls.

"Yes, yes, of course. No, I was just asking because there's a golf tournament this afternoon that most of the office is taking in. You know these lawyers. They never stop drumming up business."

"These will look fabulous on the dining room table." Pouring water into a vase, Elizabeth arranges the irises and asks him what he'd like to drink.

"The usual. Scotch."

"Three cubes, right?"

"Yes, thanks." Bernard peers through the kitchen window. "Looks like a decent crowd."

"Half the guests are Patricia's friends. It's been ages since she saw any of her old school mates."

"And your parents made it down from Edmonton?"

"Yes, they're staying overnight."

He leans against the sink, crosses one ankle over another, and takes a sip of his scotch. "You know, I never believed it would come to this."

"I know."

"But we should have seen it coming. We were naive to think that her training in intelligence would somehow spare her from being stationed over there. Particularly when she started learning Pashto."

We? Bernard could never accept that it was over between them. "You should get out there and say hello," Elizabeth says as she ushers him out of the kitchen. "And I should round up a few of the guests to have a bite to eat."

"Hey, Dad. You made it." Extricating herself from her circle of friends, Patricia embraces her father, and envelopes her hand in his before leading him outside to the table where her grandparents are seated.

Bernard shakes hands with Stanislaw and leans over to give Krystyna a peck on the cheek.

"Good to see you again, Bernard," says Krystyna. "Patricia, bring that chair from over there."

"No, I'll get the chair." Bernard plants the chair between Krystyna and his daughter. "So, how have you been keeping?"

"Fine, fine." Stanislaw passes his glass to Elizabeth who's been hovering over their shoulders.

"Did you want another one, Tata?"

"Yes. But not so strong this time."

Before getting her father a refill, Elizabeth invites the guests with whom Patricia has been socializing to help themselves to some appetizers. As they follow her inside, she's overcome by a flood of memories — of classmates and neighbourhood kids arriving with presents to celebrate Patricia's birthday, the birthday cakes graced each year with yet another candle, the chorus of young voices singing "Happy Birthday," Patricia puffing up her cheeks to blow out the flames.

She sets the scotch and soda down in front of her father, and adjusts the table umbrella so that he, having recently had some cancerous skin surgically removed from his scalp, remains shaded from the sun.

"Sit down for a moment." Krystyna offers her her chair. "I need to use the washroom. Stanley, can I bring you a plate of food?"

"Yes, please."

"Let me round up some more guests for appetizers. I'll be back," Elizabeth says as she turns toward another group of guests beckoning them inside.

Phillip Bowes, the department Chair, takes advantage of everyone's exodus to light up.

"Let me get you an ashtray, Phillip," says Elizabeth.

He grabs hold of her wrist and shakes his head. "Don't worry about it. I'll go out to the alley and dispose of it when I'm done. So, when do you leave for the Baja?"

"Oh, not for another six months. In February. It'll be good to have a month off after the fall semester concludes."

"It's good that you're going. Taking a break from the classroom. Is that Bernard over there?"

"Yes. His firm is hosting a golf tournament this afternoon. So it's unlikely we'll see any of his partners."

"I hardly recognized him."

"It's been a few years."

"Your daughter looks well. All that hard core training seems to agree with her."

"She's always been a fit person. Skiing, swimming, soccer."

"When does she leave for her posting?"

"On Monday."

"How do you feel about it?"

Elizabeth shakes her head. "Terrible. She trained in intelligence. I thought that might spare her from the worst."

"But surely you must have known that Afghanistan might be in the cards?"

"Oh, yes, she joined up to go over there, but a parent, somehow ... I know it sounds delusional, hopes that it'll never come to this."

"You know, they're trying to get the village elders on side with NATO forces. To undermine the Taliban's efforts to recruit insurgents. Help build up trust in the foreign troops. Has your daughter told you what her assignment is over there?"

Elizabeth shakes her head. "She says it's classified information."

Phillip nods knowingly. "Better that she not tell you."

"Why?"

"Then you'd really be worried."

The most politically savvy and well-travelled academic in the department, Phillip's father had been a career diplomat and had been posted with his family in consulates and embassies the world over. After Patricia's recruitment, Elizabeth had considered consulting Phil about the approach she should take to try to dissuade her from joining the armed forces. With his connections, he would be privy to more information than the general public. She wishes now that she had spoken to him. "You know something that I don't?" she asks, her brow furrowed with worry.

"No." He shakes his head. "I just know a little more about our government's handling of foreign affairs than you do. They're buffoons, or rather, I should say, we are. The government of Canada, after all, is us. The public service." He lifts his cigarette to show that it's time he extinguished it.

"I'll send Bernard over here to catch up with you. Good chatting with you, Phillip." She navigates her way through the clusters of guests, toward the corner of the patio where she'd left her parents and Bernard. Willing herself to stem the panic spreading throughout her body, she asks Bernard whether she can refresh his drink. Elizabeth holds out her hand for Bernard's glass before raising her chin in Phillip's direction at the rear of the patio. "I promised Phillip that I'd send you his way."

"I can get it, Liz," Bernard offers, rising from his lawn chair. He excuses himself by nodding towards Krystyna and Stanislaw, and then lifting his hand to signal to Phillip.

Afraid that her mother will sense her agitation, Elizabeth recedes into the celebratory ambience of the gathering.

29.

SHUTTING THE DISHWASHER DOOR, Elizabeth turns around. "Well, I think that went rather well, don't you?"

Patricia swallows the grape she's been munching on. "Yeah. It was good."

"Did you enjoy seeing your old friends?"

"Yeah."

"What have they been up to?"

"Studying. Summer jobs. The usual."

"Is *Dziadzio* taking a nap?"

"I think so."

"Maybe you want to spend some time with your grandmother?"

"I thought I'd go for a run. Is there anything else I can help you with?"

"No. It's all under control. You go ahead."

Patricia remains rooted to the bar stool. The look she gives Elizabeth seems to intimate she wants to tell her something.

"Is anything wrong?"

"No." Patricia shakes her head, smiles. "I just wanted to thank you for the party."

"I just wish you didn't have to go," Elizabeth says as she takes her daughter in her arms.

Patricia releases herself from her mother's embrace. "Before you know it, I'll be home again on leave. You'll see. The eight months will fly by."

"But I'll be on assignment by the time you're back."

"So, I'll jump on a plane and come down to the Baja."

"From one desert to another, eh?"

"Why not?" Patricia points her chin towards the kitchen window. Twilight having descended upon the city, the patio has become engulfed in shade. "I want to make it back before dark."

"Yes, of course. You go. I should check up on your grandmother."

Krystyna opens her eyes upon Elizabeth entering the living room. The television is on, but the sound is muted. Stanislaw's hearing is no longer what it used to be and her mother has obviously taken advantage of his absence by not just turning down the volume, but turning it off altogether.

"So you've finally found a moment to sit and have a little chat." She gestures to Elizabeth to join her on the couch.

A plethora of thin lines crisscross her mother's cheeks, but they don't detract from her otherwise handsome facial features — the highly placed cheekbones, smooth, unblemished complexion, hooded grey-green eyes and a delicate, feminine-shaped nose. In her younger years, Krystyna had been a real beauty and customarily wore her thick, brown hair suavely swept off her forehead. It was only in pre-war photos, though, that Elizabeth had ever seen her mother as a brunette. Red and blond hair had been all the rage in the post-war years. Krystyna still dyed it, but had begun to favour a paler blonde hue that blended almost seamlessly with the gray.

"Remember when it was the other way around? You were always on your feet, cleaning, doing something, and it was I who urged you to put your feet up."

"Yes, I remember." Krystyna nods, displays an ambivalent smile. "Are you happy about how things went?"

"Yes. I think everyone had a good time."

"And Patricia?"

"She really appreciated it. She's gone jogging."

"Always trying to keep busy, that one. Like your brother, Michael."

Elizabeth throws her mother a look of bewilderment. She'd never thought about that before. In the army, every minute is accounted for. A person is told what time to wake up, to eat, to polish their boots. Had she unwittingly raised her daughter to live a regimented life? No! Just the opposite. She'd been the one to live her life like that, under the constant, critical eye of Stanislaw, who could never sit still for very long. And Krystyna, too, after having spent her youth in a German labour camp, couldn't relax either, although old age had evidently caught up with her. Her mother looked tired. At their age, the drive down from Edmonton had been enough for one day, let alone having to make small-talk all afternoon with Bernard and the other guests.

"How is Michael?"

"Good." Krystyna nods her head. "He was on call this weekend at the hospital. Otherwise, I'm sure he'd be here."

"Krysia!" Stanislaw's demanding voice carries into the living room.

Krystyna laboriously rises from the sofa, ambles down the hallway to the guest bedroom. They are conversing in Polish about his heart medication. Elizabeth hears her mother shuffle into the kitchen, open one of the cupboards and then run the tap. She thinks about how her parents' generation does everything out of duty. Her mother's lot in life was to serve her husband and children, plain and simple. There were no choices, no options, unlike now. Maybe that's what makes for simpler times. Now there are too many choices. Maybe Patricia's generation, overwhelmed by choice, is rebelling by embracing commitment. But are they really embracing a simpler life?

Phillip's last comment, that it's probably a godsend that she doesn't know anything about Patricia's assignment, is still making her feel uneasy. She's known Phillip too long not to know that whatever he says, he says in earnest; he doesn't mince his words.

Krystyna shuffles back into the living room. "Maybe I should make some tea?"

"Let me do that, Mama." Elizabeth rises from the sofa and pats her mother's shoulder on her way into the kitchen.

"What's made you so nervous, all of sudden? It's Patricia, isn't it?"

"Yes. I don't want her to go over there. What parent wants that?"

"Even your father isn't behind this, although he would never tell Patricia how he feels. He's too much of a military man for that. He respects his granddaughter's decision. Just like he decided over fifty years ago to serve his country."

"But father didn't have a choice. He'd just graduated from the military academy."

"Yes, but it was his own decision to join the underground, which was even riskier."

"And Poland was an occupied country. This is just another integration of Canadian foreign policy with that of the U.S. An extension of the American military industrial complex."

Krystyna's face draws a blank. Elizabeth is talking over her head. When she still lived at home, as an undergraduate, she'd often discuss theory with her mother. Having to explain the theories in layman's terms helped her organize her thoughts, compartmentalize the concepts, and synthesize them later into the assigned essays that she'd spent days, sometimes weeks researching and writing. Despite having only a Grade 10 education, Krystyna is intelligent enough to grasp almost anything. When Elizabeth stopped and really thought about it, Krystyna had always been her most dedicated student.

"After the war, President Eisenhower, when he was still a general, warned that Americans were relying too heavily upon its arms industry to boost its own economy. We're now going down the same road. Canada, of all countries!"

Krystyna purses her lips. Her eyes convey a worried expression. A perennial and staunch opponent to war, her harshest chastisement of armed conflict was the inevitable loss of control over one's life. A politician's signature on a declaration of war could wipe out, overnight, the aspirations of a student, a professional, or a parent for their child. The future is erased, supplanted by uncertainty. The base side of people emerges as they struggle to survive.

It suddenly dawns on Elizabeth that there had been a hypocritical side to today's going away party. Today's milestone was nothing like the birthday parties that, over the years, Elizabeth had thrown for Patricia on the patio; and yet the mood that she'd tried to set for family and friends was in the same lighthearted, celebratory vein as a birthday, graduation, or wedding. Perhaps that had been at the root of Phillip's cynicism? Rather than hinting that there's a sinister basis for Patricia's secrecy, maybe he was insinuating that he was offended by having to celebrate Patricia's posting.

The tea kettle whistles and spurs Elizabeth into automatic action. The crowd having favoured savory foods over sweet, she's been left with twice the number of dessert trays. Bernard had taken his leave so hastily that she'd missed out on arming him with a doggy bag. But she can always count on her father to chip away at the leftover sweets. She anticipates that the whistling kettle will rouse him from the guestroom to join them for tea and cake, a longstanding family evening pastime.

"Where's Patricia?" her father asks.

Setting the tray down onto the coffee table, Elizabeth glances through the front bay window and notices that the street lights have come on. "She should be back soon. She went out for a jog."

"Good for her."

"Did you sleep?"

"I was just dreaming a little bit."

Elizabeth smiles inwardly. Her father is the only person she knows who dreams without falling asleep. His round face and ruddy complexion defy his age and growing frailty. Save for the deeply etched lines extending from his eyes, he has few wrinkles, although his hands exhibit a tremor as he lifts the mug of tea to his lips. Like a child, he's been relegated to clutching it with both hands.

Krystyna, who's seven years younger, retains a steadiness in her hands. After taking a sip, she sets down her mug and folds her hands in her lap. Her mother has always been embarrassed about her hands. The relentless air raids that had targeted Hanover and other cities in the German industrial heartland had finally culminated in the shutting down of the munitions factory where Krystyna, along with scores of other young Polish women, had been transplanted into forced labour. Assigned the chore of sifting through the rubble of bombed out buildings, without gloves, Krystyna's hands had endured frostbite and innumerable cuts and scrapes. Her hands had swelled and never recovered their normal slender shape. They still bore a permanent reddish pigment, and were an anomaly; they didn't match the rest of her body — her long, shapely legs, tiny wrists, and trim figure.

Stanislaw leans over, slides the dessert tray towards his end of the table, and selects a piece of cheesecake. He leans back into his chair, but before piercing the cheesecake with his fork, he looks up at Elizabeth. "Bernard wasn't himself."

"He's worried, just like everyone else."

"Worried about Patricia?"

"Yes, of course."

"Sometimes war is necessary."

Elizabeth catches Krystyna's eye. She shoots Elizabeth her classic preemptive stern admonishment. The perennial peacekeeper, her mother has, over the years, perfected her "let him have his say" glance.

"How so Tata?" Through the corner of her eye, she notices Krystyna's eyes subtly conveying her approval.

"There is no honour anymore, no loyalty. War is a terrible thing. But afterwards, those who survived shared a commitment to one another that you don't see anymore."

Elizabeth knows that he's referring to all his old war buddies who, like Stanislaw, immigrated to Canada, and remained throughout their lifetimes, even after they'd settled at opposite ends of the country from one another, the staunchest of friends. Their loyalties extended to the next generation. Whenever Elizabeth had travelled to Montreal or Toronto or Winnipeg, she'd been obliged to touch base with one of Stanislaw's old buddies, and their kids had been obliged to do the same. Most of them had predeceased Stanislaw. He'd grieved terribly over each one's passing. Elizabeth could never imagine feeling the same heart-wrenching grief over the death of one of her friends or colleagues.

Duty and commitment had regulated her parents' lives, and was a yardstick that they'd taken pains to instill in her. She'd always locked heads with Stanislaw, but after her decision to leave Bernard, the strain in their relationship had deepened. It was no longer a simple matter of generational differences. For Stanislaw, she'd betrayed herself and her family. By joining the ranks of other women who were divorcing their husbands, she was undermining the very fabric of society. She decides that he probably thinks that Patricia's posting in Afghanistan is her just desserts.

"You're right, Tata. Everyone, these days, seems to just be passing through."

Stanislaw nods. "Very good cheesecake." He doesn't look up from his plate and, ultimately, Elizabeth isn't sure whether his nod of approval is on account of her having agreed with him or because of the dessert.

"How was the run?" Krystyna asks Patricia as she bursts through the door.

She's perspiring heavily. Arms bent at the elbow and her hands on her hips, Patricia leans over slightly to catch her breath.

She nods her head a couple of times. "Good."

Stanislaw looks up from his dessert. His eyes narrow as he studies his granddaughter. "You're too thin, Patricia. Sit down. Have some tea and cake."

"No thanks, *Dziadzio*. I had some grapes before I went for a run."

"Grapes! You burned off those grapes in the first five minutes of your jog." He pronounces "jog" like "joke," and Elizabeth is forced to stifle a laugh. It's nervous laughter that she's holding back. Flooded with embarrassing memories of her parents struggling to make themselves understood, butchering the English vowel sounds of monosyllabic words so that with whomever it was they were speaking, even as a child, she anticipated the typical feigning of total incomprehension, followed by disdainful indifference. How could she have avoided not becoming increasingly more indignant, wary of human nature, when she'd been forced to intervene and repeat what it was her parents had said, less the funny accent?

Patricia smiles at her grandfather. "I'll have some tea, though."

Krystyna pours the rest of the tea from the pot into a mug and hands it to her.

"Thanks, *Babcia*." Patricia seats herself in the chair beside Stanislaw, crosses one leg over the other, and sighs.

"So, you're off the day after tomorrow?" Stanislaw says.

"Yes."

"How was the training camp?"

Elizabeth feels her cheeks become flushed. This is where the secretiveness has a tendency to rear its ugly head.

"Good." Between sips of her tea, Patricia nods. "I enjoyed the routine. A person didn't have to think about what they were going to do next."

"But you were training in intelligence. You must have received a lot of instruction in Afghani culture and insurgency tactics and strategies." Elizabeth is gambling that Patricia might not be so evasive with her grandparents, but the cutting glance that her daughter throws her tells her otherwise.

"Yes, of course, but that is all classified information."

"Of course," Stanislaw pipes up, turning his head hastily in Elizabeth's direction and throwing her a critical glance that seems to imply that her civilian background has rendered her incapable of understanding the most fundamental tenet of military ethics.

"What time did you want to head back to Edmonton tomorrow?" Elizabeth regrets asking this question as soon as it comes out. Her father, fortunately, doesn't connect the dots, but Krystyna does and she imagines that she hears her mother suck in her breath.

"After lunch."

"You'll probably want to sleep in for the last time, Patricia," Elizabeth smiles.

"No. I'm used to making an early start."

Elizabeth can't get over how much her daughter has changed. She never thought that she'd miss her daughter's emotional outbursts, her tendency to challenge whatever she says. When thwarting her attempts to glean some information about intelligence training, Patricia had dismissed her queries as dispassionately as a seasoned courtroom lawyer would refute the arguments of opposing counsel. And when Stanislaw had challenged her about declining dessert, she'd maintained an impassive poker face. Is this what her training in intelligence had instilled in her — to keep a tight lid on her emotions, to become desensitized to the feelings of others and by extension to herself?

30.

PIERRE SQUIRMS BACK AND FORTH on the ground, trying to get comfortable. His legs are awkwardly crossed and Elizabeth fears he's about to spill his plate of food, which he's balanced precariously onto his thighs. Thankfully, the frijoles and tortillas, onto which the goat's meat stew has been ladled, stick to their plates and are virtually slide proof. Setting his plate down on the ground, Pierre straightens his back. "Why do you think Guzman is so intent on undermining the dismemberment stage in shamanic initiation? The bobcat superimposed on the feet of the second figure is *très significatif*."

Elizabeth likes the way Pierre throws in the odd French word. She likes his intensity, finds it comforting. "I agree. The bobcat is the only feline depicted in the panel. Felines, like deer, are considered to be animals of transformation, but they are also the only animal depicted in the mural that is capable of dismembering a live human. Vultures, of course, dismember corpses."

"It is important to bear in mind that the superimposition of animal figures symbolizes transformation into spirit form. Many Aboriginal tribes believe that the shaman, figuratively speaking, gives the animals his own flesh to eat, which can be equated with dismemberment. The superimposition of an animal at the feet of a shaman symbolized travel for *los indios* as much as depicting a motif alongside a rock fissure." Picking up his plate again, Pierre scoops the rest of the food into a tortilla and rolls it up into a crepe.

"Yes," Elizabeth agrees. "But I know what Guzman would say to counter your emphasis on transformation through animal spirits." Glancing furtively across the encampment at Guzman, seated between *Señor* Morelo and Raul, she pronounces Guzman's name in a muted tone of voice. "He'd say that you're overlooking the female influence in the initiation rite. The manner in which felines mate is instructive. The female is the aggressor and initiates coitus. They are also highly revered by Aboriginals because of their strong maternal instincts. Male felines do not have much to do with their offspring."

"What about the arrow that pierces the bobcat's mouth?"

"The mouth, like all orifices, is considered to be a place of transformation. Because of the female body's capacity to receive semen and to give birth."

"So ... *peut-être* he is correct?"

"I don't think there's one right or wrong answer. I think there were many painters and there are many interpretations. *Los indios* are long gone, and we're relegated to applying whatever spiritual symbols continue to resonate with extant Aboriginal tribes."

"I'm surprised that there are no scorpions depicted in the mural."

Elizabeth winces in reaction to Pierre's reference to scorpions. "Maybe they weren't considered transformational creatures. The Maya categorized all fauna into four different groups of animals — crawlers, runners, flyers, and swimmers. Scorpions belonged with the crawlers, with snakes and other insects, which aren't depicted in the mural either."

"Have you heard about the recent discovery by a team of researchers of oil paint used in the Bamiyan Valley cave murals of Afghanistan?"

Elizabeth is startled by Pierre's sudden change in topic. "Yes, interesting how in that part of the world technological strides had been made in the medium used to paint, whereas, here, the crowning achievement is the actual symbolic portrayal of their belief system."

Pierre throws Elizabeth a quizzical glance. "But in Bamiyan the murals also depict a belief system — Buddhist monks in vermilion robes amid palm leaves and mythical creatures, sitting cross-legged, just like we are now seated."

"But the significance of the discovery is that it's shattered the long held belief that oil as a medium hadn't been used until the twelfth century in Europe."

"It just goes to show you how trade can advance technology," Pierre adds. "The Bamiyan Valley is on the Silk Road, the ancient trade route between China and the West. The paint is believed to be a mixture of walnut and poppy seed drying oils, proteins, gum, resin and other extracts. Here, in the Baja, *los indios* were *absolument* isolated from the rest of the world. They were limited in the materials they used to create their pictographs by their natural environment."

"And I take it that these Afghani murals, like others, as in the Ajanta caves in India, are believed to have been painted by the monks themselves?"

"*Probablement.* The murals date back to 650 AD, when Aboriginals were being converted. With illiterate people, images come before ideas, and converts wanted to worship images of Buddha and his incarnations. I think it is instructive for us here. The painters of our murals might have been the shamans themselves."

Nodding, Elizabeth reflects on the slideshows that she's used as an educational tool. Pictures, even for the literate and educated, can be more powerful than words. "Only twenty percent of the Bamiyan cave murals, as I understand it, are preserved. The Taliban not only dynamited the colossal Buddhist statues in the valley, but also the caves," Elizabeth comments, her tone disapproving.

Pierre shakes his head. "Yes, the Taliban are terrible, *non*? Unbelievable how savage and backward in their thinking. You must be so worried."

She considers it ironic that Pierre is the last member of the team to have broached the subject of her daughter. "Why do you think they are so regressive in their thinking?"

"Power. Control. The Taliban is a reaction to the Soviet invasion in 1980. Look what happened in Iran with the Ayatollah. Remember the hostage taking at the American embassy?"

Elizabeth nods. She'd been a graduate student at the time, immersed in her studies, but she recalled that it had taken almost a year before the hostages had been released.

"That was a reaction to the Shah of Iran forging closer ties with the Americans. After their defeat in Vietnam, the Americans needed a buyer for their weapons and found a willing partner in the Shah, who, of course, used oil money to finance his military arsenal. Iran is on the border of the former Soviet republic of Turkmenistan, and the Soviets were afraid that Muslim fundamentalism could spread to the other Muslim republics of Uzbekistan and Tajikistan, which border Afghanistan. In 1980, Afghanistan was still a *frontière*, much more backward than Iran, so it is understandable that Islamic fundamentalism took a much more radical turn there."

"Have you heard anything about plans to build a pipeline across Afghanistan?" asks Elizabeth, hoping to glean some information that might shed light on the motives for her daughter's kidnapping.

"*Oui, bien sûr.* Before 9/11, the American vice-president led a delegation of oil companies to negotiate such a project with the Taliban."

"What was the result?"

"9/11." Pierre's gaunt, weathered face breaks into a cynical smile. "The last thing they would want is to have another foreign presence on their soil."

"Perhaps the Soviets had the same idea. Those southern

former Soviet republics have a lot of oil and gas," Elizabeth adds, furrowing her brow.

"Yes, and the Soviets were always friendly with Pakistan and India. And don't forget about China which shares a sixty kilometer border with Afghanistan. It is a mountain pass, through which the Silk Road passes. In France, we look at things differently. Russia, China, India and Pakistan have nuclear weapons, and so do we, along with the English, and the Americans. But the American point of view is very egocentric: America against the world. But it is a good thing that those other countries have nuclear capability. It provides a form of geopolitical balance."

"What about geosequestration? Do you think that the pipeline was also intended to transport liquefied carbon dioxide back from India to be stored underground in Afghanistan?"

"*Peut-être*. Oil and gas running south, and liquefied carbon dioxide north. It's possible. But, you asked me about the Taliban because your daughter has been kidnapped by them, *non*?

Elizabeth swallows hard and nods her head.

"I have only heard through others, here, that your daughter is in intelligence."

"Yes."

"So, the Taliban will not regard her as just an ordinary soldier, but someone with more value. They will use her to bargain for release of some of their own imprisoned cell members." Pausing, Pierre pulls his chin down, and as though to ensure that he's caught her attention, he peers at her over his sunglasses. "I believe that she will be released. That you will see her again."

"You do?" Elizabeth feels her heart quivering, but she's afraid to smile, to release the flood of emotions that Pierre's hopeful sentiments have triggered inside of her.

"Yes. That is politics. Not bad for a dentist, *non*?"

"Not bad."

"But she will no longer be the same person," he adds.

A lump develops in her throat. "Never?"

Solemnly shaking his head, Pierre rises from the ground, pulls his shoulders back. "*Non, jamais.*"

Pablo collects their plates and cutlery, and offers them a date square for dessert. "From the date palm groves of San Ignacio."

"*Gracias.*"

"*De nada.*" Extending the dessert tray, he offers them a second helping. "My brothers will be bringing a fresh batch, this afternoon, from the village. My mother bakes them. How is your hand, *Doctora*?"

"*Mejor.*" She turns her hand over and extends it, palm raised, towards Pablo. "It's still a little swollen, but much better, *gracias.*"

She thinks back to Patricia's homecoming and going away party; how Patricia had shrugged off her suggestion that she use her last free morning to sleep in, rather than leave at the crack of dawn. Had Patricia's comment about relishing the routine of military life really been so out of character? Like her own parents, Elizabeth had fallen into the trap of failing to appreciate that children, like snakes, shed their adolescent skins and take on personalities unfamiliar even to loved ones. She'd forgotten how much consternation she'd suffered on account of her own parents not letting go, not realizing that adolescence has a definitive crowning glory and upon embarking upon the path of adulthood, she was destined to evolve, chart her own course. Notwithstanding the tendency, as one ages, to resist change, adulthood's lengthier duration militates against the status quo, demands periodic evaluation, assessment, the abandonment of certain values and beliefs, and the exploration of other possibilities.

Elizabeth realizes now that she herself has been resisting change and has been projecting that resistance onto Patricia. Perhaps she'd cut herself off from intimate relationships with men after Patricia left home to shield herself from the psychic upheavals of the second phase of adulthood as an empty nester and has been clinging too hard to her younger, now badly frayed, adult self.

31.

"ASIDE FROM THE BRUTAL clitoral circumcision rites of some African tribes, very little is known about female rites of passage." Elizabeth pauses. The backdrop of the central panel's towering anthropomorphic figures diminishes Guzman's projected authoritarian self-image, and makes him appear smaller than he is. When he doesn't say anything, she continues.

"Remarkably, there's an affinity between segregationist rites practiced in the Middle and Far East with certain North American Aboriginal tribes. As soon as a young woman begins menstruating, she's isolated from the rest of the tribe, taken under the wing of an elder woman, nurtured, and taught how to look after herself. Pierre, you've studied the Middle Eastern patriarchal view that during menses a woman is considered to be polluted, unclean, and should not prepare meals or participate in divine rituals?"

"*Mais, oui.* The chore of cooking at that time of month would have been relegated to post-menopausal women, as the cycles of all tribal women tended to coincide."

Elizabeth feels herself blush. Not long after she'd started menstruating, she'd been amazed to discover that her cycle coincided with her mother's. She recalls her embarrassment over encountering, in high school classrooms, the distinctive and pungent smell of young girls on their period. Seemingly, none of the male students had detected the odour. At least they hadn't exhibited any of the predictable facial reactions — the crinkling of nostrils, surreptitious sniffing of the air to validate their suspicions that they'd been overrun by an army of menstruating young women. Like hostages, those poor guys had been held captive, besieged by the smell of menstrual blood. No wonder menstruation was considered to endow women with too much power.

"What is it?" asks Pierre.

"Nothing." She shakes her head, but with Pierre and Guzman's eyes upon her, she feels compelled to add, "I was just thinking about something back in my school days."

"About all the young girls on their period at the same time." Guzman breaks into a mischievous smile.

"So, you know that particular smell?"

"*Si.*" Guzman nods his head. "And at home too. I had two sisters."

"And here I thought that the boys in school didn't smell anything. You know, I was just thinking... the theory that taboos against menstruating women arose because men had no control over the female monthly cycle might be too complicated. Perhaps there's a simpler explanation. Maybe the idea that the male hierarchical position of superiority was threatened by menses is entirely misplaced. It could just boil down to men feeling trapped, powerless to escape a bad smell."

Guzman breaks out laughing. "*Tal vez, Doctora.* We might be overanalyzing. But let's not forget that there is an astronomical dimension to menses. The female cycle is of the same duration as a lunar cycle, and the moon was revered for its power to affect natural phenomena — marine tides. *Los primitivos*, during their treks up and down the peninsula, would have camped on the beaches of both the sea and the Pacific ocean during the hotter summer months, when the trade winds brought some relief from the heat. They could not have failed to make the connection between the tides and the phases of the moon."

"And menses," adds Pierre.

"*Exactamente.*" Brandishing the stick he'd used in the morning as a pointer, Guzman directs it towards the bobcat, superimposed on the feet of the second shamanic figure. "The bobcat was considered to be endowed with powers of transformation because, as a predator that hunted at night, it would have been associated with the magical properties of the moon. *La luna* is associated with feminine principles, like instincts, moods, receptivity. Hunter/gatherer societies believed that light emanated from darkness, just like the male springs from the female. Women, as gatherers, retained a closer connection to the earth. It wasn't until societies evolved from primitive to primary, agrarian cultures, that women lost their right to choose a mate, accumulate and dispose of their individual property. *Independente* of influence by parents or tribal elders."

"But primitive societies are not universally considered to have been egalitarian." Unlike many of her colleagues, Elizabeth has never subscribed to the myth of the noble savage. "In some extant hunter-gatherer societies, when the male hunters embark on a hunt, it's customary to prohibit their menstruating wives from touching any of their hunting gear. They're scared that game might be repelled by the odour of menstrual blood. The taboo might have originated as an exclusionary impulse, a pretext for hunters to save face, in case they returned without sufficient game to sustain the tribe. Eventually the taboo developed into a custom for safeguarding subsistence, but originally, it allowed hunters to blame their menstruating wives for jinxing the hunt."

"*Entonces, Doctora*, you are not in agreement with the view that menstrual taboos originated with primary, agrarian societies?"

"No. Look at all the red paint in the mural. Red is the colour of menstrual blood, which metaphorically represents a loss of potential life, without threatening the woman's life. So there was probably some potential power in that too."

"I agree with Elizabeth," says Pierre. "The taboo evolved over time and culminated later into a practice of segregating menstruating women from the rest of the tribe. But primitive societies would have realized that when a woman was menstruating, she was not pregnant, and a primary concern of hunter-gatherers was the propagation of the tribe. Fear is an emotion closely related to powerlessness. *Peut-être*, the shamans projected their fear onto the mural through the application of red paint and the painting of the female vulva motif, the "v" shape, which is prolifically represented in the mural."

"*Entonces, las pinturas* symbolize *los primitivos*' respect for the female dimension in their solicitation of the animal spirits to guide them to fertile hunting grounds?"

"*Si, pero.*" Pierre raises his hand and extends his index finger. "The bobcat, when it dismembers the shaman in the second stage of initiation, metaphorically kidnaps the initiate's soul."

At Pierre's enunciation of the word, "kidnap," Elizabeth's breathing becomes shallow and her heart begins to pound. The sun, which has fallen to a forty-five degree angle, casting long shadows of their figures, has become too intense for her. Crouching down behind a boulder, she retrieves her water bottle from her knapsack and drinks greedily.

"The theory that on vision quests the animal totem kidnaps the initiate's soul can be applied, I think, also to shamanic initiation." Pierre pauses for a moment, and upon ensuring that he's regained Elizabeth's undivided attention resumes his theorizing. "After initiation, the initiate is never the same person."

"*Tal vez*, initiation rites might have originated in response to menstruation. And that is why there is no formal female initiation rite. Are you all right, *Doctora*?" Guzman asks.

"*Si*. I just feel very warm, all of a sudden."

"Do you want to take a break?"

"No, it's okay."

"*Bien*. Where were we?"

"We were discussing the male tribe members inventing their own rite of passage, in response to female menses." Pierre nods in Elizabeth's direction before continuing. "After a girl began her menses, she became a woman. Nature is responsible for this transformation, but for men it is different. They have to initiate their own rites of passage into adulthood. The initiation rite supplanted the role of nature."

"With their belief system." Guzman knocks on his head a couple of times with his knuckles. "*Con sus cerebros.*"

"So for males, the rite of passage was celebrated, but for women it evolved into a taboo." Even Elizabeth can hear the angry shrillness in her voice.

Before Pierre had interjected with the mythological belief about animal totems kidnapping the souls of adolescent initiates, she'd wanted to convey another theory about the function of menstrual taboos — to manage anxiety, health, and tribal social organization. Apart from the synchronous odour of menstrual blood playing a role in the segregation of menstruating women, the edgy mood swings and irritability that women tend to exhibit during menses might also have prompted tribal elders, in the interests of maintaining harmony and order, to deem menses a taboo. How many times, particularly since she's eclipsed the proverbial middle-age crisis, has she felt the need, at that time of month, to divorce herself from the stress of human relationships? While recovering in her tent from the scorpion bite, she'd felt relieved to have a valid reason to isolate herself from the rest of the team. Older menstruating tribal women might have welcomed the taboo. In the same vein as the taboo provided a pretext for luckless hunters to blame their menstruating wives for returning empty-handed from the hunt, segregation of menstruating women might have been a pretext for the older contingent of tribal women to withdraw from the world.

Elizabeth's own rite of passage into womanhood had been anything but dramatic. Taking her by the hand, Krystyna had solemnly led her into the bathroom where, underneath the sink, she kept a box of sanitary napkins and a belt. After fastening the elastic belt around her waist, she demonstrated how the clips kept the napkins in place. "From now on," Krystyna said, "you can get pregnant and have children."

Her mind races, and summons up her previous conversation with Pierre. Never. *Jamais.* Pierre's last words reverberate in her brain. He'd spoken them with such finality. Emotional anguish, the anxiety of not knowing, resonates deeper within her now than any hope or faith in a positive outcome. Fear. She's afraid to believe that Patricia will come home, afraid that a cruel fate will make a mockery of any hope and faith that she might muster up before finding out. Like the hunters who banished their menstruating wives from touching any of their implements, intent upon exercising some measure of control over their destiny, she's afraid to entrust her faith in fate, to resign herself to the infinite vagaries of the unknown.

32.

MAYNARD TREADS THE STEEP INCLINE from the direction of the left panel. He raises his right hand with his palm extended outwards.

It's now or never. Having at one time made decisions, even consequential ones, impulsively, Elizabeth, over the years, has steered away from making rash decisions. Resorting to sleeping on a problem, she's learned to trust the lapse of time to illuminate a solution. On this one, though, she's ruminated far too long. She needs to find out whether her instincts are correct, whether Maynard is somehow complicit in her having been followed, or whether her stressed out imagination is simply getting the better of her.

"*Que tal?*" Guzman asks, squinting his eyes.

"It's Richard. He's been bitten by a snake," Maynard gasps.

Elizabeth notices that Maynard is panting. Beads of sweat have collected on his upper lip and above his brow. Guzman and Pierre quickly pick up their backpacks and head down the path. She thinks of Raul and Bartek, who are working on the right panel, and considers running up the trail to alert them, solicit their help. A wave of panic overcomes her. She's confused. Richard. This is about Richard and not her. It's like the wiring in her brain is short circuiting. She hurries after them, anxious to see Richard. *Please, God, may he be okay.*

Pierre is in the lead and as she catches up to them, she hears him ask Maynard, "Is he suffering from convulsions?"

"Yes, I didn't know what to think, and considered maybe he was an epileptic, but then I heard the rattle. After moving him into the shade, I stayed with him for a bit, before running to get help."

"What did you do with the snake?" Lagging behind, Guzman appears to be struggling to keep up with Pierre's pace.

"The snake's gone. I made sure of that."

A cluster of boulders intercepts the diminishing, oblique rays of the late afternoon sun, casting elongated shadows upon the left panel. The light becomes nebulous, makes it difficult to see, like when a person stares too hard at the sun, abruptly turns away and lingering spots dance upon the eyes' retinas. Pierre slides his sunglasses off his face and onto his head, then slows his pace, stops, looks out onto the arroyo. Brigham points at Richard's prostrate body. Pierre hurries over to him, kneels down, and dumps the contents of his knapsack.

All the blood seems to have drained out of Richard's face. He's only sparsely shaded by the scrawny branches of an ocotillo bush, but the involuntary shiver his body emits reveals that he feels cold.

Elizabeth kneels down and strokes Richard's forehead. It's indeed cold to her touch. "We need a blanket, or something."

Rummaging through his first-aid kit, Pierre retrieves a syringe and a plastic dispenser with anti-venom. The snake's fang marks pulse red on Richard's left elbow. Grasping his arm, he turns it over. "I'm going to prick you just below the elbow, in the same spot where a lab technician would withdraw blood for tests."

Richard nods, feebly replies, "Okay," closes his eyes.

"You're lucky to have been struck on the elbow because where I am administering the injection, the anti-venom will act almost immediately."

"Pierre, do you carry a blanket with you?" asks Maynard.

Guzman unzips his vest and lays it on top of Richard. "How did he get bitten on the elbow?"

"I don't know, *Doctoro*. He was drinking some water. His backpack," Maynard points to a boulder, "was over there."

Elizabeth retreats to the boulder pointed out by Maynard and spots Richard's water bottle lying on its side with its lid agape. The ground is wet where water spilled. The nozzle is caked in mud. Stowing it inside his knapsack, she slings the bag over her shoulder and approaches the left panel. She stares at the mural but doesn't take in any of the motifs. Nothing registers. She feels numb, guilty for not feeling more empathy for Richard.

In her mind's eye, she replays the scene of Maynard trudging up the hill, raising his hand. Had it been in greeting, or was it a gesture made in distress, to beckon them to follow him back to the left panel? How had Guzman and Pierre reacted to his sudden appearance? She's been so self-absorbed, consumed by Pierre forewarning her about Patricia returning as a different person, that she draws a blank on having sensed alarm on their part.

There's no point in confronting Maynard. Just like she'd misread Maynard's hand gesture for a greeting, she'd misinterpreted his intentions when pontificating about geosequestration. Richard's complaints about Maynard obsessing about the latest panacea for climate change had only intensified her suspicions, and that's what all this amounted to — mere speculation, extrapolation. Her professional training has made her a master at connecting the dots.

But what about Bernard's partners reassigning the Kazakhstan oil company file to another lawyer? And Pierre too had postulated that the Taliban would regard someone in intelligence as harbouring valuable information about the NATO mission. Bringing up her visualization of the gun she'd imagined falling to the floor in the room next to Richard's, at the motel in San Ignacio, she dispels from her mind any doubt about being followed. But her encountering Maynard in the courtyard, after she'd left Richard's room, she now realizes, had been purely coincidental, and his inquiring about her background had been merely small talk over an early morning coffee.

Turning around, she sees Pierre and Brigham slowly lift Richard to his feet. They stand back. Pierre addresses him, probably asks whether he can make it back to camp; just like Bartek had questioned her after she'd been bitten by the scorpion. She shudders at the thought of the rattler raising its head, menacingly protruding its tongue, piercing him. What had he done to provoke it? How had he preempted a second attack?

She no longer feels as though the universe has been conspiring against her. Krystyna had always said that bad luck comes in trios. Her own encounter with a rattler on the precipitous mule trail had been her second stroke of misfortune, followed by the scorpion bite. Now it's Richard's turn. She shakes her head, curses herself.

Like her triumph over impulsiveness, she'd thought that her immersion in reasoned scientific study had disabused her of the superstitious notions that she'd unwittingly picked up from her parents. But old habits, archaic thought patterns die hard. It's easier, more comforting, to cling to illusory ideas about why the universe unfolds as it does, why some people survive, while others have their number called up; unless one confronts death and defies it. Like Patricia. God willing, Pierre is right. She'll never be the same person again.

33.

PULLING A BANDANA from his jean pocket, Antonio raises his cowboy hat and mops his brow. His hair is oily and matted down, just above his ears, where the band of his hat has left an impression. Once again, Antonio has come to Elizabeth's rescue over a wayward snake. "*Doctora*, do you have a moment to make the acquaintance of Carolina Madero?" he asks.

"*Si, muy bien.*" Aimlessly standing beside her tent, Elizabeth has purposely relegated herself to a timeout from the rest of the camp. She wishes there was a breeze, some other sound that she could latch onto to muffle the voices of the others who've been jettisoned into high gear by Guzman to erect a makeshift infirmary for Richard.

Antonio's otherwise ramrod posture appears slightly stooped. She imagines him leaning forward, over the saddle's pommel, and then straightening his back, struggling to remain alert on the narrow trail traversing the canyon, from camp to the Morelo homestead and the following day, back again. He gestures with his hand for Elizabeth to follow him.

"Antonio. Did you ask your mother whether there were any phone calls for me in the past few days?"

"*Si*" he answers obligingly, nodding his head, "*Pero*, the machine just blinked a few times and then *nada*."

"You mean the fax machine was turned on and someone called but nothing came through?"

Antonio nods his head, but Elizabeth is left with the notion that he's not sure what happened or whether anyone called, tried to leave a message, or transmit a document.

On the opposite end of the encampment, his brother, Pablo, is erecting another tent. Diverting his attention momentarily from his pounding of stakes with a rock, Pablo looks up at Elizabeth and mumbles, "*Buenas tardes.*"

Elizabeth reciprocates the greeting and then notices a small, compact woman seated cross-legged on the ground rummaging through a backpack. The woman looks up at her and nods, but then shifts her attention back to her knapsack and resumes her frenetic probe of its contents.

Antonio shoots Elizabeth an awkward smile before thrusting his chin in Carolina's direction and addresses her with: "*Maestra, por favor, la Doctora esta aqui.*"

Carolina raises her head and peers up at Elizabeth and Antonio. Standing, she extends her hand towards Elizabeth. "*Mucho gusto.* I'm sorry. I'm looking for my memory card. I hope I didn't forget to bring it." Carolina's handshake is simultaneously firm and delicate. It also feels soft to the touch, a testimony to her having only just arrived from a life replete with the amenities of central plumbing.

"*Mucho gusto.*" Elizabeth can't help but size up her new acquaintance. Unlike herself, Carolina favours a sleek hairstyle, tied back into a French knot, but which in her estimation makes her look older than her forty-odd years. Her large brown eyes exude a mischievous intensity. "Perhaps you packed your memory card in one of the pockets," Elizabeth offers. "I do that all the time. Put something in a place where I think I will have an easier time remembering where I put it, and then forget that I put it there in the first place."

"No," Carolina shakes her head in frustration, "I have already looked in all the pockets." She drops to her knees and resumes her ransacking of her backpack, tilting it to take advantage of the sun's angled light.

"*Con permiso*," Antonio remarks, nodding toward the two women before taking his leave to help his brother.

"*Gracias amigo*," Carolina calls out after Antonio. Turning to Elizabeth, she pats the ground beside her. "*Sienta te.*"

Elizabeth does as she's told, stretches out her legs and leans back on her elbows after planting then into the soft ground.

"So you are from Canada?" Carolina asks.

"Yes."

"It is cold there now, yes?"

"*Si*. And you, Carolina, did you fly into La Paz?"

"No." Carolina shakes her head. "Loreto. And then I took a bus to San Ignacio and Antonio picked me up from there early this morning."

"You must me tired."

"Not so much. Do I look tired?" She peers at Elizabeth, and opens her eyes wide as though to defy any impressions that her tired-looking eyes might have evoked.

Elizabeth breaks out into a smile in response to Carolina's exaggerated facial expression. She notices that her eyes are an unusual brown with green speckles and that her lashes are full and long.

"*Mira*, finally." Carolina holds up her memory card. "I really thought I forgot to pack it." Unzipping one of the backpack's exterior compartments she shoves it inside, heaves her knapsack away from her.

"Are you married? Do you have children?" Elizabeth asks.

"Divorced," Carolina answers with finality. "And two sons. They are grown up now, but not married yet. And you?" Shifting into a reclining position, on her side, she props one elbow onto the ground and her head onto her hand to face Elizabeth.

"I'm divorced too, and I have one daughter. She is twenty-two."

"*Maestra. Es listo.*" Pablo announces.

"*Gracias amigo.*" Carolina shoots an obliging nod in Pablo's direction.

"*De nada.*" Pablo throws the fist-sized rock with which he'd hammered in the stakes, into the desert scrub. The sound of the stone rolling along the ground coincides with a sudden hiatus in the commotion generated by the pitching of tents.

Turning back to Elizabeth, Carolina asks, "So what happened with the American professor? *Doctoro* Wellington is his name?"

"Yes."

"I heard something about a *serpiente.*" Carolina feigns a shudder and grimaces.

"Yes. It was bad." Elizabeth sucks in her breath to stop herself from crying. She can't help but notice that her distress hasn't escaped Carolina's watchful eye. Elizabeth can't hold back the tears anymore. Sitting up, she runs her fingers up and down her cheeks, wiping them away as they stream uncontrollably down her face.

Carolina leans over toward her backpack, drags it toward herself, retrieves a packet of tissues and hands one to Elizabeth. Her eyes search out Elizabeth's.

"*Gracias.*"

"*De nada.*" Carolina waves her hand in a downward motion.

Elizabeth wonders how much Carolina knows about her circumstances. She feels so exposed, chastises herself for allowing her emotions to become so transparent to a mere stranger. The breeze that she'd been hoping for has finally wafted into the valley, stirs up the air that since the morning has been morbidly still.

"Maynard, the professor from Vancouver," Elizabeth explains, "said that Richard suffered a convulsion, so *Doctoro* Guzman decided that someone should stay with him all the time. That's why they are pitching a larger tent for Richard and Pierre, who is also a dentist and has some medical training."

"I see." Carolina nods, but the look on her face conveys bewilderment, as though she'd expected Elizabeth to unburden herself about Patricia, rather than speak about Richard and the setting up of a makeshift infirmary. After a moment, she says, "You are the one who is tired, *Doctora*."

"Please, call me Elizabeth."

"Okay, Elizabeth," Carolina corrects herself, smiling. Leaning over, she sympathetically rubs Elizabeth's arm. She checks her wristwatch, and stands up. "There is a little time before *la comida*. I think I will organize myself inside my new home."

Elizabeth follows suit, but feels rooted to the ground, at a loss for words, realizes that she's been expecting to have to unburden herself, but then plays back Carolina's words, "there is a little time." She looks up at the highest peak, spots a bird with an enormous wingspan. It's not a turkey vulture. It looks like a California Condor, but from a distance it's difficult to tell. They are rare now, having succumbed over the decades to the widespread application of pesticides.

Of course there is time, time for her to get to know this latest addition to the team, time to come to terms with Richard's need to convalesce. *How silly of me to have read too much into Antonio's offer to introduce me to Carolina. It was nothing more than an old world gesture of politeness, extended as much toward Carolina as to myself.*

34.

"**B**ETTER CLOSE THE FLAP before the mosquitoes do me in."

"Oh, yes. Good idea." Elizabeth quickly takes in her surroundings, the spaciousness of what everyone refers to as the "big tent." "Wow, this tent has a floor and everything."

"Lap of luxury is what you get when you're on your deathbed," Richard smiles wryly.

"Oh, come on. It's not that bad."

"Could've died up there. Didn't know what hit me. One minute I was crouched down to get my water bottle, next I was gone."

"Have you ever had a seizure before?"

Richard shakes his head.

Elizabeth takes a sip of tequila and savours the warmth of the liquid as it oozes down her throat. "I'd offer you some, but it may not be a good idea."

He raises his arm and then drops it, as though in resignation. "Thanks for coming. How'd you arrange it?"

"When *Señor* Morelo called for a bit of a nip, Bartek suggested Pierre not miss out on his share. Like a dirty shirt, I jumped in and offered to play waitress."

"Good of you. You must be feeling better."

"Why do you say that?"

"You've been sluggish lately."

"Self-absorbed."

"Any news from the village?"

"Apparently the fax machine the Morelos have hooked up to their phone line surged into action a couple of times. Antonio mentioned how the machine's message light flashed, but no document transmitted."

Richard rolls over onto his side, plants his elbow onto his sleeping bag and props his head onto his hand. "Typical Mexico. *Muy simpatico*. They really feel for others, but sometimes it gets downright awkward."

"Like the Poles, when it comes to food and drink. 'No' in Polish means 'maybe' — an invitation to be plied with a second helping. It was good of Bartek, though, to think of Pierre."

"Nothing awkward about getting a friend a drink. How's the Mexican artist?"

"Super lady. So gracious. I felt bad for her, arriving in so much chaos."

Richard hadn't witnessed Guzman peremptorily ordering Pablo to set up two more tents — one for Carolina and the second to serve as an infirmary, where for the next twenty-four hours Pierre was relegated to periodically checking on Richard's vital signs.

"Got to hand it to Guzman. Should nickname him *el general*." Richard pronounces "general" in Spanish, with the "g" enunciated like an "h."

Elizabeth laughs. "*General* Guzman. It has a ring to it, all right. So you heard all the commotion?"

"Those poor Morelo brothers. Didn't have a chance to catch their breath after their suicide mission across the canyon and back. You getting along alright with *el general*?"

"Yes, not bad, but I'm glad Pierre's along for the ride. It'd be pretty tough working alone with Guzman. He can get pretty uni-dimensional. He's obsessed with the female dimension of shamanic initiation rites. I agree with him that male puberty initiation rites were likely adopted to mimic menses, but I'm not convinced that shamanic initiation rites originated from lunar and menstrual cycles."

Richard closes his eyes.

"Are you all right?"

"Yeah, just tired. Pierre said it would take a couple of days before I'm on my feet again. Pass me some water." He points to a small collapsible table by the doorway. "I'm supposed to drink a lot of fluids, like you did, after that scorpion bit you. To flush out the toxins."

"Sorry, I shouldn't be going on about shamanic initiation. Maybe I should get back to the fire and bring back Pierre." Looking over at the collapsible table where she'd deposited Pierre's tequila, she adds. "Poor guy's missing out on his share."

"No, stay." The needy tone of his voice catches her off guard. As though sensing her consternation, Richard's quick to add, "So, you're engaged in a bit of theoretical wrangling with *el general*?"

"You sure you don't mind me talking about this?"

Richard shakes his head.

"Sometimes I get the feeling that Guzman is trying to make a point about traditional female roles. He makes me feel as though I'm suppressing my femininity."

Richard raises his eyebrows, shoots her a look that she interprets as him thinking her introspection might be a little misguided.

"I know psychologists say no one can make you feel a certain way, but even Pierre has picked up on Guzman's preoccupation with the female dimension in the mural."

"Maybe he's trying to tell you something," Richard suggests.

"What?"

"I don't know. *Are* you suppressing your femininity? If not, then Guzman wouldn't make you feel as though you are."

Elizabeth feels like a grenade has become lodged in her chest and is about to explode. "Jesus Christ! I'm a mother whose only child's life is threatened! How can he be playing such mind games with me?"

"Hang on, hang on. Sure you're not reading too much into what's going on? You know, as well as I do, that some academics prefer a polemical approach to conducting research. Guzman obviously likes to engage in heated discussions. Would you prefer he treat you differently because of what's happening in your personal life?"

"No, of course not." She sits down on the other cot, rests her elbows on her knees, and lowers her head. Her heart, though, continues to race. It seems she hasn't only been in left field about Maynard, but also, as it turns out, about Guzman's intent in theorizing about the female dimension in the panel.

"So were you terribly disappointed the Morelos didn't have any news about your daughter?"

Raising her head, she peers at Richard for a moment, and questions why he's changing the subject. "No." She doesn't mean for her answer to come out quite so defensively. "Patricia and I are in remote places, so how could I expect otherwise?" She pauses, reminds herself that Richard is her friend, and she needn't feel threatened. "I'm beginning to realize it's a good thing I'm here, and not in Calgary where everyone expects everything to go like clockwork." As she says this, she thinks of Bernard and how hard it must be for him — enduring the awkward, pitying eyes of his partners and associates. "I'm also re-evaluating my values, trying to shift my perspective." She takes a swig of tequila and holds it in her mouth before swallowing. "Just this morning, Pierre gave me another perspective on Patricia. A point of view that totally eluded me." She pauses, takes another sip. "I've known for years about the notion that when the adolescent meets his animal totem during a vision quest, his soul is believed to be stolen, kidnapped. Maybe it's the stress. I don't know. I should have thought of that."

"Patricia being kidnapped is like an initiate meeting his animal totem?"

"Yes, absolutely." Elizabeth again hangs her head before raising it to catch Richard's eye. "I connect dots that aren't even connected and miss the obvious."

"Not exactly obvious. Don't beat yourself up too much. Even when a person's immersed in this stuff all the time, over time, you forget these theories."

"When Pierre mentioned the animal totem kidnapping the initiate's soul, it was like a light bulb was switched on in my head. I'm so scared Richard!" Her eyes fill with water. "Even if Patricia survives this, she'll never be the same person again." Elizabeth drops her head, heaves up sobs.

Richard raises himself from the cot, leans over, and strokes the back of her neck. "Come over here." He sidles his body closer to the edge.

Sitting down, she pulls a Kleenex out of her jacket pocket and blows her nose.

"It's hard to keep faith."

"Trust. I'm so afraid to trust."

Richard nods. "We think we're in control but we're not. We think we're supposed to be. Have these inflated perceptions of ourselves. I hate to say it, but the Taliban, fucked up as they are, don't suffer from any delusions. Not like us — in denial. They know this isn't all there is. They've got nothing to lose. That's why we'll never win against them over there."

Elizabeth takes another sip of tequila, tilts her cup and grimaces at how much is left.

"Sorry, can't help you with that." Richard shakes his head. "Wish I could. Shouldn't waste it, though. Could be in for a dry spell in a couple of days. Do a bottoms up." He lifts his chin for emphasis.

"No way. I may not make it back to my tent."

Richard lays back down on his cot. "Not that different from Vietnam. We were fucking doomed. When I was still in high school, I heard about Vietnamese mothers handing a basket with their newborns to American GI's being evacuated by helicopter from the jungle, with fucking explosives inside. How can you win a war against a people willing to go that far?"

Elizabeth sighs, slowly exhales, and lays her head down on his chest. Survival. Thousands of years ago, in this arroyo, it was about survival, tracking game, and soliciting, though their shamans, indulgences from a higher power that was believed to hold all the cards, wielding control over whether the tribe was fed, watered, and physically fit enough to sustain and propagate itself. For her, it's been what Patricia has railed about — a luxury problem — maintaining her sanity.

"You've been a real good friend to me Richard."

"Hey, I fell in love with you the moment I caught sight of you on that beach."

She lifts her head, peers at him. "You're just saying that."

"Hell, no. Why would I lie? I've been a bachelor for a long time." Richard's eyes dart back and forth, as though he's confused about her misgivings. "Something about you made my heart bang around so hard in my chest I thought ... I don't know what I thought." He coughs, clears his throat. "There's a cliff at that end of the beach. I was sitting on some rocks. I heard you cut the motor over the roar of the surf. Then, I saw you come up from the dunes, watched you take in the horizon with the big island. You seemed so at peace, comfortable in your own skin. I could tell you were really captivated by the sound of the surf, the water fowl, the desert."

"And here I thought I was all alone."

"I thought I'd better make an appearance before you turned around and left. You didn't see me 'til I began walking toward you."

"You must have thought I was nuts, the way I kept turning around, observing everything."

He runs his hand up and down her arm, shakes his head.

"So I was lucky?" Elizabeth muses.

Richard shoots her a quizzical glance.

"I was lucky you were there. I might have gone into that

palapa restaurant alone." Elizabeth smiles wanly. "Was meant to be."

A chorus of laughter drifts from the gathering at the campfire. Summoning up the image of Carolina's exaggerated facial expressions, when they'd spoken about fatigue and snakes, Elizabeth imagines Carolina joking with the Morelos and the other team members. She wonders whether everyone, in her absence, feels more at ease, inclined to poke fun at one another. A sudden surge of jealousy overcomes her. *When was the last time that I savoured such a feeling of lightheartedness?* She shakes her head.

"What is it?" Richard asks.

"I was such a mess in your hotel room." She looks down at her hands, folds them together into her lap. "You have no idea how glad I was when you called me two days later to ask for a lift to the orientation."

Richard looks confused. "Why do you have to apologize? You're a good mother. Holed up in your hotel room waiting for the phone to ring. As though you were sentenced to some sort of prison term."

Elizabeth thinks of Stanislaw. He felt guilty his whole life for having survived when so many perished. Patricia, thankfully, will be spared that type of survivor guilt. At least she's not vying for survival with hordes of others condemned to die.

"I was going crazy! I kept picking up the phone to ask you to have dinner with me, but stopped myself every time."

"I felt guilty," she confesses. "Even though you and Bernard kept telling me that there was nothing I could do for Patricia if I returned to Canada, I kept agonizing over my decision to stay."

He nods. "I felt at a loss so many times. Still do!"

"Oh Richard! And you're counselling *me* to be kinder to myself. You've been so understanding. Really, everyone has." With the base of her thumb, she wipes away the moisture running across her cheekbones.

A rush of wind suspends their conversation. The walls of the tent billow in and out again. Within the ensuing silence, Elizabeth catches the faint murmur of voices emanating from the campfire. She rises from Richard's cot and seats herself again across from him, on Pierre's portable bed. "But when we went down the east cape, you told me she has her own path in life. Raul said the same thing. That's the most painful part of being a parent. Resigning oneself to the reality that our children have their own path and not feeling guilty about it. And powerlessness. I feel so powerless over what's happening to her."

"No one's judging you," Richard remonstrates, shaking his head. "Man, you're hard on yourself!"

Stanislaw. Stanislaw had to be hard on himself to survive. And now Patricia's drawing upon that same well of resilience.

35

"I T'S ABOUT WATER. It's a shrine. They prayed here to a higher power for water." Maynard smiles self-consciously, exposes his long, perfectly formed teeth. It's a wolf's smile.

"So it's about rebirth?" Elizabeth asks.

"Yes."

"What leads you to believe it's a shrine?"

He lifts his cap off his brow and scratches the crown of his head. "Richard came up with the theory. The gap between the deer's head and antlers appears to have occurred naturally by a water seep washing out the paint."

The predominant motif, to which Maynard refers, is a nine foot, vertical deer, roughly the same height as the largest human figure in the central panel. It's painted black — the colour of the uninitiated — with its legs extended, presumably to mimic the central panels' giant anthropomorphs raising their arms upwards, towards the outer world. Its supplicating posture gives the impression that it's paying homage to the shamans in the adjoining panel.

"His theory made him thirsty and his thirst for water almost killed him," Elizabeth says.

Maynard shoots her a cutting glance. She senses his disarmament. "Why did you say that?" he asks, accusingly.

"I don't know. It just popped into my head." She feels edgy, perhaps because of last night's late hour and the tequila she'd polished off back at the fire, after Pierre returned to the big tent to resume his nursing duties.

"You're angry."

"I didn't mean anything by it." Despite her realization that Maynard hasn't had anything to do with her being followed, she can't help herself. When Guzman reassigned her to take Richard's place on the left panel, she'd conjured an image of rubbing her hands together. She can innocuously unleash against Maynard, more so than against any of the others, all the built-up aggression she's been holding in, projecting inward, towards herself. Apart from being the youngest member of the team, emotionally, he presents as the most vulnerable. She'd mistaken his ambivalence, awkwardness as suspicious behaviour, while all along he'd been grieving the betrayal and loss of his fiancée and best friend.

Turning back to the panel, Maynard resumes his exposition of its motifs. If he harbours any resentment toward Elizabeth for her insensitivity, he doesn't let on. "There's also that strange-looking twin with a fish-like appearance, superimposed on the front of what looks like a deer. But we can only make out its hind quarters."

"So you think the vertical deer represents a transformed shaman praying for water?" Elizabeth asks.

"Yes. The location of this motif is significant." He flips open his notepad, scans the writing on the last page. "Beneath it, the cliff base curves under to form the ceiling of a deep chamber. We measured it. It's forty-seven feet wide and thirty-five feet deep. Inverted chambers, such as this, are repositories for water that pools during the rainy season." Maynard stops speaking suddenly and appears to prick up his ears.

"What is it?" Elizabeth asks.

Shaking his head, he replies, "It's nothing. It was at this point, yesterday, that Richard excused himself to get a drink of water. I thought I heard something, but obviously I'm hearing things."

"That must have been pretty traumatic for you," Elizabeth sympathizes.

Nodding, Maynard smiles at her appreciatively. "I didn't know what to do. Stay with him ... or run and get help."

"You did the right thing."

"I was lucky. Richard was lucky. He could have convulsed again after I ran to get you guys and who knows what kind of state we would have found him in."

"You know," Elizabeth interjects, "when I was leaving to come down here, my mother warned me about the snakes and scorpions. I thought she was being overly protective, but after encountering that rattler on the trail and being counseled by Pablo about shaking my clothes before putting them on, I came to realize that my mother wasn't too far off the mark."

"We should get back to this," Maynard urges. "Where were we?"

Approaching the panel, Elizabeth points towards the inverted cliff base. "You were saying that this might have served as a repository for water during the rainy season."

"Right. Antlers are symbols of growth, rebirth. Male deer drop their antlers in April and May, the beginning of the spring drought, and the antlers grow back in July and August, when the summer rains begin. *Señor* Morelo mentioned that every spring, *los indios* risked starvation."

"So you think this represents a tribal ritual that they adopted from climatic patterns that threatened the tribe's survival? In this case the annual spring drought?"

"Yes. Stories and myths tend to evolve from death-defying events. Like the biblical story of Noah's Ark."

"Or Homer's *Odyssey,* where all the monsters and evil forces that Odysseus encounters are symbolic of strange weather patterns that threw off his journey back home."

The way that Maynard raises his eyebrows, she can tell that he's never considered the Greek epic poem as having an environmental dimension.

"Odysseus's journey, of course, is the journey of life which is always fraught with danger, misfortune, and betrayal." She pauses after the word "betrayal," and sees Maynard flinch and lower his head.

"In the *Odyssey*, the mythic hero prevails against the forces of evil. Here, too, an anthropogenic rationale is portrayed in the pictographs. The painters are telling a story about how their tribe overcame adversity, but at the same time the pictograph is a solicitation, a shrine to the powers of nature to bless them, and spare them from the ravages of the impending drought."

"So, you think it's all right to call it a shrine?"

"Yes, absolutely." Elizabeth feels a piercing regret at having taken out her frustrations on Maynard. He's more fragile than she realized. "Shamanic initiation mimics the life cycle. They believed that everything powerful flowed from that. But sadly it also transcends that, signifies man's attempt to control his destiny."

"So, as hunter-gatherers we didn't really have faith in a higher power. We wanted control from the get go."

"Yes, that's one way of looking at it. But what distinguishes modern human beings from our ancestors is our arrogance. We have a misguided sense of entitlement." Recalling last night's discussion with Richard about how the Taliban are less arrogant than NATO forces, less fearful of death, more trusting in a higher power and a hereafter, Elizabeth is indignant at the idea of women being recruited into combat missions. The female dimension in the pictographs is indeed, as Guzman has been urging her to appreciate, overwhelming. Water, the symbol of life, is a female motif. Flow. Flow of blood, water, the life cycle — suffering, dismemberment, death and rebirth. The birthing process — the female dimension — mirrors the life cycle and was celebrated, emulated; otherwise the tribe risked starvation, extinction. The cutting of the umbilical cord, a kind of death, separates mother from child. Latching onto the mother's breast, flow of milk, was a kind of rebirth.

"And our arrogance stems from there being too many of us, including women. Women are no longer revered for their indispensable role in the propagation of our species, although now in our developed part of the world, women are being confronted, as you're probably aware, Maynard, with fertility issues. Particularly women who put off getting pregnant until they are in their late thirties or even early forties. Notwithstanding, I think we harbour a misguided belief that we're above the natural order of things."

Maynard's nostrils flare. He quickly scans his notes before raising his head, and then gapes at her perplexedly.

"Don't look so mystified. Even today, when a vessel is in distress, principles of navigation dictate that women and children are the first to be evacuated onto life rafts. Men understand, intuitively, their duty, but have also been trained to sacrifice themselves for women and children." She prays that the Taliban still harbour such beliefs, albeit in a perverse way. By banishing women to hide behind burkas, they keep them out of harm's way while obsessively defending the homeland. It probably stems from the Crusades — a genocide, which included rape as a method of eradicating a different faith of people. Bloody Catholics. Stupid religion. Perhaps arrogance arose as a result of organized religion. Arrogance breeds an exclusionary mindset; only converts are entitled to a hereafter of bliss."

"You know, before coming down here, I read about a new theory on climate change," Maynard remarks.

The way Maynard is looking at her, she can tell she has rumination written all over her face. She conjures an image of a cow ruminating over its cud. Chewing, masticating, grinding its feed down to an organic mush, before it's palatable enough to swallow. "Tell me about it." Her reply has a double-edged meaning. She notices Maynard cringe. She's become impatient with this. She feels tired.

"The latest is that there was a major change of climate about six thousand years ago and over time it gave rise to the first civilizations — Chinese, Egyptian, Inca." He pauses for a moment, clears his throat. "They think that all of a sudden the world got a lot more arid, and hunter-gatherers were forced to gravitate to more fertile regions of the planet like the Fertile Crescent, which had a Mediterranean, more benign climate. The stresses of different tribes of people coming together spurred an agrarian revolution and the exploitation of man by man."

"They probably followed migrating game," Elizabeth encourages.

"Yes. But the interesting thing is, we're at the same point now, anthropologically. We're on the cusp of evolving yet again. Environmental refugees will precipitate huge demographic changes on the planet that will cause us to build new civilizations."

"The Sahel region of Africa, the countries south of the Sahara, have seen the annual rainy season diminish to the point that there is a lot of civil unrest there now."

"Exactly," Maynard concurs, appearing gratified. "Political theorists blamed the Africans for overgrazing their livestock, but now they think that the Indian Ocean has become so much warmer that the rains don't reach so far north anymore. And in Afghanistan, too, they've been experiencing drought. Winters are no longer as cold, their summers are hotter."

Now it's her turn to cringe at Brigham's mention of Afghanistan.

"So, the so-called information age is on the brink of transforming itself?"

"Yes, they theorize that it all started with computers, around the time of the Second World War. But you know, when we look back in history, the information age might be viewed as merely a stage in the fossil fuel age — referred to now as the Anthropocene." Maynard pauses as though to ensure that Elizabeth is still with him. "The industrial revolution, when coal was discovered and the steam engine was invented, really started everything. The agrarian revolution was spent. There was enough food. Surplus lead to innovation."

"So we went from starvation to surplus and now we're going back to starvation."

"Unfortunately, yes."

Elizabeth thinks back to their last conversation in San Ignacio, when Maynard had mentioned that his father had been researching geosequestration, before anyone had heard about peak oil. Maybe NATO has an idea of what the world will look like ten, twenty years from now. Why not relegate parched, rugged Afghanistan to a wasteland where carbon dioxide can be stored underground?

"Have you discussed this theory with Bartek?"

"No, I haven't had a chance to work with him yet. I'd be surprised, though, if we weren't on the same page on this. The hard sciences are the foundation for the soft ones. My father always stressed that. I wanted to be a writer. He urged me to study science. Here I am."

"And teleology is a function of the material, concrete world."

"Yes. Drought, starvation, was the impetus for this shrine. The hunter-gatherers might have been illiterate, but, like preschoolers, they could draw and paint, and tell their story pictographically."

"*Hola!*"`

Elizabeth and Maynard step back from the panel, turn in the direction of Carolina who is trudging up the rise towards them. "*Hola,*" they reciprocate simultaneously.

"*Como estas?*" Carolina drops her backpack within the shade of a boulder, stands with her hands positioned on her hips beside Maynard and faces Elizabeth.

Elizabeth senses that Carolina's question is addressed more to her than to Maynard. She also notices that unlike herself, who favours wearing a baseball cap and sunglasses to cut down on the glare of the sun, Carolina is outfitted in a wide brimmed straw hat with a chin strap. "*Bien, gracias. Doctoro* Guzman has permitted you to take a coffee break?"

Carolina laughs. "*Si.*"

"We were just talking about how the cave painters overcame their illiteracy by documenting their belief systems pictographically," Maynard interjects. "Have you ever worked on pictographs before?"

"No. It is my first time to La Baja. In Mexico we have so many archeological sites and I have worked all over, photographing and drawing artifacts and ruins, but never *las pinturas rupestres.*"

"Are there any different techniques that you'll be required to apply here with the murals?" asks Maynard.

"*No se.* So far I just took instructions from *Doctoro* Guzman. The light is not so good right now." Carolina raises her head and looks up at the cloudless sky. "I think a little later it will be better. Technology, of course, makes a lot of allowances for light but good natural conditions are always easier to work with."

Recalling Carolina's frenzied search for her memory card, Elizabeth asks, "Do you like working with digital cameras?"

Carolina shakes her head. "Not so much. When I studied photography, I learned how to develop my own pictures. I was still living at home with my parents — in Mexico DF — and we constructed a wall in my bedroom for a darkroom." Her voice takes on a wistful tone. "On assignment, when I worked with archeologists, I loved the process of first surveying the site, and then studying the light, observing the clouds, before setting up my equipment."

"It was like a ritual?" Elizabeth offers.

"*Si. Exactamente.* I loved the anticipation of how *las fotografias* would turn out." Carolina lowers her tone of voice, as though in nostalgic reverence for another time. "The process allowed me to think about what I was doing. Now, there is no time for anything, for contemplation. It is no longer an art form in the traditional sense."

Stepping back, Maynard leans his torso against the outcrop and crosses one ankle over the over. "So from an aesthetic point of view, what do you think about the artists who painted these murals?"

"*Doctores!* So many questions. *Doctoro* Guzman sent me here to have a break." The inflection in Carolina's voice has risen again, but Elizabeth knows instinctively that she doesn't expect to be taken seriously.

"Sorry!" Maynard says, throwing his hands up, as though unsure what to make of Carolina's sudden outburst.

"It's okay. I understand," Carolina replies reassuringly. "You want a different perspective." Hesitating before answering, she casts her eyes upon the left panel, turns her head slightly from right to left and then back to the right before settling her gaze upon them. "I think they were like all artists. They wanted to leave an impression of what their lives were like."

"For posterity," Elizabeth sums up.

"So that people like us will have something to latch onto. To understand what was going on back then," Maynard clarifies.

Nodding, Carolina translates the word into Spanish. "*Posteridad.* They wanted to leave a legacy."

"Yes," agrees Maynard. "But, tell me ... why is it important for people to leave some evidence of their lives behind for future generations to discover?"

"*Tan muchas preguntas, Doctores!*" Carolina rolls her eyes and smiles. "This is too much work, for a simple artist like myself." Again, she takes her time in replying, positions herself beside Maynard, prompting him to move over a little so that she too can lean her back against the boulder. "*Porque*, like all of us, they didn't want to be forgotten. They didn't want to accept that after they died, it was the end." Crossing her arms before dropping them onto her thighs, she shakes her head.

"*Los primitivos* were not like *los animales*. They understood about death and couldn't accept that they had to die. That there is an end to everything. Even though with the end, there is always a new beginning."

"Do you think they thought very much about what they were painting, or that it was a spontaneous creative endeavour?" Elizabeth asks.

"Absolutely, it was spontaneous. I think they were having a lot of fun. They were painting with their hearts." Carolina points to her left breast. "And not with their heads. Even though they wanted to leave a legacy, later generations didn't care so much about what was already painted here. They painted on top of paintings. That is why there is so much overlapping of figures, so much superimposition."

36.

PABLO THROWS ANOTHER PIECE of choy onto the fire. Sparks fly and fizzle in the enshrouding blackness. A glow seeps from behind the mountain that shades them in the early morning. The sharp edge of a new moon creeps over the summit. Patricia used to call such a moon a "banana moon." Elizabeth hadn't corrected her, hadn't told her that it's known as a crescent moon — a symbol of Islam.

The red-blue embers lick the replenished kindling and coalesce into a wreath of fire. The pile of choy, collected in a communal effort from the arroyo, is nearly spent. They'll have to wander down the canyon to scavenge more. Richard, having recovered from the snake bite, is seated next to Elizabeth. Bartek is on the other side of her, beside Pierre. *Señor* Morelo hasn't yet called for a nightcap. It seems the day will end as a dry one. They have to conserve their supplies. According to Felipe, too much water was consumed during the day, no doubt on account of dehydration precipitated by last night's drinking.

The choy ignites and transforms everyone's faces into cryptic proportions. Noses acquire an eerie prominence. Those with hooded eyes, like Guzman's, appear hollowed out, more recessed. Carolina's wide mouth and thick lips appear fish-like, almost grotesque.

Turning to Bartek, Elizabeth points to the crescent moon. "How ironic that they would choose a new moon as their symbol."

"Why? Because they are backward? While Europe was stuck in its dark age, Islam was flourishing. Everything changed after the Crusades." Bartek bites his lower lip before changing his tone. "Why do you think of such things now?"

Bartek's retort cuts like a knife. She has the urge to protest that Patricia, when she was small, called a crescent moon a banana moon, and that she was just making conversation, but she simply nods, crawls inside herself, and stares at the fire.

On the other side of the campfire, Maynard extends his legs, leans back, and plants his elbows behind him. In the firelight, his red hair shines as though gilded. Elizabeth thinks back to their conversation about how civilizations evolved, thousands of years ago, as a result of climate change. She thinks of the Incas sacrificing children to appease the gods, throwing them from mountain tops in the hope of forestalling another drought that had brought the hunter-gatherers together in the first place, along the more humid coastal spine of the Andes. Scarcity had precipitated conflict, until one tribe of people prevailed over another, and enslaved them.

She resists the urge to shake her head. She doesn't want Bartek to intuit that she's still at it — wracking her brain, trying to make sense out of what's happened. Faith. That's all there is. From the get go, since the painters documented pictographically their belief system, human beings have been trying to control their destiny. Perpetually sitting on the fence, harbouring faith conditionally. Faith, trust, comes so much easier when the gods smile down upon us, and human beings, forever arrogant, hardwired to survive, forget their past errors, mistakes, and revel in the deception that they deserve their good fortune, have somehow earned it. The gods are to blame when things don't go the way that humans envision. The ultimate price: That is what a soldier has to be prepared to pay. She scans the faces of her other colleagues — Raul, Guzman. None of them, thankfully, had been so brazen as to tell her what she didn't want to hear.

She'd felt so distanced from Patricia before her deployment. That one awkward moment in the kitchen after everyone had left, when Patricia had been eating grapes, just before she'd gone for a run, she'd sensed something. There had been just a hint of despair, and instead of picking up on it, she'd squandered the opportunity to reconnect with her, choosing instead to fulfill her own needs, not wanting to accept that her little girl had grown up and had her own path to follow. No wonder Patricia had disengaged from her embrace.

She senses Richard's gaze fixed upon her. Wondering for how long he's been observing her, she smiles back at him. She's been absorbed in her own thoughts. How patient he's been with her. Patience, or to express it as Carolina did yesterday, we have a little time.

She recalls Krystyna having commented about Patricia keeping busy all the time. She'd never noticed. They'd been in the habit, throughout their lives, of keeping busy. Elizabeth's heart feels heavy, aches with regret. But what about what Pierre had said? That Patricia would be released, that she'd see her again?

Elizabeth searches her heart for an inkling of an answer, some sense that everything will work out. She looks up at the moon. It appears smaller now, its initial glow has dimmed and has become shrouded in a mist.

Acknowledgements

I'd like to express my gratitude to Inanna Publications, for providing *Mirrored in the Caves* with a home, and particularly to my editor, Luciana Ricciutelli, who shared in my vision and tirelessly encouraged and guided me to realize its potential. Apart from my publisher and Luciana, it is impossible for me to name all the people to whom I am indelibly indebted for their mentorship, support and wise counsel. I will, however, also mention the cave painters of Baja California, Mexico, whose murals inspired me to weave a story about life in the twenty-first century of the Anthropocene epoch, and to explore the last remnants of any affinity between (wo)man in the Age of Man and (wo)man in Neolithic times.

Barbara D. Janusz is a mother, an environmentalist, a lawyer, poet and an educator. Born and raised in Edmonton, Alberta, she has also lived on the west coast of British Columbia, in Calgary, in Paris, France, and in La Paz, BCS, Mexico. A contributing writer for *EnviroLine: The Business Publication for the Environmental Industry,* she has published poetry, short stories, editorials, and essays in various other magazines, literary journals, newspapers and anthologies across Canada. Barbara Janusz lives in Crowsnest Pass, Alberta, with her partner, Garry, and son, Olek. *Mirrored in the Caves* is her debut novel.